PRAISE FOR THE
CLYDE BARR NOVELS

'**NOTHING SHORT OF DYING** may be **the
year's best debut thriller**. It leaps at you like
a wolf, sinks its teeth in, and won't let go'
William Kent Krueger

'Contains **furious, NON-STOP action**
that paints the mountains and gorges of
Western Colorado red with blood'
CJ Box

andly cinematic . . . What makes Clyde
rr great isn't just that he's **HAUNTED,
iven and lethal**, but that he's paired
th a strong, independent and capable
oman who refuses to be a victim'
ylor Stevens

'A thrill ride . . . buckle up and hang on
because **you're in for one hell of a read**'
Craig Johnson

'Takes you into the underbelly of the
American West, where some things haven't
changed since the gunfight at the OK
Corral . . . Clyde Barr is **the quintessential
man's man**, a modern version of every
Wild West cowboy, sheriff, and drifter
you've ever admired in books and film'
Nelson DeMille

'In this modern-day gunslinger classic
everyone is a bad guy and **Clyde Barr
is the BADDEST OF THEM ALL**'
ott Sigler

ALSO BY ERIK STOREY

Nothing Short of Dying

ERIK STOREY

A PROMISE TO KILL

**SIMON &
SCHUSTER**

London · New York · Sydney · Toronto · New Delhi

A CBS COMPANY

First published in Great Britain by Simon & Schuster UK Ltd, 2017
A CBS COMPANY

This paperback edition published 2018

1 3 5 7 9 10 8 6 4 2

Simon & Schuster UK Ltd
1st Floor
222 Gray's Inn Road
London WC1X 8HB

Simon & Schuster Australia, Sydney
Simon & Schuster India, New Delhi

www.simonandschuster.co.uk
www.simonandschuster.com.au
www.simonandschuster.co.in

A CIP catalogue record for this book is available from the British Library

Paperback ISBN: 978-1-4711-4692-3

Printed and bound by CPI Group (UK) Ltd, Croydon, CR0 4YY

Simon & Schuster UK Ltd are committed to sourcing paper
that is made from wood grown in sustainable forests and support the Forest
Stewardship Council, the leading international forest certification organisation.
Our books displaying the FSC logo are printed on FSC certified paper.

For the world's indigenous peoples

"There are not enough Indians in the world to defeat the Seventh Calvary."

—George Armstrong Custer

A PROMISE TO KILL

CHAPTER ONE

The second time I saw the old Ute, he was dying.

It was late summer, hot and drier even than usual. I was riding a new mare and leading a reluctant mule named Bob across the lowlands of northeast Utah that lay between the hump of the Book Cliffs and the higher Uinta Mountains to the north. When I saw the old man's truck idling in the bar ditch, I let go of Bob's lead rope and kicked the mare into a half gallop. Jumped off and let the reins hang as I checked on the old man.

He sat slumped against the steering wheel of his rusty twenty-year-old pickup and was complaining that his arm hurt and that he had some serious indigestion. I told him to hang on, rummaged in my pack, and pulled out a bottle of expired aspirin.

"I'm fine," the old man said. "Just ate a bad lunch. You don't need to worry about me."

"No, you're not. Here, take these."

I shoved a couple of pills in his mouth and made him chew. He grimaced, which made his aged face look even older.

"Tasty, huh?" I said. "I'm no doctor, but I think your ticker's

1

giving out. Try not to die for a second. I'll be right back." I tied my mare and the mule to some nearby piñons and went back to the truck.

The old man looked like he was concentrating, trying to control his breathing. He rubbed his arm and clutched his shirt. "Ain't my ticker. I have the heart of a warrior. Strong." He thumped his chest feebly, and the grimace returned.

I dug back into my pack and found my cell phone, which was dead. Of course. There aren't many places to plug a charger into a horse.

"We need to get you to a hospital."

He nodded, grunted, and tried to unbuckle his seat belt. I slipped my knife from its sheath and cut the strap before he could struggle it off, then ran to the other side of the vehicle and helped him into the passenger seat.

Once I got him halfway comfortable, I hopped in the driver's seat and tried to remember how to drive an old ranch pickup. The gears were sloppy, the clutch slipped, and the engine loped like a panicked Appaloosa I once owned. The knack of relying on *mechanical* horsepower, not the animal kind, came back to me a few miles later. As the old codger and I rattled down the dusty, narrow highway, I thought back to the first time we'd met, twenty minutes before.

I'd been sitting atop my horse, trotting across the gray asphalt, when the old man had stopped and waved me over.

"Nice pony," he'd said. The clipped way he said it, combined with his dark, wrinkled skin, told me he was a Native. That was the politically correct term these days. I remembered playing Cowboys and Indians as a kid. These days, I guess kids played something PC, like Good Guys and Bad Guys.

According to the map in my pack, I was getting close to the

Uintah and Ouray Indian Reservation. This old man proved I was closer than I'd thought.

"She's a little tall to be a pony," I said as an understatement. The mare stood at least sixteen hands.

The old man laughed, his skin a map of deep canyons and craters. "I raise ponies just like that," he said. "On my ranch. Quarter horses. Not as full of fight as the ponies my great-grandfather rode into war, but pretty good." He laughed again, then asked where I was going.

I shrugged. "North, I guess." It didn't much matter where, as long as I was moving. Although it would be nice to get up into the range that I'd been riding toward the last couple of days. The cold granite, crystal water, and tall, fragrant pines would help fix what was eating away at me.

"You should come by," he said. "Cook me dinner and I'll tell you some stories."

I told him I would, and I'd planned on it, but I'd barely ridden two miles before I came to his idling pickup.

Now, as the sun sank low in the sky and the surrounding stubby juniper and piñon trees cast grotesque shadows across the road, I divided my time between trying to keep the old beater of a truck on the pavement and glimpsing over at this man I barely knew, whose condition seemed to be worsening.

"You still with me?" I asked.

He grunted and motioned vaguely with his hand. "Go to Wakara. Straight ahead five miles. My daughter works at the clinic there. She's a doctor—a good one. She'll take care of me."

I did as he said, driving through a long narrow cut that had rock walls rising up on either side, but I had to stop a couple of times to remove some debris that had probably fallen off a flatbed and would have shredded the truck's tires. When we finally got into what barely passed for a town, the sun had disappeared behind the rocky horizon and the clinic was closed.

"Where's the nearest phone?"

He shrugged, pointed to the only building out of the ten or so in town that had a light burning. I drove there, told the man to sit tight, and walked toward the door.

As I neared the slumping building, I heard the rumble of laughter and jeering. The place looked like it wouldn't make it through the winter. The outside walls were a mix of peeling plaster, missing windows, and artful graffiti.

The inside was worse.

CHAPTER TWO

Once I opened the front door, my nose caught the pungent scents of dried leather and manure, and my eyes took in the sight of rows and rows of haphazardly placed goods for sale. On one wall were tightly packed clothes, and on another was an assortment of hunting and fishing supplies. Occupying the room's center were stacked cases of canned goods and packaged food. Where the back wall should have been was a recessed area that featured a bar. And in front of that bar were at least twenty loud, burly bikers in leather jackets and chaps. Surprisingly, all were white. No Natives in sight, despite the fact that I was officially now standing inside an Indian reservation.

There was no one manning the small checkout counter by the door, so I waded into the boisterous room.

"Hey," I yelled, barely able to make my voice heard above the drunken racket. "Is there a phone here?"

The room went quiet. Which gave me time to notice details. Like the patches on the bikers' jackets. Their club was apparently called the Reapers, and they were one-percenters, what they call the hardest of the hard. I'd met bikers before and seen outlaw patches similar to these. Normally they wouldn't have bothered me. What *did* bother me was the way these men held themselves. Most were leaner and more muscled than the bikers you see on TV or in the movies. But more important was their eyes. They were full of menace. For some reason, this crew reminded me of the Janjaweed—a deadly horseback militia in Sudan that I'd once made the mistake of upsetting.

The biggest of the men, a giant who must have topped six foot six, shoved his way ahead and moved to stand in front of me. His patches said he was the club's president, and that his name was Jury. "No phone. Store's closed for a private party. *Leave.*" I could feel his hot breath on my beard.

His men smiled. I said, "I've got an old man outside—he's in bad shape. I need to borrow someone's phone."

Jury grabbed a beer bottle out of the nearest biker's hand and slammed it to the floor. Glass shattered and tinkled against my boots. "Let him die."

For an instant I tried to assess how much of this stone-cold-killer response was an act. Maybe he was just testing me, waiting to see if I'd offer the secret "bad guy handshake" or whatever. *Should I say something clever?* At that moment, I couldn't think of a single comeback other than "I can't."

At that, Jury's friends' eyebrows all raised like coordinated curtains, and twenty heads shifted slightly to see what the president's next move would be.

"I think you will."

"Won't." I didn't move. Instead, I matched his stare.

"Listen, bumpkin," he said. "When our club rolls into a little town like yours, we own it. We make the rules, and we make the demands." He stared hard at his men, paying special attention to a couple of the sloppier Reapers wearing Nomad patches—the only ones who weren't yet coiled for action. "We also say who lives and who dies. And if you don't leave in the next three seconds, you and your friend outside will both be dead." Time slowed as I fought to control my adrenaline. Twenty bikers continued to stare at me like hungry hyenas at night, waiting to see if they could feed. My hands shook. I wanted, more than I'd wanted anything in a long time, to pop Jury in the throat and wade into his friends with chin jabs. But there was an old man dying outside. So I put my hands up and backed away.

"That's right, walk away, bumpkin. Go play with the Indians. And if you *ever* interrupt us again, I'll stomp you into six kinds of flat."

CHAPTER THREE

It was full dark when I hurried back outside and climbed into the truck. In the glow of its overhead light, the old man seemed paler. Beads of sweat broke off his forehead and ran into his eyes. He didn't wipe them away. "Still hanging in there?" I asked.

It took him a moment to answer. "Don't worry about me. Even at eighty, I'm stronger than you."

"Probably," I said. "Where's the nearest hospital?"

"No hospitals. They're full of Mormons who poke you with needles and try to convert you at the same time. Take me to my house."

"I could, but then you might be dead in an hour. We're going to the hospital. Point the way."

This time, I noticed, he didn't put up any fight. For all his stubbornness, he probably knew he was in a bad way. He pointed north. "Thirty miles that way, in Vernal," he said, then curled up tighter and clutched his chest.

I shifted into drive and was about to pull out when a teenage Ute boy ran around the corner of the building and grabbed at the truck's door handle. He tried to talk, but his run had left him breathless. He wore a dishwashing apron and a flat-brimmed ball cap over his long hair.

"What's wrong, kid?" I asked, wanting to get out of there.

Panting, the kid pointed at the old man and said, "My grandpa. I heard you say an old man was hurt, and I hoped it wasn't him, but I came out to see, and . . . and it is."

The old man mumbled, "Taylor?"

"I'm here, Grandpa."

"This guy wants me to get poked by Mormons."

The boy looked at me for an explanation and I said, "Your grandpa's heart is giving out. You want to come with me to the hospital or not?" He hesitated only a second before jumping in the back. The rear door was just slamming shut when I peeled out and pushed the rattling pile of metal up to its max speed of sixty. Above us, the stars shone brightly in the thin desert air.

The old man groaned again and looked over at me. "Why are you helping me?"

My eyes never left the road. "You offered a fellow horse lover dinner, right? If you die, I'll never get to eat it."

I thought about what would happen when we got to the hospital. Some insurance lady would probably have us fill out ten forms while the old man was taking his last breath. It seemed smart to phone ahead. I called into the backseat. "Hey, kid, you got a cell phone on you?"

In the rearview mirror, the kid's face looked genuinely anguished. "It was almost dead when I got to work. I need to charge it. Damn, my mom should know what is happening."

I sighed. Why is it that all the machines that are supposed to make life easier go on the fritz when you really need them? I pushed my foot down harder on the gas pedal and hoped this machine I was counting on to eat up the miles wouldn't give out, too.

CHAPTER FOUR

We made it. *Barely*. The insurance lady must have been on break. The blond nurses who took the old man away on a gurney told us if we had been five minutes slower, he'd be dead. They said he was going into intensive care, and to take a seat in the waiting room for God knows how long. So we did. The facility was much bigger than I'd expected. Acres of shiny floors and clean walls and beeping machinery. It smelled of cleaning products. I hadn't been in a hospital this modern in my life. Most of the times I'd been patched up, it was in some godforsaken place, with foreign languages being spoken and people screaming in pain from lack of anesthetics.

Taylor and I found open chairs with plush cushions and took a seat. Magazines of every variety were splayed in a circle on a table in the middle of the room, but most of the people waiting were glued to the television hanging from the wall by the entrance.

Taylor looked away for a moment and wiped at his eyes, hoping I wouldn't see. He knew his grandpa wasn't out of the woods, and he was obviously rattled. I stared at the ceiling tiles and consciously tried to drain away some of the adrenaline that had been surging for the last hour. When I looked back at the boy, he was borrowing someone's phone charger and plugging the device into the wall. He wandered back over to me, having put on his toughest mask, and asked, "Is my grandfather going to be okay?"

I wasn't going to tell him there was nothing to worry about. "Intensive care is never a good thing. But your grandpa seems pretty stubborn. I wouldn't bet against him."

He nodded, seemed lost in thought. Then he pointed at the giant screen. "Have you seen the news?"

The display showed a newscaster I'd never seen before talking in an excited rush about something big. Words ticked across the bottom of the screen as he spoke. The guy continued for a few minutes, describing an escalating event somewhere two hundred miles south of us. He mentioned a terror alert, and the moving words at the screen's bottom reported that all major concerts and sporting events would be canceled until whatever was occurring to the south was resolved. I shrugged, looked away, and picked up a fishing magazine.

Taylor, however, continued staring at the TV. "That's just south of here, man. Down by Green River, on the interstate. I canoed all the way there once. Sounds like the government is looking for something there, and that terrorists might be involved. Can you believe it? In Utah?"

I shrugged again and returned to the article I was reading about catching lake bass. My ho-hum response must have reminded Taylor where he was, because a few seconds later, he took his partially charged phone into an alcove, presumably to call his mom. If her car was faster than the rattletrap truck I'd driven, she could be here in twenty-five minutes.

As I surveyed the waiting area, I noticed that most eyes were still focused on the TV. This terror news was exactly what I was trying to get away from by going into the mountains. Death, fear, and worry—what was the point of brooding on all that stuff anyway? The situation would all blow over eventually. Even if you were caught in the middle, you'd deal with it then. Why spend your life stressing over *might be*'s and *could be*'s?

I finished the lake bass article and was just beginning a story that rated the best rods and reels when I noticed that Taylor had wandered back and was once again staring worriedly at the TV. "Hey, kid," I said, "you need a diversion. Why not grab some fine reading material?" I reached into the pile of magazines, pulled out an issue of *Cosmo*, and handed it to him.

"*Cosmo*, man? Really?"

"It's got lovemaking tips. Plenty of pictures of good-looking women, too. Read up."

The kid smiled for the first time, and riffled through the pages. "Ugh," he said, pointing to a model who seemed to be pitching moisturizer. "Too skinny." He flipped through more pages for a couple of minutes, then tossed down the magazine. "I hope my mom gets here soon. She was trying to sound calm when I told her, said how they really know what they're doing here and everything would be okay. But I could tell she was barely holding it together."

"Is she really close to your grandpa?"

"They have this running thing. Each pretends that the other is exasperating. Grandpa is always pushing the old ways, and my mom reminds him that the old ways didn't work out very well. But you can tell that they both love each other, you know?"

"Family is important," I said evenly. For me, family was simultaneously lots of great memories and lots of horrible ones. Sometimes I preferred not to go there.

"Hey," Taylor said, brightening, "my mom asked what your name is and I didn't know."

"Clyde Barr," I said, and stood to stretch my bad left leg.

"My mom says to tell you thanks, but you don't have to stay. She says you can borrow my grandpa's truck to get back to town, if you want."

"I'll stay," I said, taking my coat off and stuffing it under my chair.

"Why? You don't know us."

I shrugged. Why *was* I staying? I guess that, after seeing so many people who crossed my path end up dead, it felt important to see someone survive.

There was something else, too. "Your grandpa reminds me of a man I used to sit up late with, watching the campfire die. He told stories about his people, and I listened."

"Who were his people? Ute?"

"He was Mayoruna. Met him in Peru, near the Brazilian border. Good guy."

"You've been to Peru?"

"I've been around." We were killing time, so I took him on a ten-minute tour of the countries I'd visited, especially places in Africa and South America. I emphasized the cheery sights I'd seen—the marketplaces, the temples, the festivals. I left out the bodies lying bloated in the streets, and the fetid smells that hover over battlefields long after the last life has been snuffed out.

"Sounds cool," he said.

I smiled. I'd been like that once, always believing that what lay over the horizon was way more satisfying than my current surroundings.

Maybe I was *still* like that.

CHAPTER FIVE

I'd just finished leafing through a magazine called *Southwest Designs*, which seemed very focused on something called "Native American accents," when I heard a woman's voice call out, loud enough to be heard by everyone in the waiting room. "Taylor!"

Obviously, Taylor's mother had arrived. I looked up to see a slender woman smothering her son in a bear hug. "How's he doing?" she asked breathlessly. In the embrace of his mother the boy could no longer hold back his emotions. He sobbed into her chest. She looked over at me. "You the one who drove him?"

I nodded, suddenly feeling self-conscious about my unshowered, dust-caked appearance. She was beautiful: unusually tall, with long hair the color of a wet crow. "Thank you," she said. "Have you talked to a doctor yet?" I shook my head and she took off, determinedly marching in search of her peers.

Taylor tried to hide his wet face, and I sat down and pretended not to notice. I patted my pockets, an old habit from before I'd given up smoking, and remembered that even if I'd had cigarettes on me, nowadays you couldn't smoke indoors—

certainly not in a hospital. Taylor's mom came back about ten minutes later and filled us in. "Myocardial infarction," she said, wiping at tear-reddened eyes. "He's stable now, and his prognosis is good. He'd be dead if you hadn't found him, Mr. . . . ?"

I stood, offered my hand. "Clyde Barr, ma'am," I said.

She shook my hand firmly, with more strength than I expected. "Lawana Nicholas," she said. "Thanks again. Did my son mention you could take the truck?"

I nodded and once again said that I was staying. She didn't argue, say no, or ask why. She just put her arm around her son and led him to a seat in the waiting room.

To give them space, I wandered outside and looked up at the stars—at least, those that I could see against the glare of the streetlights. Then I took a quick stroll across the lawn just to feel the soft earth under my boots. The walk was surprisingly calming.

When I came back inside and took a seat, I overheard Lawana and her son talking in worried tones about the family ranch. Apparently the three of them—grandfather, daughter, and grandson—all lived there. Lawana was saying that she'd now have to add to her duties at the clinic daily trips to the hospital to check on her father, whose name, I'd learned, was Bud. Taylor had school and his part-time job, and the man whom Bud had hired to care for his horses and get the haying done had up and quit only two days before.

What can I say? I'm an impulsive guy. I walked over and said, "Uh, I couldn't help overhearing. It sounds like you need help working the ranch. I'm available."

Lawana and Taylor seemed somewhat surprised that I was still there.

"Why?" Lawana asked warily. "You aren't family."

"No, but you need help, and my calendar is clear."

For Lawana, my eagerness was apparently suspicious. What did she know about me anyway? "It's generous of you to offer, but—"

"I know a lot about horses," I cut in. "Heck, I was riding a horse when I met your dad." In that moment, I remembered that I'd left my animals tied up to some piñon trees by the highway. I wondered if they'd worked themselves free already and were wandering around.

"Being able to ride a horse is not the same as running a horse ranch," Lawana said dismissively.

"Actually, I've worked on a few ranches." I didn't tell her that I'd done that type of work in Zambia, Zimbabwe, and Uruguay. Nor did I tell her that I'd once pulled double duty in Argentina, in the vast grasslands of the Pampas, as both cowboy and security guard. The country had been spiraling downward, and crime had spilled out of the cities into the rural areas. I'd agreed to work for room and board, as long as I promised to carry my rifle every time I rode. It came in handy.

Taylor stood and said, "Let him help, Mom. He saved Grandpa, and he's been all over the world. I'll bet he—"

I cut him off. "I've been in trouble myself before, and I know what it means to have someone help out."

"We can't pay you much," she said with a look on her face that said, *I'm going to regret this.*

"I'm not *asking* for anything. Just to help."

She still wasn't quite ready to yield. "The hired man was sleeping in an old tack shed we fixed up with a bed and an outside faucet for showers. It's pretty basic."

"So is the bedroll on my horse. It'll do just fine."

"And another thing. You don't go in my house without permission. I catch you there once without my say-so, you're gone. And I do keep a shotgun by my side at night."

Taylor rolled his eyes. "Mom, he's not John Dillinger."

Lawana was cold steel. "Mr. Barr, my son seems to have confidence in you, but I just met you, and I've already decided that you're not like most men around here. You still have some proving to do, okay?"

I was liking her more and more.

CHAPTER SIX

After I was sure the old man wasn't going to croak, I took the truck and retrieved my horse and mule, who were a little peeved I'd left them for so long. The next day I began the glorious work of shoveling horse manure and slinging hay at the Nicholas's ranch. Through Taylor and Lawana, I learned that the family name was a corruption of the name of their great war chief ancestor, Nicaagat. He'd led his warriors in one of the last actions against the U.S. government, right before his people were forced out of the mountains of Colorado and into the alkali desert of Utah.

The place had a beauty of its own, though. In the mornings, the dew balled up on the sage, and when the sun rose the light refracted through every small drop of water, turning the flats into a brilliant kaleidoscope. At night, when the sun dropped below the rocky mesas to the west, the higher hills and mountains to the east would bleed red in the alpenglow. I fed horses and cut hay during the day, and frequently I'd be visited by ravens and magpies and deer. It definitely wasn't like the high alpine meadows that I was headed toward, but at least I was outside.

Also, the physical labor of tossing hay bales and digging post holes helped to ease the pain that I'd been keeping bottled up. The exhaustion dulled memories of my rough childhood, the wars I'd fought in the third world, my time behind bars because of a mix-up between the Mexican government and the cartels, and the people I'd loved and lost along the way. One person in particular—a girl who'd thrown in with me and didn't make it.

My third day on the ranch, I had some unexpected help.

Lawana had left early, when I was drinking my first cup of coffee, but Taylor hadn't gone with her, as he'd done on previous days. Instead, he poured himself a cup of the black stuff and leaned against the counter, mirroring what I was doing. "It's Saturday," he said. "No school, and my boss at the store told me to take the day off. I think his business is hurting with all those bikers hanging around. The people in town are mostly staying away."

I sipped the hot black coffee and asked, "So, are you going to play video games in your room all day? I hear that's what kids do these days."

He shook his head and grinned. Over his grin were the beginnings of a scraggly, half-grown mustache. "Nope. I'm going to show you how to work."

Fair enough. We finished our coffee, then went out and started working.

He helped me pull the final ditch dams out of the last irrigated fields, then helped me close the headgates on the ditches, officially shutting off the water for the season. While we did this, he never stopped talking.

Until we saw a mare lying down. Taylor ran to the small pen, threw open the gate, and rushed inside. "Damn it," he said, then grabbed a halter hanging on the fence. "Help me get her up!"

"What's wrong with her?" I asked as I helped him push and prod the older chestnut-colored horse to get up. She continued to stubbornly lie on her side, her barrel chest struggling with each breath.

"Colic. Or founder, or something," Taylor said, tugging on the sick horse's lead rope. "I don't know for sure, but Grandpa said if Seeley laid down, I had to make her walk."

A couple of tugs and prods later, the feeble animal managed to pull her front feet under her and stagger up. Taylor yanked the rope again and made her take a few steps.

"Sounds like he knows what he's talking about," I said.

"He does. He's the best. He helped raise me the past five years, and I learned everything about horses from him."

"Yeah?"

"Yup. My dad died when I was ten. He was in Afghanistan— an army captain. The plan was for him to come back here when his deployment was up. He was going to help run the ranch while Mom ran the clinic." He looked down so I wouldn't see his eyes grow moist. "The guy who came to the house to tell us—he had a note with him. It was from Dad's commanding officer. It said that he"—his voice caught for a second—"it said he died trying to save his men."

"Sorry, kid," I said. "Rough."

He kept the horse moving and said, "Yeah. I try not to think about it too much, because it's something you can't undo, you know? Anyway, it's pretty nice here—on the ranch, I mean. The rez isn't so great, but I got a couple friends. Mom, though, it's pretty bad for her. She's sad all the time. I think that's why she works so much. It takes her mind off things."

He panted and pulled the rope, his feet dragging with each step. I took the lead from him and kept walking the horse in a slow circle. "Hey," I said, "no disrespect to your dad or the beauty of this place, but why doesn't your mom move you guys to the city? Must be a lot of smart fellows there who'd pay attention to someone like her, an educated, beautiful woman."

Taylor climbed and sat on the fence, rubbed his arms. "Way before I was born, two of my aunts killed themselves. Which happens a lot here. Three kids in high school did it last year. Anyway, Mom went to school to become a doctor just to show our people that there's hope—that we Utes can be anything we want, make something of our lives. Most people don't care, but she does. She works her ass off helping everyone and trying to make this place better."

I nodded and kept walking. Half an hour later, Taylor decided the horse would be okay, and we took the halter off and went on to the next chore, making sure to check on her occasionally throughout the day. Taylor kept talking as we made our rounds, telling me more about his mom and life on the rez. The way he told it, his mom was a saint and the rez was a hole. I didn't know enough about either to argue, not that I wanted to. He seemed to be a good kid, and the more he talked and kept up with me as we worked, the more I liked him.

When the sun disappeared, I went back to the old tack shed to clean up, and Taylor did the same in the main house. About a half hour later, he came out with a tray of food. By now I knew the drill. Lawana wouldn't be returning until much later—something that happened every day so far. Taylor seemed unusually quiet as I forked up a plateful of leftover casserole, then washed it down with a few swigs of water. As

I ran a napkin over my mouth and began loading my glass, utensils, and plate back onto the tray, Taylor said, "Thanks, Clyde."

I shrugged. "No problem."

"No, I mean, thanks for staying and helping. When that lazy-ass Virgil Peters lit out of here, Grandpa said he'd quickly find someone else. That's Grandpa—he always wants you to know he's got it handled. But then a couple days later, he had that attack. There's just too much to do around here for Mom and I to handle it ourselves."

"Well, I don't know about that. You set a pretty good pace."

"Yeah, and you'd better keep up." He laughed and picked up the tray, but I caught him with a wadded-up napkin as he reached the door. He laughed again. After that, I lay back on my bunk for a long while and listened to the night sounds.

CHAPTER SEVEN

The next morning, after I'd trimmed hooves on twenty of the ranch's hundred and fifty horses, I drove into town to pick up the horseshoes I'd need later. Wakara in daylight looked far worse than it had at night. Trash was piled in heaps in many of the yards, half of the windows on most buildings were boarded up, and I counted no less than ten feral dogs roaming the streets. The so-called downtown consisted of the bar/general store that I'd been in that first night, across the street from the school. To the south was small tract housing that I guessed was built for and run by the tribe. A few scrubby cottonwoods and scraggly Siberian elm trees grew randomly along the streets and in yards. In some places there *were* signs of revival and care. The medical clinic and community center had both been recently renovated and painted, and the grass around them recently mowed.

As I moved farther into town I heard a sound drifting from somewhere to the west: the thump of drums and the high-pitched notes of people singing. The music's steady beat called to me for some reason, so I decided to drive to where it was coming from.

It didn't take long to find the music's source. Pickups and older-model cars were lined around the block surrounding a circular pavilion. A large pole in the center of the hard-packed dirt held strings of waving flags that flapped above the arena and were tied off at the edges. A crowd was gathered on the dirt field next to the pavilion, and underneath, in the center, women were swirling and stomping and waving what looked like feathered batons. All wore colorful beaded clothing and feathers. Off to the side, four men beat large drums and sang. I got out and milled with the crowd, just as taken with the music and dancing as the rest of the onlookers. Mixed in with the beats was the jingling of bells strung around the dancers' ankles.

After the first song, a man came on the loudspeaker and announced that the men's fancy dancers would be next. A rumble of excitement passed through the crowd, and I couldn't wait to see what the hubbub was about.

But instead of the drums starting up again, we heard the unmistakable roar of Harley motorcycles. Along with most of the crowd, I spun and saw five Reapers ride through the onlookers and park in the arena. The men dismounted. I recognized them from the store, but their leader, Jury, wasn't with them. Four went right to the women who'd finished dancing and grabbed them. The biggest biker, a mountain of a man wearing a bandanna and sporting a collar-length beard, took advantage of the sudden quiet and yelled, "Don't stop on our account. This is a dance, for God's sake."

Nothing happened. No one moved except the Reapers who were trying to keep the women from squirming from their grasp.

"Play the goddamned drums, Injuns," the bandannaed biker

said. "We're gonna dance with you, even though you forgot to invite us to this shindig."

Still nothing.

The big biker pulled a pistol from under his jacket, racked the slide, and pointed it at the drummers. "Play . . . the . . . *drums*," he said.

The drummers resumed. The biker put his pistol away and started stomping and spinning by himself in the middle of the arena. He threw his hands up and started screaming in a grotesque imitation of the Ute singers. The rest of his men grabbed the arms of the protesting women and swung them around in circles.

I bit my cheek, rubbed my chin, and watched to see what the members of the murmuring crowd would do. I didn't have to wait long. Some of the younger men began rushing forward, shoving aside the people in front of them. None made it far, though, before the elders in their midst yelled for them to stop.

That's when six more bikes roared into the arena, with Jury in the lead. These bikers didn't dismount; instead, they rode in circles around the other Reapers who were on foot. Jury slowed and stopped. He stared hard at the bandannaed biker and called him out.

"Gunner, get your Nomads and pull out. Back to camp, now!"

Gunner hesitated, sweat starting to drip from beneath the bandanna, but then he sneered and grumbled his way back to his bike. His friends left the women and hopped on their own bikes, at which point they roared their way through the parting crowd.

"What the hell was *that*?" I asked a large Ute wearing a cowboy hat who'd been in front of me, bulling his way forward.

He turned, looked me up and down. "Asshole white men.

Like you." Then he walked away. Realizing I was the only Anglo left in the area, I pulled my hat down and drifted back to the truck as quietly as possible.

After that I headed to the general store, back on my quest to find horseshoes. The wiry man behind the counter glared at me until I explained that I was working on the Nicholas ranch. While I was telling him what I wanted, two Reapers came in, grabbed a case of beer from a cooler, and left without paying. "They do that a lot?" I asked the counter guy.

He nodded.

"You going to call the cops?"

He shook his head.

"Why not?"

The man said nothing, just shrugged. I thought about letting it drop, but my curiosity got the better of me. I asked again.

"You wouldn't understand," the man said. "You're like them."

"You mean white, or an asshole?"

He shook his head, sighed. "White. Not from here. That's what I mean. Say I *do* call the cops. Which ones, huh? Local? This lawman we have here, Arrowchis, he won't do anything. He's been looking the other way lately, probably made a deal with them. But even if he wanted to do something, he can't. We don't have any rights when it comes to white men. They can't be arrested or tried by Indians, not even on our land. It's a shitty law."

What century had I stumbled into? "Well, there's *somebody* who keeps the peace on the reservations, isn't there? The Bureau of Indian Affairs? The FBI? What about them?"

The Ute crossed his veiny arms and shook his head, like I was a child who needed instruction. "Those outfits can't do much, either, even if they want to. Which they don't. It's too political to get involved with us Indians. People see it as interfering with our self-governing, or some shit like that, so they're not going to send a federal prosecutor down here over a stolen case of beer."

I stared back at the man, trying to think of something helpful to say, but no bright ideas were occurring to me. Once the law leaves, things go downhill pretty quickly. I'd learned that years ago in places like Burundi and Chad, and later Argentina. I thought I'd left behind all that chaos when I came back to the States more than a year ago. But apparently I was mistaken.

I waited a few minutes while the guy found the horseshoes I needed, then wandered back out to the street. Whatever tranquillity I'd felt when I first entered town less than an hour earlier had entirely disappeared.

CHAPTER EIGHT

Back at the ranch, I shod two horses, then carried my rifle into the adjacent desert to look for dinner. It only took an hour to track a mule deer buck up a dry wash and drop him as he bounded over the sandstone and into the greasewood. I didn't have a license, and it wasn't deer season, but it was subsistence hunting, so as long as we ate the meat I didn't care if I broke the law. After I'd field-dressed the buck, I slung it on and headed back to the ranch.

Outside, I showed Taylor how to marinate the meat and cook it on an open grill so it'd be tender. I left him contentedly stabbing at the steaks with a long barbecue fork.

When Lawana got home about twenty minutes later, Taylor had venison steaks, salads, and biscuits on the table. As I found out eventually, he'd begged his mom to let me join them for dinner, and seeing as how I'd provided the main course, she relented. It didn't take long for Taylor to find me out by the wood bin and bring me to the ranch house.

It was a very strange feeling to be sitting down to dinner with a woman and her son. Other than a couple of meals I'd shared with my sisters a year prior, I hadn't done anything so

ade. I'd been on my own for so

got that other people live like this.

, Mom? Is your son a good cook or

roudly.

he mother of invention," Lawana said some-

cally. "I'm afraid I've left you to fend for yourself

ights."

r straightened up and seemed to puff out his chest, as if mocking the suggestion that he was anything but self-reliant. "I'm fine—you know that. Besides, Grandpa was around till just this week."

"How *is* Bud doing?" I asked.

Lawana put down her fork, looked at Taylor and me both. "I think he's going to come home soon," she said, "but it'll be different. No more chasing horses for him. He's got to take it easy."

"Your father seems like a guy who follows his own rules," I said, smiling.

"As do you, apparently," Lawana shot back. "You know, it's a felony to poach on the rez. We can hunt, but it's poaching if you aren't a member of the tribe."

I tried to look remorseful, didn't quite pull it off.

"He doesn't care," Taylor said. "He's been around the world, and I bet he's done things a lot worse."

"Is that so?" said Lawana. She gave me a searching look. I could see she was wondering what stories I was telling the boy. Time to change the subject.

I cleared my throat. "Uh, what's with those bikers in town?"

"They just showed up," Taylor said.

"Eat your dinner," Lawana said. Then to me, "They got here last week. Bunch of oafish idiots."

I told her what I'd seen that day, then asked, "Why did the elders hold the younger men back?"

Lawana chewed silently for a while, then set her fork back down. She gave Taylor a look that meant, *Zip it*, and said, "I doubt you'll understand. It's different here than out there."

"Try me."

Taylor said, "Welcome to Indian country."

"Shut up and eat," Lawana said. "I'll try to explain." She glanced at her salad, then said, "Okay. You know where you are, right? The Northern Ute reservation. Once upon a time our people roamed over all of Utah, half of Colorado, and parts of New Mexico and Wyoming. Now, what's left of us is mostly split between southern Colorado and this part of Utah." She went on to describe how her people had fought and resisted, which I remembered reading about many times as a kid. "So now," she continued, "it's us against the outside world. Especially on the north rez. The Southern has a casino, and money. We don't. Does any of this make sense?"

I nodded. "But I still don't get why you don't run the bikers out. Or call the cops."

Lawana gave me a look that resembled the one I'd gotten from the counter guy in the general store. "The legal situation here is different. We have one tribal cop, Fred Arrowchis, and I think the bikers are paying him off. But even if they aren't, he can't arrest a white man on the rez. Federal law enforcement won't get involved for small stuff, and even some of the bigger stuff. Last year a girl was raped, and the federal attorney refused to take the case, saying it lacked sufficient evidence. I think he was scared he'd look bad, trying to help us poor little Indians, and even more scared that he might lose."

"Of course," Taylor said, "we got Mormons and other white

people living on our rez who think the land's theirs. They got their own cops, but even they don't come around much. Clyde's right, we should run them all off."

Lawana looked at him tolerantly. Fifteen-year-old boys are always excited by the idea of action, especially a boy living on a ranch where each day is pretty much like the one before. She saw her son's hand reaching for another steak and grabbed it. "Taylor, you've already had two—and by my count, about five biscuits. I think it's time to go do your homework."

"You can't just send me to my room anymore, Mom. I'm a man now."

"Uh-huh. Well, it's time to man up and do your algebra homework. I want something better for you than to be cleaning out horse stalls for the rest of your life."

Taylor apparently knew when it was time to concede. He grabbed his dirty plate and marched into the kitchen.

"He's actually a good kid," she said, "but you might be a bad influence on him."

"Turning him on to a life of crime as a deer poacher?"

"You know what I mean. He thinks you're cool. You could tell him to do a handstand on the roof right now and he'd probably do it. There've been a couple guys in my life since . . . well, since I lost my husband, Brian. I've seen it before."

"Taylor told me about what happened. I'm sorry."

She nodded slightly but didn't seem to want to go there.

"Bud seems like a good influence on the boy," I ventured. "I can tell there's a lot of mutual love and respect there."

She looked up, smiled wryly. "My father is trying to raise Taylor to be a good Ute warrior, and a great horseman. Totally impractical. But that's Dad—he's too drum-and-feather."

"Drum-and-feather?"

"Traditional. He still believes in smudging—you know, burning sage—and that primitive ways are better than the hospital."

"They have their place."

She glared. "I didn't go to eight years of school to come back and practice magic. We need the modern here if we're going to survive."

"Sure. But sometimes it's smart to respect the old ways. It's not the modern that keeps the tribes in the Amazon around."

"That's just what my father would say. You two aren't very different, which is good and bad."

I wanted to ask about the bad, but what was happening in town was still nagging at me. "So no one is going to do anything about the bikers, even when they do crap like they did today?"

"We've waited out the white men before. We've been putting up with them for hundreds of years, so what's a few weeks or months until the bikers leave?"

I couldn't answer that, and we finished our meal in silence.

CHAPTER NINE

The next day I was up at dawn and on a tractor, hoping to get some work done before it became unbearably hot. Lawana had left earlier for the clinic, and Taylor was just dragging his adolescent hide out of bed as I started running the swather around the fields, cutting the tall grass that would be raked by another tractor and then bunched into bales and put away in a hay shed to be fed to the horses during the winter. The ranch—which consisted of a main house, a barn, a corral, the old tack shed where I was staying, and a building containing some horse stalls for animals that needed special tending—was surrounded by 120 acres of irrigated fields that needed cutting. I'd finished bumping and banging around the first field and had started on the second when I noticed that the sickle bar was missing teeth and wasn't cutting worth a damn. To continue this job I'd need to replace the teeth, so I headed back into town.

On the dusty drive, I tugged my hat down against the glare and started musing on the bikers. *Why are they here?* The question was driving me crazy. Why would they be hanging out in this small, poor town in the middle of nowhere? I should have asked Lawana for her theories the night before, and now

I regretted it. It made sense that the Utes were waiting out the bikers, hoping they'd clear out when they realized there was nothing here for them. But what had brought them in the first place? I vowed to ask Lawana that night.

My second trip into town caused me to notice even more details about Wakara's layout than I had previously. Except for the cluster of tribal housing to the south of the general store, most of the residential buildings were haphazardly placed, and many of the other structures and trailers were abandoned. The uncared-for jumble of it all made me wonder why the people who stayed did. Were they traditional folks who firmly believed in the power of the tribe, or had they simply given up any hope of a better life? As an outsider drifting through, I'd never know.

As I slowly drove down the potholed highway, I reflected on how much this place reminded me of hundreds of small towns in the third world—forgotten settlements where the people had obviously been abandoned by their government but were desperately trying to survive, and to cling to old traditions. Rounding a corner, I passed a weathered church with a broken sign out front, then two abandoned gas stations, then I hit the small downtown.

Just before I reached the store, I saw Lawana's car parked in front of one of the only buildings with a brand-new paint job. Obviously, some of the people were taking pride in their town, and the doctor was one of them. So was whoever was running things at the small school. The grounds were immaculate inside the fence, whereas outside the dead weeds stood six feet high. I stopped in the center of the highway to let a group of high schoolers cross on their way back from buying lunch from the store, then found a parking space.

As I walked around the corner I was almost run over by two young men. Both were tall and skinny, but with muscular arms that sported plenty of tattoos. One was using a skateboard to slalom the broken sidewalk, and he almost skidded into my legs. He jumped off the board, kicked an end and flipped it into his hand, then said some words I couldn't make out but that were obviously not complimentary. The other kid stared at me in surprise, then menace. He wore ripped jeans, a T-shirt with the sleeves cut off, and a red baseball cap turned backward.

"Get out the way, white man," he said. He brushed past me and followed his buddy into the store. The skateboarder flipped me off from behind the swinging front door. I followed them inside, more amused than anything at their bravado.

That's when I found out how bad the biker problem really was.

After the two young toughs walked to the refrigerated drinks section and pulled out a couple of energy drinks, they walked to the back of the store, kidding each other about looking for girls who didn't eat too much fry bread. They casually walked by a biker and his five buddies arguing in the corner, and the kid holding the skateboard accidentally swung it backward and grazed the biggest biker's vest.

Jury's vest.

I forgot why I'd come into the store and watched in horror as Jury reached out with a massive paw and grabbed the boy's shirt, pulling him around to face him. "Apologize," he said to the shocked kid, who now held his board between himself and the giant like a shield.

"S . . . sorry, sir," he said, suddenly looking much smaller than before.

Jury didn't let go. The second kid, who'd spun around to watch his friend, now spread his feet and lifted his chin at the bikers. "Let him go," he said, his voice cracking slightly. "He said he's sorry."

The giant grimaced and shoved the kid away. The other five bikers, all standing straight and tall beside Jury, laughed. I noticed that all five had the Nomad rocker underneath the big Reaper patch on their jackets. The man standing next to Jury—the one he'd been arguing with when we entered, the wall of flesh named Gunner—said, "Go run home, boys. Your mama squaws are waiting for you at the tepee."

Jury shot him an angry look, and the braver kid, the one wearing the ball cap, gathered whatever resolve he had left before replying, "Go to hell, asshole."

"What?" Gunner said as he jumped past Jury and went after the kids, who'd turned and rushed toward the door. In a final act of defiance, the skateboarder flung his board backward at the bikers, shouting, "This is *our* town!"

And hit Gunner in the face. Which started bleeding. Jury stood still and furious, but the other four bikers beside him took off out the door behind their now bleeding comrade, knocking cans and bags of chips off shelves along the way.

Well, this wasn't going to be good.

CHAPTER TEN

As much as I wanted to, I couldn't stand idly by. I moved to the doorway, blocked it, and tried to dissuade Jury, who was starting to stomp after his men. "Leave them alone," I said. "They're just kids."

He stopped, inches away from me. His looks could have made a Viking tremble: a smoothly shaved skull, decorated on either side with what looked like a tattoo of the devil riding a chopper; a four-inch long goatee; battering-ram shoulders; and enormous chest muscles poking out of a leather vest. He shoved me hard with both hands and I fell like a rag doll into the doorjamb, then onto the ground.

"Those kids just made everything worse," he said, then followed his men into the street. I heard a shouted argument, then the sound of the kids screaming apologies. I pulled myself to my feet and rushed outside.

The brilliant desert sunshine shone almost directly down, making it hard to see without sunglasses. So I pulled down my hat brim even farther, and saw the friend of the skateboarder sprinting away toward a house opposite the school. The other kid, the one whose board had collided with Gunner's face, was down on the dusty ground, in the fetal position, with his arms hugging his head. Gunner and his friends were kicking the kid in the stomach.

Jury rushed up alongside him, "Head back. *Now.*"

Gunner didn't stop kicking. He grunted out, "After we teach him some respect, yeah, we will."

The sound of boots smacking flesh made me sick. Scanning the street, I saw a big Ute in shorts and a tank top near the only restaurant in town throw his cigarette down and jog toward the ruckus. Across the street, by the police station, a skinny little white man approached, waving his arms.

The big guy in shorts shouted, "What the hell are you doing?" and "Get off him!" He kept jogging, finally reaching the ruckus, and pulled a kicking biker away. That's when Gunner delivered a hard uppercut to his belly. The big Ute staggered, but didn't go down. I sat my hat down by the store's door.

This was the kind of thing I'd tried to avoid ever since coming back to the States after being released from prison. So far, I'd been spectacularly unsuccessful at it, getting into more brawls than most people will in ten lifetimes. I tried telling myself, *again*, that incidents like this always escalate, that this wasn't my fight. But sometimes the opportunity to ring an asshole's bell is just too tempting.

I grabbed the ponytail of one of the kickers and ripped him backward, where he tumbled over my outstretched foot and fell into the dust. When he shouted, the bikers going after the big Ute turned to look at me, and the Ute punched one in the eye, then ran for the kid. I stood over the prone boy while Gunner came at me. He threw a punch that I slipped, and I saw Jury stop arguing with the little white man and rush over to help his men. The white man yelled for us to stop, but the bikers ignored him, instead focusing on the big Ute and me.

A wall of leather, tattoos, and bad facial hair rushed in, and on instinct I started shoving palms in faces and elbows into heads. I caught a couple of wild fists in the gut and forehead, two real good hits in the ear, but kept going.

They were all good. Veterans of hundreds of brawls. None of 'em made rookie mistakes, none hesitated or missed a well-placed strike. But I'd been in at least as many scrapes, so I kept calm. If you're not—if you worry or think—then you stall. And if you stall, you die. So I took some blows and tried to dish out more.

Out of the corner of the eye that wasn't blood-filled I saw the big Ute wrestling with a fat biker, both of them down and rolling. One of the men I was dealing with, an older guy with almost no teeth and lightning-bolt tattoos on his neck, tried to land a slow haymaker. I stepped into the swing and shoved a palm under his jaw, lifting all two hundred pounds of him off his feet an inch or so. He fell to the ground, his breath leaving in a *woof*, and I turned to the other biker, who'd been trying to punch me in the kidney.

He tried to get in a couple more shovel punches when I whirled, but his knees gave out after I slapped him in the ear. Before he could recover, I grabbed a handful of mullet and pulled his head into my knee. Twice. The dude crumpled, and I was feeling pretty good about myself until I felt arms bigger than a mountain gorilla's wrap around mine from behind. I left the earth, and my breath left me.

As I struggled to breathe, I saw the big Ute get up and kick the man he'd been wrestling with. He went over to the prone kid and cradled his head in his big hands, then looked up and saw Jury trying to crush my ribs and squeeze out my guts. If the Ute hadn't left the kid to help me, Jury might have succeeded.

As many melees as I'd been in over the years, I'd never been bear-hugged by someone as strong as Jury. Actually, I didn't know someone could *be* that strong. I smashed my head back, trying to hit his nose, but hit nothing but forehead. That, combined with the inability to breathe, made my vision dim. The world was going gray, close to black, when I was suddenly dumped to the ground.

Grainy dirt filled my nose and an ear. I heard Jury grunting and the sound of the big Ute swearing. Heard a crack, and the Ute went down next to me. I pushed off the ground and slowly got to my feet. Jury was shaking his already swelling hand, but when he saw me get up, he set his feet to lunge at me. I braced for impact, trying to come up with a plan.

"Jury!" the skinny man from across the street shouted. "That's enough. Stop this silliness now. Get your brothers to camp."

Jury stopped his charge, considering. He looked over at the little man, who was walking away, then swung his gaze back to me. "This isn't over, bumpkin. Me and you? Next time I see you, I'm going to kill you." He spit at my feet and went to his fallen friends, helping them up. He dragged them, limping and swearing, in the same direction the small man had gone.

On the ground, the big Ute was groaning. I limped over and helped him up. He rubbed his jaw and said, "Damn. I haven't been hit that hard since I was inside."

As we dragged ourselves over to check on the boy, I said, "Where'd you do time?"

He scrutinized me, looking at my old green tattoos and the scars that weren't hidden by my T-shirt. "A dime in Draper."

I nodded, crouching down to check the unmoving boy. "You mean Utah state pen?"

"Uh-huh," he said, bending down next to me to get a look at the kid. "Not a good place for an Indian. Where'd you do yours?"

I felt for the kid's pulse. Still strong. There were growing lumps under his eyes, an avulsion on his scalp that was bleeding pretty badly, and plenty of soon-to-be-nasty bruises. I hoped that none of his bones were broken. "South of the border. Three years in lockup." I held out my hand. "I'm Clyde, by the way."

He took it and gave it a strong shake. "Name's Colorow. You think the kid's going to be okay?"

"Hope so. We need to get him some help." I took my knife out of its sheath, cut the cleanest part of my shirt off, and pressed it to the rip on the kid's forehead. "Help me carry him to the clinic."

He took the kid's legs and I took his armpits and we waddled our way up the street to the clinic a block away. During our trek, a blue-and-yellow Tribal Police SUV rolled down the road but didn't slow or stop.

"Goddamned Arrowchis," Colorow said, grunting as we walked. "Hasn't done a damned thing about those assholes since they showed up. Used to be okay, for a cop, but now he's turned his back to his people. Anyway, the town owes you one for helping this kid. *Tog'oiak'*."

Curiosity made me ask. "Was that Ute?"

"It just means 'thank you.' I only know a few dozen Ute words. There's probably only a thousand people left who speak the language."

It made me sad to think that a language tens of thousands of people had once spoken was going to die out soon. The same thing was happening in Africa. One of these days I guess the whole world would be speaking English—or maybe Chinese. That's one of the reasons I enjoyed being out in the wilderness. In nature, differences are preserved.

We made it to the newly painted clinic without collapsing or dropping the kid, and headed inside. In the distance, we heard the diminishing rumbling of Harleys.

"Those bikers will bleed for this," Colorow said.

I grunted. I hoped it didn't come to that. Hoped they'd leave before things got any worse. Hoped I wouldn't have to be here to see it if it did. But I'd promised Lawana and Taylor I'd stick around for a while, until they didn't need me, and I never backed out of a promise.

CHAPTER ELEVEN

The front room of the clinic consisted of a simple waiting room with four soft chairs of different designs and a table. Also, a young Ute lady's face in a glassed reception window. The woman stared aghast as we carried the kid past her and tried to make him comfortable in the largest of the chairs. Colorow smacked a meaty fist against the glass and said, "Get Lawana, *now*." The face disappeared into the back. Colorow and I took seats on either side of the boy. I checked his pulse again. Still strong. And he was breathing. His eyes fluttered occasionally under swollen lids, and I knew he wouldn't be able to open them if he wanted to.

"Stay with me, kid," I told him. To my surprise, he groaned.

"Adel is tough," Colorow said. "As long as there isn't a lot of internal bleeding, he should be okay." He let loose a stream of obscenities intended for the absent bikers, then said, "I know you ain't one of them, so why are you here? You work in the patch?"

I shook my head. "Never been on a rig. Just passing through. Or I was until I met Lawana's dad, and now I'm helping out for a while at their ranch."

"Bud's a good man. He took me to a sweat once, taught me some of the old things, before I went away." He rubbed his puffed-up jaw and looked at the ceiling. "You know," he said, beginning to slur his words, "some of the history he passed along to me, about the way our people used to be, might have kept me alive when I was inside. He made me man up, get tougher, you know?"

I did, sort of, but right then I couldn't take my eyes off his swollen jaw. It looked as if he'd stuffed a baseball into one side of his mouth. He began mumbling again and I started laughing.

"What?" he said. He followed my gaze and tenderly felt along his jawline. "You don't look any better, man." He laughed and pointed at my chair. I looked down and saw blood dripping from my torn ear onto the scratchy fabric. There was a lot of it. Blood, not fabric. What was left of my formerly blue shirt was now tie-dyed with red. I looked like a front row fan at some rock show.

I patted myself down, found new bruises on my elbows and some very sore ribs. My back felt as if I'd been kicked by my mule, which was bad. It meant I might be pissing blood for a couple of days. I grabbed some tissues from the dispenser on the table and staunched the bleeding ear. The other injuries would heal in time.

Just then Lawana came through the only door other than the one we'd just pulled the kid through. She was dressed in blue scrubs, her long hair put up in a braid. A young man and younger woman, also in scrubs, followed closely behind. They were pushing a stretcher, and rushed past Lawana to ease the kid onto the rolling bed. They whisked him back through the door as Lawana said, "What happened?"

"Reapers," Colorow said.

Lawana nodded, her face pinched. "Sit tight. We're short-handed. Once I get him stable you guys are next." She spun and ran to find her nurses.

Colorow stared at her fit form as she disappeared. "You gonna live until she gets back?"

"Probably. You?"

"Might." We laughed, then Colorow mumbled, "She's good. Worked in Salt Lake City in a real hospital. ER, I think. Good-looking, too."

I lifted my eyebrows to acknowledge that, yes, she was very good-looking. "So why did you run over?" I asked. "Most people watch, or take videos with their fancy phones. Some call the cops. But you jumped right in. Why?"

Colorow shrugged, and winced. Something other than his jaw was hurting, too. "I could ask the same question. Only difference is—he's my people. Not yours. Why would a white man help an Indian kid?"

I shrugged, not really having an answer for him. The silence lingered for a few moments, then Colorow said, "We got lucky."

I tried to laugh, but my ribs wouldn't let me. "Yeah? How so?"

"In Draper, I met a couple Reapers. They base out of Vegas but are from SLC originally. They still run in Utah, and occasionally get popped. Inside, I learned that these mothers never get messed with. Not by the Aryans, not by the Hells Angels, not by the Mexican Mafia. Word is, they're tougher and meaner than most of the cartel guys. Anyone messes with them ends up cut into little pieces for the prairie dogs to eat."

"I've never been a fan of *any* biker," I said, then remembered their patches. "What's a Nomad? Some of the Reapers have patches that say SLC, and some say Nomad."

"Biker club stuff," Colorow mumbled, patting his jaw again.

"They call 'em clubs and not gangs because they have a president and vice president and all that shit. And they're regional, like a club in each city. These guys must be the Salt Lake City club. The nomads are guys who are official Reapers but don't have a home base. So they can't vote or be president or anything. They run with the rest of a club if the club needs help."

"Man, you're a biker encyclopedia," I said. "So answer me this. Why are the Reapers here, on the rez?"

"Don't know," he said in words I could barely make out. "But they need to go."

I nodded, worrying what I might be tempted to do if they didn't. I'd found over the years that I didn't coexist well with people who like to hurt others. Eventually it was either them or me.

The door swung open again and Lawana came back out with a clipboard in hand. She looked at Colorow and said, "He's going to be okay. In a couple of days. This is the worst one yet."

Colorow shook his head and was about to respond when Lawana motioned us through the side door. She directed us down a narrow white hall and pretty much shoved us into a small room with a paper-covered table and a shelf with Q-tips and cotton balls. She made Colorow sit in the chair and had me lie on the table. The paper crinkled as she messed with my ear. "You're both lucky you're not dead," she said.

"Luck only carries you halfway," I said. Then I remembered something else: "Who was the short guy? Jury's master?"

Colorow mumbled something, but his jaw had become so swollen I couldn't understand him. Lawana said, "Orval? I've seen him at the restaurant Colorow cooks for, talking to the big biker, Jury. No one knows why any of these troublemakers are here, little guy included."

Curiouser and curiouser. Lawana wrapped my arm in Velcro and pumped a plastic ball. Felt around on my arm with her stethoscope. She wrote something down on the clipboard. "Adel and you guys make ten since the Reapers showed up. They're keeping me busy, and that's not a good thing."

"They roughed up *seven* other people?" I asked.

"Probably more. That's just the ones bad enough to have to see me."

"And you're still keen on waiting this out?" I said.

Colorow slammed a fist into the chair but regretted it immediately. He grunted in pain.

Lawana threaded a surgical needle, told me to lie back. As she started pulling the coarse thread through my skin, she said, "I'm doing plenty." She shoved the needle hard, adding an exclamation point to her statement. I tried to nod, but that was a bad idea, because she hadn't anesthetized the area first.

She tied off the stitches and told me I was done. "Take some ibuprofen and stay out of fights." Colorow switched places with me and she went back to work. I must have dozed off. When I woke, Colorow could talk again. At least, well enough to argue with Lawana. "We *have* to run them off," he was saying.

"I agree with the goal," she said. "I just don't see the means. You two look pretty bad after taking on only six guys. There are many more of them than that."

Colorow stood up and moved to the door. "We'll see," he said, and stomped out.

Lawana turned to me. "You can go, too."

I picked up my hat and stood. As I was heading through the doorway, Lawana grabbed my arm. "Don't make this any worse, Clyde," she said. "I don't want you two playing vigilante and sending more patients my way. We'll figure out a smart way to get rid of them. Promise me you won't do something stupid to make more trouble."

I tipped my hat and started walking down the hall.

"Promise me," she said.

"Thanks for the stitches," I said, and walked out of the clinic.

CHAPTER TWELVE

I caught up with Colorow as he tromped down the cracked sidewalk. The mosquitoes were out, trying their best to swarm and feed. I slapped them off my arm and asked, "What now?"

"I should be back at work," he said. "But I'm gonna talk to Arrowchis first. This crap has got to stop."

I told him I'd go with him. I probably should have been finishing the cutting, but this seemed more important. The grass wasn't going anywhere.

The police station was a five-room, multi-story concrete building at the corner of the main highway and the road that led south to the tribal housing. It sat squat and menacing beneath the only ash and maple trees in town. The thick, wide leaves shaded the gray cinder blocks, almost hiding the structure. Inside, I followed Colorow as he marched up the three steps to the front desk. The desk, which was more of a window to the receptionist's office, was the only thing in the room other than three chairs and a rack of brochures and pamphlets.

"Tabby?" Colorow said. There was no answer, so he dinged

the tiny silver bell on the desk hard enough to send it over the side. "Tabby!"

I leafed through the pamphlets while we waited. There were the usual maps and don't-dig-before-you-call flyers, but there were also booklets that explained all the tribal programs that were set up to help kids stay off drugs. Plus a surprising number of leaflets focusing on suicide and diabetes. A couple of minutes into Colorow's yelling, a very large woman appeared in the desk window, wearing a beaded jacket and black dress. She had a beaded brocade in her hair and thick glasses. "Jesus, C," she said. "I was eating. What you want?"

"We need to talk to Fred."

"What's wrong?"

"Fred. Where is he?"

"Out. Should be back soon."

"We'll wait."

Tabby shrugged and walked slowly away, into the depths of the building.

We went outside to wait, where we both paced restlessly, lost in our own thoughts. I thought about the town, and the bikers, and the doctor. Couldn't help it. Something about the way her steady hand ran a suture needle, and the way she truly cared for her people. I was wondering vaguely what her deceased husband, Brian, had been like when I noticed through the shimmering heat wave the form of the tribal SUV. It was parked across the street.

"How many cop cars are there in town?" I asked Colorow, who was staring at a raven in a nearby tree.

"Just the one. Why?"

I pointed to the parked vehicle. Colorow squinted, saw it, and spun back into the police station. I followed. Inside,

Colorow pounded on the door next to the front desk and started yelling for Tabby again. His outrage worked, in a way. Tabby never showed, but a sturdy older man in a uniform unlocked the door and came out.

"Colorow. You don't look so good." He laughed, then put his policeman's mask back on. "You want me to call your parole officer and explain how you're disturbing the peace?"

Colorow shoved his defiant chin in the air and said, "And do *you* want to explain why a biker gang is beating up high school kids and you aren't doing a damned thing about it?"

The officer, who I assumed was Arrowchis, shook his head sadly and said, "I haven't heard about anything like that."

"Bullshit," Colorow said. His angry outbursts were aggravating his recent injuries, and his jaw was starting to swell again.

"Watch your mouth," Arrowchis said. His hand drifted down toward the Taser on his overweighted Batman belt.

I stepped forward and tipped my hat back. "You saw us packing the kid to the clinic."

The hand drifted lower and touched the Taser, then moved to the pistol. He shook his head again. "Don't know what you're talking about. And you are?"

"Clyde Barr. Working at the Nicholas ranch. And you're a liar. Want to tell me why?"

"You have ten seconds to get out of my station. Both of you."

Both of us shook our heads. Colorow spoke first. "People in town think you're taking money from the Reapers to look the other way. That true?"

The cop's eyebrows lifted. "That what you think, too?"

"Starting to," he said.

"Listen," the officer said, hitching up his belt. "I'm going to stop the rumor right now. It's not like that at all. Here's the thing: My hands are tied, and you know it. I can't arrest white men. And it has to be a felony crime before I can call the BIA or the FBI. And then they have to want to come and investigate. Which they haven't for the last three major crimes. We've been on our own. I could call the sheriff's office over in Roosevelt, or Duchesne, but that would screw up a twenty-year lawsuit aimed at giving us legal jurisdiction over all the towns on the rez. Even the Mormon ones." He sat his considerable bulk in one of the chairs and sighed. "The *good* news, though, is that the Reapers are leaving in a day or two, no more. Let's just drop the whole thing."

"How do you know they're leaving?" I asked.

"I was assured." He pushed off the chair and headed to the door. "Let's leave it at that. Now get out."

Colorow said, "Fine," and left the room in a huff. I didn't. "Who assured you? Jury?"

Arrowchis stopped and turned at the door. "I told you to leave."

"I didn't hear you. Tell me who, and explain what's really going on, or I'll go through the town telling everyone you're betraying your own people."

The cop sighed. "If I explain, will you let it drop?"

I nodded.

"Fine. A man came to see me last week. Little white guy. He said that it would be in my best interest to look the other way when his friends rolled through town. As long as I did, there wouldn't be trouble. He said they'd camp outside of town and be gone in a day. Then the guy comes back and says there's been a delay, and they're going to be a few more days, and his men are going to have to come into town occasionally for supplies. I didn't like it, but he said if I didn't cooperate, they'd burn the town—all of it."

"And you believed him?"

"This man is actually quite talkative. He likes to tell stories. Unfortunately, his stories are persuasive. I checked a couple of them out, found out about some incidents. Nothing that could be tied to him. Nothing I could go to BIA with. But it seemed wise to not test his veracity."

"So far, they've hurt ten people in town. Some bad. That doesn't bother you?"

"Of *course* it does!" he shouted, slamming the door shut. He turned and pulled his shoulders back. Stood as straight as a boot-camp marine. "I care about my tribe, and this town. Lived in Wakara all my life. But when you've worked this job as long as I have, you learn there are no perfect solutions. I'm just trying to keep the maximum number of people safe."

Tabby came to the window then, saving us both from an awkward conversation. "Everything okay, Fred?"

"Right as rain," he said, waving me off as he went back through the door.

It was a pretty apt expression, I thought as I walked back into the searing heat of the desert. It looked like this town hadn't gotten rain in years.

MY NEXT STOP WAS THE store, where I bought the parts I needed for the swather. I grabbed a six-pack of Coors from the cooler, paid, then headed back out to my truck. Leaning against the door, clipping his fingernails, was the little white man.

I almost laughed. He was trying to look nonchalant and tough, but his pale skin, wispy mustache, glasses, and fancy pants made him look like he spent most of his time tapping on a keyboard.

"Orval," I said, nodding.

"It would be best if you forgot the name." He put his clippers in his pocket and smiled. Or tried to, but it looked more like the pinched grin of a recently divorced salesman.

"Yeah? Well, it would be best for you if you got out of my way." I moved to the truck door, and Orval stepped aside. He was still smiling. I got in the truck and started the engine. Orval moved to the open window. "That little altercation you had with my guys?" he said. "It will be worse next time. But I hope, for your sake, there won't *be* a next time. I'm sure the cop told you, but we're leaving soon. I'd appreciate it if you'd stay out of our way until then. Sound good?"

"And if I don't?"

Orval's thin-lipped smile widened. He looked across the street to an abandoned house. Three Reapers stood in the overgrown and dying grass, all sighting down the barrels of AK-47s. "So far, we haven't killed anyone. You'll be the first, if you don't leave us be. Understand?" I stared into the little man's eyes, not moving or showing emotion. For some reason, Lawana's words when I left the hospital whispered to me right then: *Promise me you won't do something stupid to make more trouble.*

"Fine," I said. "Can I go back to work now?"

The smile stayed on Orval's little face. "I figured you'd see it my way. Have a good day." He walked across the street, showing a stiff-legged, sore-backed gait that verified my assumption that his usual work involved sitting on his ass. I watched as he and his men disappeared behind the old house, then I pulled away and drove back to the ranch.

CHAPTER THIRTEEN

That afternoon, as the temperature settled into hellish, I found myself back on a tractor, back to the simple routines, and it helped me forget the day's earlier events. There's nothing better than simple labor to empty your mind. The only bad part was the bumps. As I made my way through the last field, cutting the grass in circles, the tractor seemed to be hitting every clump of grass and rock on purpose. And every time it did, it sent searing jolts of pain through my ribs. I guess that also helped keep my mind off the bikers, and my recent past.

I'd spent all summer driving along the West Coast, direction-less, wandering just to wander. But the time in civilization hadn't been good. I'd thought that maybe some time around people would be fun, but it turned out the opposite was true. Everywhere I went I was advertised to. There were the inane billboards on the highway, there was the gas station TV, the ads at the ATMs, even ads over the urinals in the bars I stopped at. I'd come to the conclusion that those with nothing are pleased with anything that falls into their lap, while those with a lot think they'll only find happiness if they get more. Modern life had become about getting more. That's what drove the people I met. So I'd come back to Colorado, checked on my sisters in Grand Junction, then sold the car and bought the mare and Bob. I was sure that a long trip in the wilderness would calm me down.

It *did* help, to a point. The wilderness was the closest thing I'd ever had to a church, so my mind was more at peace. It was just the loneliness I couldn't stand. There came a day when I realized I was talking too much to my horse and mule.

I WASN'T ALONE *NOW*, THOUGH. Taylor had arrived home from school and he'd offered to walk the fence line with me, checking for breaks. Sweat poured off his face, dripping into the sandy soil, until he dunked his head in the horse tank. He let out a war whoop as he whipped his head out and back, his long, wet black hair sending spray into the air.

"Goddamn, it's hot out," he said, wiping water from his eyes. A few drops stayed on his wispy mustache.

"Could be hotter," I said, thinking back to some hellholes I'd spent time in.

"Like the Sahara? I'm going to see it someday."

"I wouldn't recommend it."

"Yeah? You sound like my mom. When I told her I was going to join the marines, she went ballistic."

I started heading to the shed to get grain for the older horses. "I wouldn't recommend that, either," I said.

"Whatever." He followed me to the shed. "I'm gonna do it anyway. It's the only way to get off the rez, see the world. Mom doesn't want me to, because of what happened to my dad, but I don't care. It's in my blood. Warrior spirit, you know?" He thumped his chest with a fist.

"Warrior spirit gets you killed, kid," I said. I tried not to smile but couldn't help it. The boy was so much like me at that age—full of piss and vinegar, immortal.

"So what?" he said. "We all die. It's an honor to die for your country, just like it was an honor to die for the tribe back in the day."

I had a lot to say about honor and valor, but I was from a different culture, so I held my tongue and grained the horses. We finished the last of the chores, and Taylor went to the house to rustle up some dinner. I stayed out in the barn to repair a few bridles, and was almost finished when I heard the sounds of vehicles pulling up to the main house.

Not Lawana's car, my senses told me immediately. Rather, it was the throaty exhaust of three or four trucks. My memory flashed on the sound of pickup convoys in Algeria, mostly "technicals" armed with fifty-caliber machine guns. Then I heard Colorow's voice drift through the corrals: "You home, Barr?"

I left the darkness of the barn, emerged into the setting sun. Three jacked-up Dodge pickups sat idling in front of the main house. All three of the cabs were full of Utes. So were the truck beds. I counted twenty men, all scowling and carrying hunting rifles. Colorow and another Ute in a ball cap walked around a truck, each carrying a rifle. Something was very wrong, and my stomach sank. I hoped this wasn't a white man lynching.

"What's up?" I asked, one hand instinctively reaching behind my back for my pistol.

"Everything's gone bad, that's what," Colorow said. "Barr, this is Rob Goff." Rob nodded, still scowling. I tipped my hat with my free hand. Colorow continued. "His daughter is in trouble."

Goff jumped in. "She went out camping at the Olives with her friends. They do that some nights, to drink a little, smoke.

They think we don't know. We do, but we let it go. As long as it's all kids from the rez, and as long as they come home in the morning, we don't care. But a couple hours ago . . ." He looked away.

Colorow took over. "Late this afternoon, a lot of the kids went out there. They made a big bonfire, cranked up the music, you know? But, according to Lawana, the bikers must have spotted them. Seen the campfire smoke, heard the music—something. Ten or so rode out there. There was a little scuffle, not much because the kids couldn't stop that many men. And then the bikers rode away."

"And took my daughter," Goff said. His whole body trembled with rage and sadness.

"They took her friend Dianna, too," said Colorow. "She and Rose are gone."

This was a lot to think about before dinner, after a very long day. "Wait," I said. "How does Lawana know what's going on?"

"Because it's even worse than that," Colorow said. "Lawana said that when the bikers showed up, a couple of the kids called Arrowchis. He drove out there to break things up. He was shot."

I let go of the pistol, took off my hat, and wiped the sweat off my forehead. It was probably seven o'clock and still in the eighties. "Is he okay?"

Goff said, "He took one in his vest. Broke ribs and his clavicle. He'll be okay, but he'll be in the clinic for a while. He told Lawana everything that happened, and she called me. Told me about Rose."

"And then he called me," Colorow said. "And we called a few others. Dianna's dad and some friends. We grabbed rifles and are going to get our girls back. God knows what those bastards are intending. I thought . . . well, I thought you might want to come along. You seem pretty handy at this stuff, and *motivated*."

I tried to remain poker-faced. Meanwhile, my mind was working furiously, trying to think of a way to get the girls back without letting twenty angry men start a war. That's when Taylor came outside.

"Go back in the house, kid. Wait for your mom. Tell her I went to town."

"What's going on?" he asked, looking at all the trucks and men, his eyes as wide as an owl's.

"Trouble. You and your mom need to stay here at the ranch."

"No," he said. "I'm going with you."

"The hell you are."

"You can't tell me what to do, at my place." The way his voice rose in pitch made him sound more hurt than angry.

"I can, will, and did," I said, then used the same tone I would if I were issuing orders in a sweaty jungle war. "Go *inside*."

His face collapsed, his shoulders slumped, and he turned and shuffled back through the front door.

I walked back to the trucks and motioned Colorow over. "Okay. Here's what we do." I hurriedly laid out a makeshift plan to get the girls back, based on the little intel we had. The rest, I guessed, we'd figure out on the fly. "Give me five minutes to get my rifle and gear. Don't leave without me. We need to all get there at the same time, or the plan won't work." The men seemed irritated but agreed.

At the tack shed I grabbed my new Winchester Model 70 .375 Holland & Holland magnum rifle and my pack, and I was about to jump into the ranch pickup when Lawana's car pulled into the drive.

CHAPTER FOURTEEN

"**W**hat's going on here?" Lawana asked when she saw me toting my rifle and pack and walking toward the ranch truck. It was parked about a hundred feet from the three idling pickups. "What are you guys planning to do?" I shrugged as if to say, *Well, what do you think we're planning to do?* "You're going after those girls, aren't you?" I could see her wrestling with it in her head, debating whether she should tell all of us to calm down and wait for things to work out. I don't think even *she* was buying that, though.

"Wait right there." She disappeared into the main house, and I considered leaving. Thought better of it, then double-checked the contents of my pack. She came back out with what looked like a large tackle box.

"I'm going, too," she said. "To make sure you guys don't do something stupid. And you're driving. I don't want to take my car out into the desert." I didn't argue. The look on her face suggested that would be unwise.

"What about the cop, Arrowchis? And Taylor?"

"What about them? Fred will be fine. The nurses are handling it. And Taylor will be safe here. God willing, we'll be back soon."

"What's in the box?" I asked as she strode around to the passenger side of the truck and hopped in. She set the tackle box on the seat between us.

"Medical supplies. Someone is bound to get hurt in this thing."

I grunted and got in. I turned the key in the ignition and we joined the convoy of trucks. For the next several minutes Lawana didn't say anything more. I drove the ranch truck behind the three bigger vehicles, trying to stay on the road, mostly unable to see due to the dust. The road from the ranch to town was paved, but there were no street sweepers in this part of the world, so the fine sand and dirt from the desert accumulated in drifts on the asphalt. Half of them felt like speed bumps when the truck drove over them at fifty miles per hour, and the other half busted apart when we hit them, filling the air with thick red clouds.

Colorow and the others had said the bikers were camped ten miles north of town, on the main highway, at the mouth of Henry Wash. The wash was a deep cut in the Wakara bluff that loomed just west of the main road. The camp was supposedly tucked up against the base of the bluff. Our plan called for us to stop at the last dip in the road before the camp, out of the bikers' sight, and split up. As we neared the dip, my mind began conjuring all the ways things could possibly go wrong. They were legion.

I also couldn't help thinking about the determined woman sitting beside me. I didn't really know her yet, but I got the distinct feeling she didn't like me much. I decided to work on her a little. "This wasn't *my* idea," I said.

"I know. I heard some talk. But why are *you* involved at all? This isn't like staying to help with horses."

"I have a bad habit of volunteering."

She didn't say anything at first, then she let out a long sigh. I looked over. "What's that sigh about?"

She gave me a hard stare. "You know, when you first showed up—at the hospital, I mean—I knew you had this past, something about Africa and South America, but I told myself that I wasn't going to ask about it. Truth is, I didn't *want* to know. I figured you'd hang around for a couple weeks and my father would be back and that would be it. No need to download, you know?"

"And now?"

"There's a woman in town, Julie Pinto. She's all eyes and ears, the town gossip. She lives across the street from the general store. Spends too much time staring out the window. She saw that fight you were in today. I ran into her just after you left the clinic. She was there to pick up a prescription. Anyway, she couldn't stop talking about the way you fought. She thinks you're ex-military or something. Who are you *really*, Clyde Barr?"

Oh boy. I didn't expect that. I fidgeted with the steering wheel and stalled for time. How could I sum up my life? How can *anyone* sum up their life? It's a feat, bundling all the wrong turns, detours, and breakdowns into a story that makes sense.

Lawana was still looking at me, so I gave her just a taste. "It started out with me hunting—after I left Colorado and went overseas. I was working for some villagers in Senegal, bringing in bush meat to supplement their food supply in a year of bad harvests. I stayed for a while, fell in love with the Jola people. Nights were filled with dancing by the Gambia River, listening to music played with these cool lute-like instruments, and flirting under the mangrove trees with this girl I met. On the days I didn't hunt, I took fishing trips on the river. Until the bad times started.

"Some of the Jola people thought the government was taking all of their wealth, and somehow I got swept up in the movement. I worked as a scout for months, slipping in and out of the forests, keeping an eye on the government forces. I got spotted a couple of times and had to fight. Unfortunately, I kept volunteering for nasty little wars all over the continent, anytime I found an underdog. And I began to get good at it."

"But . . ." she prompted.

"Yeah, there's a 'but.' But at night"—I took a deep breath—"at night I see a lot of people who were close to me who didn't make it. After Africa, there was South America, and after South America there was Mexico, where I wound up getting grabbed by corrupt local law enforcement and tossed in prison. When I finally got back to the States, something terrible happened—"

"Your sister got kidnapped."

How the . . . ? My hand jerked slightly on the steering wheel and I nearly drove the truck off the road. "How do you know about that?"

"I don't know much," said Lawana. "But just before this whole thing with Arrowchis blew up today, after I talked to Julie Pinto, I tried Googling you. I found only one article, a really cryptic one in the *Denver Post*. It said something about a huge meth dealer being shut down, about a kidnap victim, Jennifer Barr, being rescued, and unconfirmed reports that her brother, Clyde Barr, may have had a hand in bringing down the operation. The story said that at least twenty-five people in the employ of the meth dealer were either dead or reported missing."

I gripped the steering wheel tightly, wouldn't allow myself to look at her. "Like I said, I got good at it."

"And that's it?" She seemed angry at my neutral tone, the matter-of-factness of my concession. "You're what . . . like, a *killing machine* or something? You just visit towns and figure out who needs to be eliminated?"

"The opposite, really. I try to forget. That's what I was hoping to do here."

We both sat in silence, eyes fixed on the rear bumper of the truck in front of us, contemplating the nature of this new emotional terrain we'd entered.

"Sweet God," she said, her eyes wide. "I'm having trouble processing this."

I nodded. I was just glad she was still talking to me. "We can discuss it more later. Right now, I think we should focus on getting these girls back."

Luckily, we arrived at the rendezvous point before the awkwardness could continue. The jacked-up trucks had pulled off the road at the bottom of what must have been the widest section of Henry Wash, where the road dropped down to cross it. In other parts of the state, folks might have built a bridge over a wash this deep, but not here. I pulled the ranch truck behind the bigger ones and cut the engine. I got out to talk to the men, and Lawana stayed in the truck, her face a mask of determination, or resignation, or both. It was hard to tell. The men milled around the vehicles, checking their rifles and murmuring. There was a sense of urgency that bothered me, as though these guys were seconds away from rushing the plan and blowing our chances of helping the girls. If they moved up the timetable, a lot of people would get hurt.

Colorow was the first to speak. "You'll want to drive up

the wash. You can go almost a mile before it gets too narrow. Then you'll have to hike to the top of the bluff. From there you should be able to look down into the camp and cover us. We'll give you thirty minutes, then we're going in to get the girls."

"We wait for full dark," I said. "I'll be set by then, and if it works like we planned, I'll be the only one shooting. They'll fire back at me, and you guys should have a simple grab-and-go."

Everyone nodded and murmured consent, though none seemed too keen on waiting. I got back in the truck and headed up the wash.

"Where are we going?" Lawana said, finally showing worry as we left the main group. She watched the men standing by their trucks disappear in the mirror.

"Higher ground," I said. "We'll cover them when they run in and grab the girls."

"Let me out," she said immediately. "I need to stay with those guys, in case one gets hurt. Stop the truck."

I let off the gas, touched the brake, and then thought better of it. "You'll be safer with me. We'll be out of the range of their assault rifles and pistols, and if my plan works, the men down there won't need you."

"I don't want to be safe, I want to help. Stop the truck."

"No. You can't help them if you get hurt, too. Stay with me, we'll cover the rescue, and then we'll come right back down. I promise."

She stared at me, probably wondering if she could trust me after our discussion of a few minutes ago. But I held her gaze until she looked away. "Fine," she said, peering out the passenger-side window. "I'll go with you. But if this plan back-fires and people start getting hurt, I'm running back down to help." She turned to look at me again. "Do you have *any* idea what you're doing?"

"An idea, yeah. Will it work? Don't know."

She returned to staring out at the desert, which was draped in a dwindling light that made the shadows crawl across the sandy soil. I turned the truck up the wash, jammed the transfer case into four-wheel drive, and kept busy trying to navigate around the sandstone boulders that had rolled to the bottom of the deep cut.

"Something about this feels very reckless," Lawana said.

FIVE MINUTES LATER WE WERE out of the truck and weaving through the fragrant maze of brush and trees, climbing as fast as our heaving lungs would allow up the steep red-clay hillside. La-wana passed me halfway up, telling me to hurry my lazy ass. "Shh," I said, whispering. "From here on out, we need to be ghosts." I saw her roll her eyes, probably thinking I was being overly dramatic. As she disappeared in the junipers, tightly gripping her medical box, I consciously tried to limber up my bad left leg, reaching down every so often to rub the top of my thigh.

I caught up with Lawana at the crest of the mesa, maybe a half mile above the truck, as the twilight began edging into night and the temperature dropped to tolerable. We eased along the edge of the flat top, carefully placing our feet on solid sandstone and avoiding making any sound. When the bikers' camp finally came into view, we found a gray rock wall that resembled a giant exposed brain and settled down behind it.

"How are you going to see them when it gets pitch-black?" Lawana whispered as she sat down next to me.

I pointed to the east, where a mostly full moon was rising. After I arranged my pack against the rock—making sure it was open and that the boxes of extra shells were on top—I stood and surveyed the biker camp through my rifle scope.

In the last of the twilight, I saw the tents and bikes—many more than I'd expected. This biker crew was far larger than I'd thought. I remembered seeing about twenty Reapers in the bar that first night. Obviously not all of the club had been in attendance. Now I gauged the Reapers' strength at twice that number. Parked among the rows of Harleys was a chase van—probably for hauling gear and supplies when the bikers were riding. The tents were clustered against the base of the mesa, the bikes were parked in long rows near the road, and the majority of the bikers were on their feet, milling about in the center of a small clearing surrounded by stumpy juniper trees. I searched the crowd and saw the girls. They were standing, tied to a post sunk in the middle of the clearing. Both seemed to be okay—for now.

Not for the first time, I wondered why so many bikers—these ones, certainly—derived such sick pleasure from abusing women. Didn't they have mothers and sisters? Wasn't there at least some awareness in these Reapers' small brains that what goes around comes around?

After checking the girls, I scanned around the outside of the camp, looking for sentries and roving guards. I found one standing and smoking where the camp's dirt road met the paved highway, and two more behind a semitruck and trailer parked just off the main road. All three of the guards seemed bored and fidgety, probably because they were missing out on the festivities back in the main camp.

As the moon rose higher in the sky, the jumbled sounds of

laughter and drunken revelry faintly drifted up to us. Every time someone cheered, the guards stomped around angrily. I kept my scope on the truck watchers for a few moments, trying to figure out why the vehicle was so important, and I was surprised when Jury's large form marched into view. He smacked one of the men in the ear, then turned to the other and screamed at him. I couldn't make out Jury's words, but it was clear he was ticked.

I was still trying to figure out why a tractor-trailer was parked near the camp when headlights rose up from a low spot on the main highway and pointed down the road.

Game on.

CHAPTER FIFTEEN

"**H**ere they come," Lawana whispered. I nodded, keeping the rifle trained on Jury. When the trucks turned off the main road and killed their headlights, I swept the scope back to the camp, found the bikes, and pulled the trigger. The rifle bucked against my shoulder, and the night air split with the sound of the report. The first bike in the row fell over, a thumb-sized hole in its gas tank leaking fuel.

Lawana held her hands over her ears as she turned from staring at the approaching trucks to glare at me. "You could have warned me," she hissed. Then, "Don't kill anyone. Don't make it worse." I grunted and swung the rifle back to where Jury had been. He was on the move, running back to a camp that was swarming with confused bikers. I put the crosshairs on the bikes again and sent two quick rounds into the next ones in line. Reloaded and did it again. By then a couple of the bikers had gotten themselves together enough to return fire. I heard the pops, but none of the whizzing that comes from lead getting close. I put the last round in the magazine into the dirt by the foot of a firing biker.

Meanwhile, the three trucks loaded with Utes were getting

closer and closer to the camp. The bikers were too focused on us to notice. For the moment. While Lawana watched the goings-on in camp through my binoculars, I reached into my pack and pulled out three rounds that I'd hand-loaded for times like these. I thumbed them into the .375, ran the bolt, and took aim just over the fallen bikes. After gently squeezing the trigger, I watched the white glow of the tracer round fly through the gasoline fumes. Fire burst out, quickly engulfing the bikes on the ground. The already angry bikers stopped in their tracks, not fully believing at first, then rushed to find blankets to smother the flames. One grabbed a shovel and frantically began scooping dirt, trying to keep the wall of fire from spreading. *That should keep most of them busy.*

I swept the scope through the crowd, looking for Jury as Lawana muttered, "Sweet Jesus."

"Yup. Watch the bikers, and I'll cover the trucks." She nodded, and I kept searching for Jury. I found him running like a rhino back to the camp, yelling orders to his brothers. He grabbed a cooler from the back of the van and was lugging it toward the fire when I put a bullet through it. Lawana nudged me and told me that more bikes were on fire. From this distance, Jury looked like a bear getting swarmed with wasps. He swatted the air, screamed into the night, and stomped his size-twelve feet.

Just for fun, I fired the last of the tracers next to his head, trying to set his greasy goatee on fire. It didn't work, but it sure as hell pissed him off. He ducked into a tent and came out with a shiny black rifle, maybe an AR. I kept the scope trained on him as I reloaded, and watched him fire horribly inaccurate rounds in my direction.

He changed magazines and kept firing, hitting trees and rocks below us, while the trucks driven by Colorow and the other Utes eased to a stop just outside the camp. As I'd suggested, the men had turned off their headlights, and I put the scope on them as they piled out of the trucks and worked their way into the camp. The bike fire raged on the camp's outskirts, turning the surrounding sage and junipers into a soft glow of yellow and orange. Until the cheat grass, dead and dry this time of year, caught fire.

When the ground started flaming, the bikers doubled down on their firefighting. They poured all of the camp's water on the flames and shoveled sand with every implement they had, barely managing to slow the conflagration. The few Reapers not fighting the fire were either shooting wildly in my direction or trying to work up the side of the hill to where Lawana and I were positioned. That didn't work out well, either, since the slope was steeper than it looked. Those who made it more than a hundred yards up the hill were sent running back when I put a round in a tree next to them.

The result of the bikers' distraction was that no one was guarding the girls in the center of the clearing, a situation that Colorow and Rob Goff took immediate advantage of. They snuck through the tents to the south, ran to where the girls were tied up, and cut them free. When one of the bikers, a skinny young guy with a Mohawk, noticed what was happening and turned in the Utes' direction, reaching into his belt as he did to grab a ball-peen hammer, I put a 250-grain bullet in his leg. Instead of shouting an alarm, he screamed louder than a gut-shot hog, then fell to the ground and passed out.

Lawana gasped and said, "They have the girls!"

I nodded and watched as Colorow and Goff put arms around and under the girls' shoulders and ushered them back to the trucks. I took a couple more shots to stir up the hive, then watched the Utes make their way back to the trucks through the darkest parts of camp. They piled back in, and when I was sure they were about to turn on their engines, I started firing into every bike and vehicle in the camp, pulling the trigger and reloading as quickly as possible.

When the trucks turned around and rattled off back to the main road, I felt the briefest sense of victory. Until I realized I couldn't find Jury anywhere in the confused crowd of bikers. Lawana and I wouldn't be out of the woods until we were back in the ranch truck and on our way to town.

I fired again at an armed man running toward the base of the mesa, then felt in my pack to reload. *No more shells.* "I'm out," I told Lawana as I lowered my rifle. "We need to go."

Lawana grunted and stood. I did the same, slung the pack and rifle on my back, and started weaving through the trees toward our pickup, hoping we'd make it.

CHAPTER SIXTEEN

Through the dark silhouettes of the trees, as we huffed and puffed our way down the hill, I spotted our truck bursting into flames. I stopped and thrust out an arm to halt Lawana's downward descent. She hit my elbow hard, muttered a curse, and then saw the truck. "How?" she said, panting.

"Not sure," I said, panting even harder. "Looks like Jury spread out his men along the base of the mesa. The ones farthest east found our truck. They're probably humping up the hill on both sides of us. We have to go back up."

A lot of people in this situation would have panicked. Most would, actually. But I saw that determined look in Lawana's eyes. Saying nothing, she pivoted and began climbing at a furious pace.

Struggling to keep up with her, I found myself bear-crawling on the steepest section. *Damned* knees—my ligaments had taken a pounding from running downhill. When Lawana ran into a circular open area between the low trees, I whisper-shouted, "Stay in the trees. Don't make a shadow." She stopped, confused, and a rifle cracked to our right. Lead thumped into a piñon in front of her that looked amazingly like a gnarly old man. Lawana dropped to the ground and covered her head.

My mind raced, trying to see what was happening from a bigger, bird's-eye perspective. While I'd been happily setting fires and causing distractions, Jury must have rallied some of the better men and spread them out. He'd sent them crawling in a line up the hill, using a classic pincer movement, hoping to catch us in a semicircle and then cut us to shreds. If the men hadn't found and burned the truck, they might have done it. Now we had a slight chance of outrunning the line and hiding in whatever lay beyond the rim to the north.

I stumbled and crawled to where Lawana lay swearing in the fallen needles and cones. "We gotta go," I said. I grabbed her by the arm and pulled her to her feet. Just as we made it under the first scraggly branches, another rifle fired from behind, somewhere to our left. A ten-round burst cut into the tree's smaller branches, sending pieces of bark and wood flying.

Lawana looked at me from her half crouch and said, "Damn you." I knew what she was thinking. She'd trusted me to know what I was doing, and now we were very close to not making it.

By this point, I'd shifted almost entirely to muscle memory, my movements dictated by a hundred similar jams I'd been in. I grabbed her hand, found a faster gear in my jog, and whispered, "Shh."

We moved as quickly and as quietly as possible through the trees, and as we did I felt my adrenaline surge. My vision narrowed, sounds turned sharp, and the smells of the fragrant forest intensified. It was like running down a tunnel sprayed with pine perfume.

Lawana slowed to whisper in my ear. "Hide," she said.

I was thinking the same thing. We ran north, hoping that

the men pursuing us would tire enough that we'd lose them. Of course, I was cursing myself for not being fitter. I'd once walked the length of South America, humping over mountains and slogging through jungles with a heavy pack on my back. Lately, though, I'd spent too much time riding my horse. And there was that slight limp in my left leg, the result of a hungry hyena years ago. The one thing in our favor was that Lawana seemed amazingly fit. It was me who was struggling to keep up with her.

As we crested the top of the mesa and took off across the flat sandstone and into the taller piñon trees that led down the other side, I registered that the firing behind us had tailed off. That's when something caught my eye. "Wait," I said. Lawana slowed and gave me an exasperated look, seemingly annoyed that I was delaying our progress. Off the edge of the path I'd noticed a small hole where a tree had fallen over and pulled out its roots. In the hole was a flat red sandstone rock, with another depression under it where water had run off the mesa and moved the softer sand. It looked like the perfect place to hole up, at least until we caught our breath. And by *we*, I meant *I*.

I crawled into the hole and waved her down. She hesitated, noticing how little room there was left for her, but she scrambled next to me when she heard another report of gunfire coming from what might have been a few hundred yards away. "We'll wait here for a bit and see if they're following," I whispered. "When we're sure it's safe we'll sneak off the side of the mesa and try to get to the road." I heard her sigh. I'm sure she was still angry at me, but it was too dark to make out her face. I did feel the heat coming off her body where our hips touched. I also smelled the faint scent of her perfume.

Neither of us said anything for a long while. Instead, we sat in the dark, waiting and listening. I strained to hear footfalls or the muffled voices of men, but it seemed that the bikers had taken a different route, moved off the mesa's top along an alternate path. For some reason, a memory came to me of being ten years old and hiding amid a bunch of old blankets in my room while my mother's violent boyfriend raged down the hall. It had been so peaceful bundled into all that softness that I never wanted to come out. I just wanted to curl up in those blankets forever. I remembered that I'd pulled a thick green wool one over my head and fallen asleep.

"Hey," Lawana whispered, tugging me back to the present. "You think they're gone?"

Our body heat in the small semi-enclosed area had kept the night chill off, which was important. Around us, we heard the sounds of crickets and dead tree limbs rubbing in the wind, but nothing else.

Decision time. "The way I read these guys," I whispered, "they're not the type to deploy in various places on the hill, sit tight, and watch out for us. They don't have the patience. I'm thinking that after they lost us, they headed back to camp to pick out an easier target."

"You mean the people in town?"

"*That* seems more their style."

"Then we've got to find a way back . . . fast."

CHAPTER SEVENTEEN

We made it off the mesa without incident, other than a couple of missteps due to the dim moonlight. Once we were back on the flats, I stopped to try to get my bearings. Around the mesa, to our left, I could see the dim orange glow from the still burning camp. Off to the right was seemingly endless desert scrub. In front of us lay the shimmering thread of the main highway. That meant that the mesa was between us and the town. The only way to get back to town was to either stealthily work toward the highway and try to flag down a rare motorist, or skirt the base of the mesa and hope we weren't seen by the bikers. We could then go back up and cross the mesa again to the east and head on foot down into town—but I didn't think we had the energy.

Unlike me, Lawana didn't hesitate for more than a second. After spotting the far-off strip of asphalt, she started heading in that direction.

I decided to follow, thinking that might be the fastest and easiest way back. But I stopped when I heard the growl of motorcycles and saw the flashes of single headlights. It meant that the few bikes that had survived the attack were out and about, and it also meant that the road was no longer an option. The Reapers might be patrolling, or they might be going into town to make their displeasure known. If it was the former . . .

Lawana must have been thinking the same thing. She turned to me and asked, "What now?"

I stared off into the middle distance, thinking. It seemed like there was only one play. "We have to steal us a vehicle."

She rolled her eyes. "I'll bet you hotwire cars, too, right? Well, if you haven't noticed, there aren't any parking lots around here."

"Actually, I did notice," I said, smiling. "That's why we're going to the Reapers' camp. Maybe we can make off with their van or truck."

Now Lawana glared at me. "I think you're absolutely out of your mind."

I put my hands up defensively. "Just trust me on this. We'll scout things out. If there's no safe way to do it, we'll figure out something else. But I'll bet most of the hornets have left the nest. They're riled up and they want to plant their stingers in as many Utes as they can."

She sighed again. That sound was getting familiar. "Why do I keep listening to you? You obviously *like* danger. You *like* risking your life."

"No, that's where you're wrong," I said, meaning it. "And you're the last person I want anything to happen to."

I don't know, maybe she felt my sincerity. Maybe she felt as though she didn't have any other option but to tag along. Reluctantly, she fell into step beside me as we headed toward the shifting glow of the fire that still lit the Reapers' camp.

About ten minutes later we were working our way through the greasewood and rabbit brush when Lawana stopped so fast I nearly ran her over. When I pivoted slightly around her to avoid a collision, I saw why she'd brought both hands to her mouth.

On the ground lay two corpses. Both were clothed in what looked like blue military fatigues, and the stink emanating from them was worse than week-old roadkill. But there were no roads here. No vehicles. So how had they wound up in this ditch? By the glow of the fire in the distance, I guessed the camp to be less than a mile away, and I figured this grisly scene probably had something to do with the bikers. I bent down to inspect the bodies.

"Don't *touch* them," Lawana said, grabbing my shoulder with that strong grip of hers. "It's a crime scene, Clyde. You can't mess it up."

I looked up at her and said, "Your cop is in the clinic, and you said the Feds don't come here. I'm going to find out what happened." With my left hand pinching my nose against the smell, I knelt down next to the corpses and looked them over. Two males, both young, had been shot in the back of the head with a small-caliber weapon. They did have uniforms, and the patches told me that Jenner and Kardin were both in the U.S. Air Force. *Were*. Before they were murdered.

"This isn't good," I said, standing. I walked about twenty feet away from the smell and asked, "I don't suppose your cell phone has service?"

"No such luck," she said, without checking.

"Why?"

"Because the cell companies don't want to spend money putting in towers and fiber in places that don't have any money."

I nodded. Made sense, sort of. In Africa I'd seen cell towers in a lot of remote places, but it was probably because there was no other infrastructure. If we couldn't call, we were definitely on our own. "These men were executed," I said.

"What?"

"Both shot in the back of the head, and the angle looks like they were kneeling when it happened," I said.

She went over to the bodies, gagged, swallowed, then bent down for a closer inspection. "So, what does it mean? Air force?"

"I have no idea," I said, trying to think. I wasn't too familiar with the area. "Is there a base anywhere close?"

"No."

Bikers, air force, that strange little guy named Orval—something was going on, something bigger than just a group of assholes messing with some Natives. And now I was curious. "Where's the closest one?"

"Hill Air Force Base, I think."

"Huh. These guys are a long way from Salt Lake City. We need to find out what's going on," I said.

Lawana shook her head. "No. *We* don't. *We* need to get back to town and *we* need to call in outside help, because of *this*." She waved at the bodies and toward the bikers' camp. "This is too much. The Feds, as lazy as they are, will have to step in."

"Ah yes, the town." It reminded us both of what we needed to do.

WE LEFT THE BODIES AS they were and moved to a spot maybe a hundred yards from the camp. The bike fire had burned itself out, leaving a blackened spot in the brush that looked like a bottomless hole. We couldn't hear any bikers, which was encouraging, so we crept closer. It looked as though most of the bikes were beyond repair, and the ones I'd left alone were missing.

I began whispering to Lawana about whether we should try to steal the van or the truck, but she shushed me.

"What?" I asked softly.

"Listen." She pointed to the bikers' tents. I didn't hear it at first, and wondered if too many rifle shots had damaged my hearing. Then the mumbling of voices turned to actual words in the wind. It was Jury, yelling at his brothers.

"Who told them they could go into town?"

Indistinct murmuring.

"Goddamn unacceptable. Take the van and go get them. Tell Gunner his Nomads won't get a cut of any of this if they don't come back now."

Someone spoke up, almost as loud as Jury. Gravelly voice, determined. Had to be his second-in-command, a sergeant or vice president or however the chain of command ran in the biker world. "What do we tell Orval if we run into him?"

More murmurs, then Jury's outraged voice: "Tell him I have everything under control. The truck's been repainted, it's secure, and I'll make sure Gunner and his guys don't pull any more shit. We'll be ready whenever the buyer finally shows up."

Even more murmuring, then Jury said, "I know. This should have been over a week ago. Some Customs bullshit. The guy got held up. We just have to keep a leash on the Nomads for a couple more days, tops."

The voices went back to a low mumble, lost in the wind and the other desert sounds of far-off coyotes and crickets. Soon after, we heard the van start and rumble down the road.

I looked at Lawana, who was already looking at me, and said, "We're taking the truck."

CHAPTER EIGHTEEN

Getting to the truck wasn't a problem. Just a simple matter of crouching beneath the tall sage and running quietly back toward the main road, following the rabbit and cow trails. It took maybe six minutes for us to work back to where we'd first seen Jury and his cronies wandering around the semi.

Now there were three guards circling the large Peterbilt truck hitched to a fifty-three-foot-long box trailer. It took the men a while to walk a perimeter around the vehicle in the pale moonlight, and we watched them from a low spot of prairie dog holes behind more tall sage. We couldn't talk, not this close to heavily armed men who were definitely a little pissed off, but we could both wonder about each other's thoughts.

If I were betting, my money would be on Lawana thinking, *No way* the instant she saw those three men circling. With no effective weapon to use against them, since we were out of ammo and the pistol had been in the ranch truck, it wasn't realistic to think we could make off with the semi. Then Jury marched into view.

I looked over and saw Lawana scrunch her face in either

deep thought or hatred—it was hard to tell. Before I could signal to her, Jury started yelling at the guards.

"Thumper, Chow, get back to camp. Keep an eye on the tents, and watch for those shooters if they're stupid enough to come back around. I'm staying with Stank to watch the truck."

Two of the guards started slowly back to camp. "Get your ass in gear!" Jury shouted, and the men started jogging.

The last guy left, Stank, asked, "You want me by the road, or here?"

"Road. Don't let anybody in, or I'll stick my foot so far up your ass you'll taste boot leather."

Stank looked more than a little intimidated. "You got it, boss."

And with that command, the truck was again an option. Stank wandered into the darkness, down the dirt road toward the pavement. And behind cover in the thick brush, I took off my boot.

Lawana looked at me as if I'd lost my mind. Her thin eyebrows rose even higher when she saw me take off my sock and put my boot back on. In simple sign language, I tried to tell her to stay put while I went after Jury. She shook her head frantically, obviously not convinced I was likely to prevail. I handed her my now useless rifle and pointed at the holey ground we were sitting on. She nodded, but gave me that look all doctors do when you tell them you smoke: deep concern mixed with bewildered disbelief that people make such horrible choices.

I smiled, found a baseball-size rock, and stuffed it in the sock. I stood and took my improvised blackjack with me as I worked through the brush toward Jury. Of course, what I was about to do might have been easier if I'd held on to my pistol, but I'd left it in the ranch truck, which was now burned to a crisp. And besides, firing a shot would have alerted the other Reapers.

Placing my feet ever so carefully, I felt a little bit like David with his slingshot about to take on Goliath.

At that moment Jury was standing by the back of the semi's trailer, his tattooed arms folded, staring at the moon. He was wearing only his vest and jeans. A soft, warm breeze rustled his goatee, and he somehow looked even bigger in the gray light.

Seeds and pollen from the sagebrush fell like snow as I worked my way closer, covering my shirt and hat brim. I wiped some stray ones from my face and focused on the muscular man twenty feet in front of me. He was still staring up, grumbling something to himself, and I moved from the brush to the wide-open spot where the truck was parked.

I gingerly took two steps, being careful to put my foot down softly and feel for anything that would make noise. Three more steps and I'd be right behind him, where a well-swung sock would drop him. But sometimes luck isn't on your side.

Just before I took another step, a jackrabbit leaped from beneath the trailer and ran on its extra-long legs around Jury and right beside me, chased by some unknown night predator. Jury watched it pass, his gaze following the long-eared critter's blur as it raced by me, then his eyes narrowed. He reached into his jacket and I ran at him. I've heard that if you're within twenty feet of an opponent with a gun, you can get to them before they shoot. I was only six away and made it to him well before that happened. He'd barely gotten his hand around whatever was in his shoulder harness when my sock connected with his jaw.

I'd swung from down low, and used my momentum to

add some oomph to the smack. A normal person would have dropped like a dead man, but Jury only staggered a couple of steps sideways. He shook his head as I brought the sock around for another swing. This time I went from high to low and whipped the sock between Jury's legs. Another shot that would drop a mortal. Jury's face went slack, turning the closest shade to green you can get in the moonlight, but he still managed to get the pistol out of his shoulder rig.

He brought the gun around, raised it to sight with a barely shaky hand, and I hit the hand with the rock-in-a-sock. This time it didn't matter how strong he was. The nerves in his hand must have all been going haywire, because the gun dropped to the ground. I stomped at his knee while whirling the sock back around for another whack. He took the stomp without a whimper, then lunged for the fallen pistol. He was just about to reach it when he heard the sound of the semi's engine turning over. For an instant he paused.

I paused for a millisecond, too, wondering who was starting it. That frozen moment almost cost me my life.

Jury swept his long arm down and snatched up the pistol with his better hand. Brought it back around and took a quick shot.

I'd forgotten the truck and was already attacking. His aim wasn't as good with his off hand, and the bullet sped by my left ear, maybe a foot away. I moved around the outstretched gun arm and brought the rock down on the bridge of his nose. Another crack and blood flowed from both nostrils. He didn't drop the gun, but he didn't shoot again, either. This time he looked genuinely stunned.

So I whipped the rock up and around, put my hips into it, and thwacked it into the side of his neck. The pistol dropped, and a half second later the big biker did, too. I dropped the sock, searched Jury's pockets, grabbed the pistol, and ran.

Then I was in the cab of the semi, watching Lawana's rear as she scooted over to the passenger seat. "Where the *hell* did you get those keys?" I said. I'd gone to all that trouble to liberate a set of keys from Jury's front pocket and here she'd accomplished the same feat without breaking a sweat.

"A guy in town, Bear—he drives long haul. Says that truckers lock themselves out all the time, and that a lot of 'em zip-tie a spare key under the hood."

"Good to know." I reached for the clutch to get us the hell out of there, but didn't find one. I studied the dash and the cab, and was shocked to see that it was an automatic. All the big rigs I'd driven had between ten and eighteen gears, and you either had to be good or not mind the sound of grinding gears. This would be a hell of a lot easier. I punched the button to release the air brakes, heard the hiss, put it in drive, and dieseled out of the wide spot, heading for the main highway.

CHAPTER NINETEEN

We'd barely made it to the highway and Lawana was saying over and over, "Please hurry." I glanced at her and she didn't look so good.

"Hey, you okay?"

She seemed glassy-eyed, in shock almost.

More loudly, I said, "Are you *okay*?"

That seemed to snap her out of it. Her eyes refocused. "I can't believe I did that," she said. "Making a run for the truck and starting it up. What was I thinking? If you hadn't taken care of that guy . . ."

I'd seen this before: an ordinary person finds themselves in tough circumstances and discovers an ability to run *into* danger rather than away from it. Afterward, when they realize what they've done, what was at risk, they get real shaky.

"You did good. You saved us some time. I guess you've got that warrior spirit Taylor talks about."

"Taylor?" Her face clouded over. "He'll be so worried about me. We've got to get back. Please go faster."

"Sure," I said, "I'll just turn on the turbo boosters." I made a plane motion with my hand and added a little buzzing sound. I thought it was funny. Lawana didn't.

"Just drive, okay?"

"At your service, ma'am." I'd looked around for Stank as we pulled out. That shot Jury had taken at me had to have alerted the other bikers. But somehow we'd made a clean getaway. I wondered if the Reapers had any working vehicles left to pursue us.

A few minutes later, Lawana was staring at what seemed to be dozens of gauges and digital displays on the truck's dashboard. "Pretty fancy rig," she said. She ran her hand along the console, found the radio dial, and turned it. The station, X96, had just ended a song by a group called Rise Against when an announcer cut in:

"The Level 5 terror alert for the western U.S. remains in effect, with few details coming from federal or local authorities. We *have* been told that all major sports and entertainment events will remain canceled, pending further notice. Also, a twelve p.m. curfew remains in effect for all but police and public safety officials. Our correspondent Ned Marshall reported an hour ago from the FBI's field office in Salt Lake that counter-terror agencies are conducting extensive helicopter sweeps of Utah, eastern Nevada, southern Idaho, and western Wyoming. We will provide more information as soon as it is available. This concludes this special report." With that the music resumed.

There it was again. This terror thing seemed to have been the backdrop to everything I'd been doing since riding my horse into Ute country. It felt as if someone was sending me a message but I was too stupid to understand it. As we continued barreling down the highway, I kept gnawing on it. What was I missing? Then it came to me. *Of course.*

I stomped on the big brake pedal, heard more hissing, and eased the behemoth to the shoulder.

"Why are we stopping?" Lawana asked.

"I have a bad feeling about this truck."

"What do you mean?" She looked frightened.

"I think this rig is what the government is looking for." I reached behind the seat, grabbed my pack, and began digging inside it, shoving aside the pistol I'd recovered from Jury and pushing my fingers into an inner pocket to find a small tactical flashlight. Then I crawled down out of the cab. Lawana appeared beside me.

"Shouldn't we be getting to town?"

"I just want to take a peek," I explained, "see what's so important. It could affect what we're doing."

For a moment she seemed ready to object, but then she nodded.

No traffic appeared as we walked in the moonlight to the back of the rig. The heavy doors were locked. I ran the light over the side of the trailer, looking for placards. There weren't any, but there were the telltale indentations of former ones. A few seconds later, I confirmed that the trailer had been recently painted.

"Yeah, we heard Jury say something about that," Lawana said. "They wanted to hide it. You think the bodies we found were the drivers?"

"It fits. A truck that a group of psychos is protecting, a couple of dead military personnel, a man in town threatening me."

"But if they've got helicopters looking everywhere for a truck, wouldn't one parked out in the middle of the desert all by itself attract attention—new paint job or not?"

I ran my fingers through my beard. "Well, we haven't seen

any choppers yet. The government doesn't seem to be looking here for some reason. Anyway, I get the sense from what we heard that someone threw a monkey wrench into the bikers' perfect plan, even before *we* showed up."

She shrugged. "So you want to see what's in there?"

"Uh-huh."

I opened my pack and grabbed my lock tools, then examined the locks. Easy and cheap padlocks that didn't seem especially secure. But I also saw what seemed like broken welds. I had a feeling that there'd been different locks on here before, but that the bikers, after destroying them, had swapped in some Kmart specials. It only took a couple of minutes to rake open the locks, drop them in the dirt, and throw open the doors. When I stared inside, I wasn't sure at first what I was looking at.

"What are *those*?" Lawana asked, squinting.

I wasn't sure. They kind of looked like three metal flying dinosaurs, all padded up and secured to the side walls. I hopped up inside the truck and swept my flashlight over them. They appeared to be small planes.

Each was three feet tall, maybe eight feet long. They cast strange shadows on the stacks of steel boxes that were positioned in front of them. Lawana climbed into the trailer with me, and we checked the planes more closely. They looked like little polymer versions of the Russian-made bombers I'd seen laying waste to towns and villages in Africa. Except these had no cockpit, and there was a strange camera-looking thing on each of their bellies. The wings, which just barely fit inside the trailer, had mounts underneath to hold God knows what.

I stepped over the wings and made my way to the front of the trailer. As I did, I asked Lawana, "Drones?"

She knelt by one, ran a long-fingered hand over the wing. "I think so. God, this is bad."

I'd heard about them, on the radio and in the papers I picked up in random towns, but I hadn't paid much attention. I'd just recently learned how to turn on a computer—barely, when a nice lady in a library showed me how—and the majority of the tech stuff was beyond me. That's what living in the third world for sixteen years will do to you. "You know anything about these things?" I asked Lawana.

She gave a little shrug. "They didn't teach us about drones in medical school, but I remember Taylor watching a TV program about them one night. The newest ones can take pictures, drop bombs, shoot missiles. I don't remember seeing any that looked like these, though."

I shook my head. "It doesn't make sense. I mean, yeah, I get it. These contraptions would be lethal toys for someone to get hold of—*if* that person knew how to pilot them. Stealing them is serious, but . . . why is the government putting the entire western U.S. on lockdown?"

"You think we're missing something?" Lawana asked, sitting on one of the steel boxes.

I looked at the box beneath her and something shifted into place. "You mind getting off that for a second?"

She gave me a puzzled look and stood up.

I bent down and tried to turn the box, which was unexpectedly heavy, so I could see the rear.

"Oh boy."

"What?"

I motioned her over and pointed at the box's back surface. There was an elaborate digital combination lock system and a blinking red light. Also a sign stenciled in white: EXTREMELY

HAZARDOUS: AUTHORIZED PERSONNEL ONLY. "I'm betting that whatever missiles these mechanical birds fire are inside these boxes, and I don't think they're garden-variety bombs."

"What are you saying? That they might be chemical? Or nuclear?" When I shrugged, her eyes widened further. "But if these things are that dangerous, why just a single truck driven by two men?"

I ran a hand through my hair. "Just a theory, but this truck might have been traveling as part of a convoy. Maybe there was some sort of deception, a switch. Who knows? The only thing we know for sure is that if the government is as freaked out as they are, that means these birds can be put in the air pretty quickly and kill a lot of people."

"So you're saying . . . what?"

I looked Lawana in the eye. "I'm saying we have to hide the trailer."

"What? *Where?*"

"Don't know," I said. "You know the area. You tell me." I was already backing up and hopping down out of the truck, afraid that I'd accidentally make something go boom. This much technology in such a small space made me nervous. I wanted out, back under the stars.

Lawana followed right behind.

After we'd gingerly closed the doors, I looked expectantly at Lawana and saw that her face was filled with a mix of emotions. Part of her, I'm sure, wanted none of this. She just wanted to get to town, verify that a war hadn't started. But another part was probably saying, *We can't let the wrong people get this truck.* After a few moments, her face settled into that familiar look of determination I'd come to recognize. "Drive north for a mile," she said, "then take a right at the widest gravel road. It leads to the gas fields. We can hide it there."

For once, it felt good to follow someone else's plan. As I turned the truck around and began driving back the way we'd come, Lawana explained what she had in mind. "In the field, they park trailers all the time. On most of the pads. They don't look any different from this one, so no one will notice it for a couple of days."

It made sense to me. I kept my foot on the pedal for another minute until I saw her pointing ahead.

"That's the one. Take that road," she said.

Yes, ma'am. We rumbled and bounced down a heavily graveled road that led into an even drabber desert. Here, there wasn't even the prolific sage or greasewood. Just fist-size plants I didn't recognize popping out of the clay, making the ground under the moonlight look macabre and desperate.

After another ten minutes on the same bumpy road, Lawana told me to take a left onto a thin strip of asphalt leading to a flat spot. I spun the steering wheel and wheedled the truck down the narrow path, stopping at the graded pad next to a couple of cylindrical tanks. In the center of the pad were a series of connected pipes, which I assumed to be the wellhead.

"Back up over by the other trailer," Lawana said as she rolled her window down and stuck her head out. A single blue-and-white trailer was jammed against a dirt pile on the far side of the pad. I wriggled the truck around, lined up, and watched the ass of the trailer as I attempted to back it next to its friend.

Didn't work. Not the first time. Or the second. It took me four tries to back the long trailer close to its cousin, maybe due to lack of practice, or to my being better on horseback than behind the wheel of a big rig.

Lawana shook her head when I finally pulled the air brakes and went about dropping the trailer.

"Finally, something you're terrible at," she said, giving me the smallest smile. "So Clyde Barr *isn't* perfect."

I wanted to tell her I was terrible at a lot of things, but she kept going. "The fighting, the shooting, the lock picking, the sock thing? It's nice to know you can mess up."

"Actually," I said, "I'm pretty good at *that*, too—messing up."

CHAPTER TWENTY

With the trailer behind us in the gas field, the truck engine was responding more obligingly to my foot on the pedal, so I tried to make up ground once we were out on the main highway. I watched the speedometer as it inched up to seventy miles per hour, and fought to ignore my empty stomach. It must have been eleven o'clock by now, and I hadn't eaten since returning to the ranch from town about nine hours earlier. Plus, I was bone tired. It took a conscious effort to keep my eyes on the dark road.

Lawana, by contrast, seemed jumpy. There was a plastic storage compartment between us, so she occupied herself for a minute investigating the interior, coming up with a first aid kit, a can of chewing tobacco, and a tire gauge. She next turned to the glove compartment and a second later let out a whoop of triumph.

"What?" I asked.

She looked like a little girl at Christmas as she held aloft a king-size Baby Ruth candy bar. "I just found dinner!"

I struggled to not rip the candy bar out of her hands so I could eat all of it. Instead, I teased her a little. "Wait a minute, you're a doctor. Isn't all that sugar bad for you? That's packaged diabetes you're holding."

"You saying you don't want any?"

"Well, I didn't say *that*."

Carefully, she separated the bar into two even pieces and handed me one. As we both happily munched I noticed the wind picking up strong enough now to push the truck around. Dried thistles and mustards tumbled across the road in front of us.

"A storm?" Lawana said, stating the obvious.

"Looks like," I said, shaking my head. "We can't catch a break."

Lightning began flashing in the distance, turning the basin a baby blue. Occasionally, sand blasted the side of the truck, the gritty scraping drowning out the sound of the diesel engine. It looked like we might be in for a hell of a weather event.

"Does this truck go any faster?" Lawana asked, growing concerned now.

"It does, but if I push it any harder in this windstorm we'll end up in a ditch."

Rain started splattering against the windshield, mixing with the dust and making the glass muddy. The engine and the bowling alley sounds of the thunderheads were the only noises to crack the quiet. In the now almost constant flashing of lightning I saw the clouds bunching up against a nearby mesa like cattle on a fence. The storm was ratcheting up to a scary crescendo, but luckily it was happening miles away.

We rounded a corner near a narrow bridge spanning a wash, and I saw headlights. My heart fell into my stomach. They'd found us.

"Don't worry," Lawana said. "It's another truck. Probably an oil field tanker."

When the yellow lights drew closer, I relaxed a little, realizing she was right. The truck barreling toward us was a dirtier, older version of the one we were riding in, but pulling a water trailer. Trouble was, the driver was taking up all of the road, running his rig down the middle of the asphalt.

"Let him by," Lawana said, an edge of fear in her voice. It came out as more of a parental command.

I pulled the wheel to the right and worked the brake. The back end of the truck, without the weight of the trailer, fishtailed in the loose sand near the edge of the road. It was a Herculean effort to keep the truck from rolling, but I at least managed to slow down a little while keeping it straight.

"Move over, for God's sake," Lawana said again as the oncoming truck charged closer.

"Trying." I couldn't move farther off the road because of the deep bar ditch and the upcoming bridge, so I worked on slowing us down, jamming the brake to the floor. Hissing filled the cab as the air that kept the brakes off released. The back eight tires locked up, and I almost pulled the wheel from its mount trying to keep us from spinning around. I managed to get over just enough for the other truck to pass. It didn't matter, though, because instead of roaring past us, it swerved to slam into us.

CHAPTER TWENTY-ONE

We managed to slide past the angry truck, but flew off the opposite side of the road, bounced off the bridge's guard-rail, and slammed into the wash.

The sound of thunder mixed with the wail of crunching steel and the popping of tires as the smell of fuel oil and wet earth filled the cab. My safety belt dug into my shoulder as the roof crumpled and shoved me into my seat. There was a brief, sweet blackness, then I came back and went into emergency mode. Time slowed and the steps seemed easy and simple. I cut off my seat belt, then reached over and cut the belt securing Lawana, who was, thankfully, conscious. We didn't fall into the roof, so we weren't upside down, and that made punching out a window and sliding out into the rain that much easier. After I escaped the truck, I helped out Lawana, who seemed a bit shaky. Then I reached in, found my pack, and slipped it on.

"You okay?" I asked as I stepped toward her and looked her over.

"I think so," she said in a voice that seemed uncertain. She became her own patient for a moment and patted herself down. When she was positive she was okay, she said, "My God, that driver is worse than you."

At almost the same time the driver was mentioned, we heard the unmistakable sound of a vehicle braking. Then the backup alarm from a large truck.

"That driver is a Reaper," I said, wishing to hell I still had my rifle. In the chaos of stealing the truck, Lawana had left it in the bushes. Oh, well. I reached into my pack and grabbed the pistol I'd taken from Jury. I dropped the magazine: five shells, plus the one still in the chamber. It made me feel a little better, but not the same as having a tool to reach out with.

"No way," Lawana said. "How—" She didn't get a chance to finish her question. Gunshots boomed in unison with the thunder. I had no idea how close the bullets came, because the rain pissing into the puddles drowned out any whizzing I might have heard. I grabbed Lawana's arm and started dragging her toward a bend in the wash where we'd be hidden from the road. "Come on."

She pushed her long, wet hair out of her eyes and followed a step behind.

I led her to a narrow deer trail that zig-zagged out of the gully. Once we were up and out of the small stream of run-off, I found a piñon big enough to shelter us from half of the rain. Underneath was at least a year's worth of sheep pellets, meaning that it was a popular place to take refuge. I turned to Lawana and touched her lightly on the shoulder.

"Okay, here's the plan," I said, slipping out of my pack. "You hold on to my pack and wait here. Also, take this," I said, handing her the pistol, "and shoot at anyone you see who isn't me."

She stared uncomprehendingly at the pistol as I began walking off. "Dammit, Barr. Where are you going?"

I stopped and turned. "Wait for me. I'll end this, and then we'll find a way back. I promise."

Her eyes bored into me. "Like you promised to keep us safe?"

"Just wait."

WHEN I WAS MAYBE TEN yards from the bridge, I stopped, feeling the thick mud and debris flow around my legs. "You want us?" I yelled up to the vehicle above. "Then come and get us."

Over the cacophony of the storm and shooting, I heard a voice—Jury's!—shouting orders. *Of course* he was here. Who else would be so persistent? He ordered his men into the swelling gully.

I sloshed under the bridge, hoping that the bikers would run to where I'd been, then I worked my way up the slippery slope. I had to use stringy rabbit brush and sage as handholds and rope, but I eventually pulled myself up to the road. And just in time.

In the next brief flash of lightning, I saw the wall of water and mud that I'd known for minutes was inevitably churning its way toward the bridge. I'd heard it coming, knew what it was, and I hoped that Jury didn't. I was right.

Flash floods are the single most unappreciated event in the desert, until you're the one caught in one. Thousands of gallons of rain, running off rocks and sand, turn into mud that is funneled into narrow gullies and washes, eventually picking up trees and more rocks. The force of the roaring water pushes the whole mess at a speed faster than most would expect, and catches unawares anyone and anything that stands in its way.

Thankfully, I was aware.

The bikers weren't.

A long string of flashes illuminated the flailing bodies. I thought I spotted two of them—their leather-clad arms reaching for a sky they'd never see again. Even over the roar of the rain and the crashing of thunder, I heard the shouts, which were soon muffled forever by mud.

Now the odds were a little more even.

I worked my way through the dripping rabbit brush to the bridge. Jury was swearing, leaning against the steaming radiator of his oil-field truck. He was alone. He'd been overconfident, sending his helpers into the wash to take us out, and now he was going to pay for it—*if* I could figure out a way to beat a monster of a man holding an assault rifle.

I crawled through the soggy cheat grass, under sodden brush, until I was close enough for Jury to hear me shout, "Hey, ugly!"

He answered with a burst of rifle fire that ripped into the mud to my right. I rolled to the left. "Put down the gun," I shouted, then rolled farther left. He fired again, hitting the spot I'd yelled from. My pants and shirt were now soaked, and a chill had started to creep into my bones. "I'll put the sock away and we can settle this like gentlemen."

He fired a couple more rounds, then I heard him curse and the shooting briefly stopped. I crawled forward as fast as I could to a tall clump of sagebrush. Huddled there while he reloaded. "That you, bumpkin?" he said, his voice muffled by the pouring rain.

I didn't answer. Instead, I slithered through the mud to the road.

"I'll put the gun down if you come out and play," Jury

said. I could still see him through the brush at the edge of the road, and he sure hadn't put the gun down. He slammed another magazine into the weapon and pulled the charging handle. He moved to the guardrail and looked to the brush where I'd been a minute ago. Water poured down his goatee and onto his slick vest.

While Jury was busy searching for me, I jumped up and ran to his truck. He was on the passenger side of the vehicle, still looking for me, as I padded to the driver's door. I creaked it open, using the thunder to conceal the sound, then crawled into the seat. The truck was still idling. I put it in gear, but had to grind the transmission to find first, and Jury heard it. He wheeled around and fired into the engine and the windshield. The glass shattered and alarms buzzed as coolant and oil started leaking from the truck. Didn't matter, because by then I'd found the gear and popped the clutch. The truck jumped and I spun the wheel, trying to pin Jury against the rail.

He was faster than I thought, and jumped away like a startled hyena. I braked, tried to find reverse, and Jury unloaded the rest of his magazine into the cab. Lead ripped through metal and plastic and seats. I felt a bullet graze my right arm as I ground the truck into reverse and sensed it leap backward.

With rain pouring into the cab from the shattered side windows, I found first gear and jammed it in. Jury was fumbling with his rifle, trying to reload, but the gusts of rain made both the metal and his fingers slick. I gunned the engine and made another run at the big man.

He swung the rifle up and got off two random shots before he had to turn and run. He dashed and splashed down the middle of the road, trying to get off the bridge, out of the narrow guardrails, and off the pavement.

I skipped a couple of gears and the truck jerked slightly but kept moving forward, gaining on the biker. Alarms buzzed as gauges for oil pressure and engine temperature spun wildly. As I pulled up beside the sprinting Reaper, I felt the truck's engine cough and the vehicle start to slow. When it did, I jerked the wheel and stomped the brake, crashing the front into the rail, but stopping before it broke through. It was a maneuver that succeeded in cutting off Jury's escape route.

He stumbled to a stop and raised the rifle again, and I ducked behind the dripping and steaming dash. No shots. Just the sound of thunder. Then swearing from Jury as he rushed over and grabbed the door handle.

Before he could get the door all the way open, though, I mule-kicked it with both feet and heard the big man grunt and swear.

I jumped out. He was staggering back as I dropped from the cab and ran at him. He recovered just before I reached him and tried to swing the rifle like a bat, aiming for my head.

I ducked, let it swing past, then grabbed the end of the rifle and shoved a palm under the big man's chin. He didn't want to lose control of the gun, so he didn't defend the jab. His head shot back and I kicked him in the knee. He didn't flinch, but his grip on the rifle loosened, and I shoved the stock farther back. Once I ripped it out of his meaty paws, I tossed it into the diminishing flood beneath us.

When I looked back at Jury, I noticed that his entire head was a mass of bruises. I also noticed that he was smiling.

He took a step forward, saying, "Not this time," and I hit him. I hit him harder than I'd hit anyone in a long time. I twisted, pushed off the back foot, and landed a balled-up hammerfist on his ear. The smile disappeared. He faked a huge haymaker and shot a jab out with the other hand. His fist smashed into my stomach, and it felt like I'd been kicked by a Belgian draft horse. The air whooshed out of my lungs, and I almost fell. If I hadn't been in hundreds of these little spats, I would have.

Instead, I let myself get mad. I swatted away a couple of bad punches and started thinking about how this guy I was fighting was to blame for everything I hated in the world—for the boy the bikers had put in the hospital, for the way they'd treated the women in town, for whatever had been in that air force truck that was stolen and maybe had the potential to kill thousands of people, for the painful life my mother had led, for my sister Jen, who deserved better, and for a certain girl who'd trusted me too much and paid for it with her life. I also thought of every child I'd seen who'd been forced to close their eyes for the last time in a hundred villages across the third world because of some greedy bastard somewhere who wanted *more.* I used *all* of it—all the anger—and I laid into Jury with everything I had.

But Jury hadn't gotten to be king of the jungle by being a pushover. Somehow, he bulled through my hammering fists and caught me in one of his lung-crushing bear hugs. He pushed me down, and as I felt his bulk settle on me I also felt a rib crack. A moment later, a hand was reaching up to clutch at my windpipe, and that's when I felt him suddenly jerk back. There was blessed relief as my rib cage was finally able to expand enough to breathe.

I shook my head, groaned, and pushed up to an elbow. Jury was struggling in a sitting position, both of his hands around his neck, fighting with something that was choking him. It took me a second to realize that the moon was back out, and then a little longer to realize that there was a rope closing tighter and tighter around his neck.

Six feet behind Jury stood Lawana, pulling hard in a two-man tug-of-war and wrapping the end of her rope around the bumper of the tanker truck. When my eyes adjusted further, I saw that the rope wasn't actually rope. It was thinner. I gave up trying to figure out what it was and decided to use the advantage Lawana had given me.

I thought about sending my foot crashing into Jury's head, but worried that would be too little. Almost by reflex, my knife appeared in my hand. I was scooting forward to grab the biker's jacket and drive the blade into his chest when Lawana called out.

"N-o-o-o, Clyde. Not that!"

I raised the knife anyway and was about to swing it deep when Jury gave a sputtering cough and his body suddenly relaxed. He'd passed out.

CHAPTER TWENTY-TWO

The rain had started to move north. Under a desert sky lit with patchy stars and a brightening moon, I rolled to my back and watched Lawana drop the rope—or whatever it was—and run forward. For a brief instant I thought she was going to grab me and ask if I was okay. Instead, she ran straight to Jury's unmoving bulk, where she knelt and felt for a pulse. I didn't understand, and rolled to my side to look at them both.

"Leave him," I said.

She looked frantic. "I'm worried I killed him."

I spat blood on the ground. "You should be worried that you *didn't* kill him."

She stood in a half crouch and grabbed at his shoulders. "Well, at least help me move him out of the road."

Again, I was a little confused. "Uh, that guy was trying to kill us. He almost killed *me* just now. And you're worried about him getting run over?" If I didn't feel completely busted up, I might have laughed.

She tried dragging Jury's bulk to the truck, but she may as well have been pulling on a giant slab of granite. She gave me a pleading look, as if to say, *You owe me one.* I supposed

I did. Slowly, I staggered to my feet and shuffled over to the sweaty mass of flesh that was sitting in the middle of the road. "I'll take the arms," I said, "and you, Florence Nightingale, can help by picking up his feet." Together, we managed to get the bulky body to the truck. The dragging almost did me in, and it definitely didn't help my grating rib, which might have been more than cracked. It took the rest of my energy to work the big man out of his vest and stuff it in my pack.

"Why'd you take his vest?" Lawana asked.

"I might have a use for it," I said, declining to elaborate.

"Thanks for the full explanation," she said, rolling her eyes. She watched as I crouched over Jury's body and shoved it under the truck. "He may have a skull fracture," she said worriedly.

"One can only hope."

She looked at me, exasperated.

I decided to change the subject. "You know, I had it handled before you came along and did your lariat routine. I was just beginning to tire him out."

She smiled. "You are so full of shit, Clyde. It's a good thing I found that cord in your pack—*and* that I did a lot of roping as a kid."

So that's where she got the rope. I looked on the ground near her feet and for the first time registered the twenty-five-foot paracord that I usually kept with me. "I hesitate to ask, but . . ."

"I know what you're going to say. I'm sorry—I lost the pistol."

"How?" I asked, making no effort to hide my frustration.

"Well, after you left I heard all those gunshots, and I got scared, and I was making my way up the gully when I tripped and the gun fell into the water that was rushing through. I tried reaching for it, but it was dark and—"

"No more gun."

"Uh-huh." She watched as I stuffed the paracord back into my pack and slipped the pack's wide straps on my shoulders.

"So, what now?" I asked. "We're stuck here with two dead trucks and it's the middle of the night."

She nodded and looked around, considering options. "We've *got* to get back to town. And it doesn't seem safe to take the road."

"So that means?" I asked, dreading the answer. It was past midnight and all I wanted to do was sleep.

"We head through the desert."

CHAPTER TWENTY-THREE

In a dream that seemed impossibly real I was a little boy again, maybe eight, sitting crouched by a campfire, feeling colder and colder as the flames dwindled. I reached down and clutched at a pile of twigs, throwing them into the flames, but the twisty orange tendrils didn't seem to want them. The twigs just lay there, failing to catch. I grew colder and colder. As the last ember was about to fade, a fog bank suddenly moved in, bringing with it much-needed warmth. The mist seemed to envelop me like a blanket, and I felt myself reaching toward the blanket and bringing it closer. Its surface seemed especially soft, like the touch of a woman's skin.

I woke up to realize I was lightly touching Lawana's face. Damn. How long had I been asleep?

We'd started off on our five-mile journey through the desert hoping that, despite both of us being bone tired, our progress would be steady and the ordeal short. After all, the desert looked relatively flat, other than the big bluffs in the middle. But what we found when we started hoofing it was a mess of wrinkles, as if someone had taken a map, wadded it up, and tried to smooth it out. But not very well.

The downpour we'd experienced had cut deep into the soft sand, leaving the harder rocks but creating a maze of dry streams and riverbeds. If it were the grassy plains we'd been crossing, we might have averaged three or four miles per hour. But here, cutting cross-country, climbing up and down the washes and dodging brush, the journey felt endless.

After only a couple of miles, with my rib hurting like hell and both of us knocking into each other out of fatigue, I suggested we sit down for a short while to recharge our batteries. Lawana didn't exactly put up a fight. The last thing I remembered was her sitting about a foot away from me as we nestled beneath a big boulder.

Now, in the gray predawn light, I caught a glimpse of a snowshoe rabbit bolting out of its hiding place, which reminded me that I hadn't eaten anything besides that candy bar in what seemed like forever. What I would give right now for some rabbit stew.

I glanced at Lawana, still fast asleep. Unsurprisingly, both of us were filthy after clambering through the mud in that confrontation with Jury—me especially—but for some reason the splotches of mud on Lawana's face and her tangled hair didn't diminish her beauty. Fact is, I could have happily contemplated that face for another few minutes, but I made the mistake of shifting my position and that was enough to stir Lawana awake.

"Where are we?" she asked, rubbing her eyes. As she did, she realized how close she'd squirmed to me for warmth, and drew slightly away.

"Guests of the Desert Inn," I said, "with sand for a bed, and the muddy clothes we're wearing for linens."

"Oh my God," she cursed, balling up her fists. "We were

just going to stop for a few minutes. How long have we been asleep, do you think?"

I squinted at the rising sun. "Hard to say. Four or five hours? It might be as late as six thirty in the morning, give or take a half hour."

She looked depressed. "Tell me last night was just a nightmare."

I stood and dusted myself off. "Afraid not. A whole lot of Reapers are probably mad as hell at us—those who're left. Bad enough we shot up their bikes. But when they realize we took their precious drones . . . Hell, before Jury charged after us, he probably sent someone into town to tell the little guy about our bad behavior."

Lawana's face clouded. "That could mean Taylor is in danger. If they link him to us—"

"I'm truly sorry," I said, and I meant it.

She frowned and stood up to face me. "Why is everything so complicated with you? You're like Superman come to save the day, except you make things worse."

"What *should* I have done?"

She sighed. "My husband, Brian—he used to be like you. The unit he sacrificed his life for—he'd only been given command of it a few days prior. He'd just rotated in. Those men were strangers to him. And he bled out on the battlefield trying to protect them. After I got the news, it ate at me. Those *strangers* got to go home, but I lost a husband and Taylor lost a father. I told myself after that to just take care of my own."

I picked up my pack, slung it over my shoulders, and began walking. "I'd say that you're doing a lousy job of that."

She followed right behind, nudging up close to my ear. "What does *that* mean?"

I turned and gave her a gentle look. "I'm just saying that you sure do spend a lot of time caring for everyone in town, working at the clinic, toting around that medical bag of yours. Hell, you even stepped in to save me, and then you made me drag that piece of crap Jury off the road."

She pushed past me, quickening her pace. "Okay," she said, "I'm bad at following my own resolutions. But you have me beat when it comes to suicidal self-sacrifice."

BY THE TIME THE SUN edged over the brown eastern mesas, we'd marched another two miles. Lawana made sure to tell me that she would have went farther if she didn't have a wounded man to take care of. I ignored her, sure that fear and worry were putting words in her mouth. Instead, I decided to direct her attention to something we both badly needed: water.

"I think it's time we find something to quench our thirst," I called ahead.

She stared back at me like I was crazy. "No lemonade stands out here, Clyde."

"How about the next best thing, then?"

She turned and stared at me, hands on her hips. I had her attention now.

"All I'm saying is, if we want water, we need to climb," I said. "I say we steer for that little mesa over there with those scraggly trees. It's not too high." I pointed slightly to the east.

She wiped the sweat off her forehead. "You *do* know that if you make me walk up there and we don't find anything resembling water, I will kill you."

"I would expect nothing less," I said, smiling.

Nine minutes later we were at the top, looking for places I knew would hold water. Lawana stood at the edge and stared. The yellow early-morning light lit a face wrinkled with worry and doubt.

"Found it," I said, kneeling on a flat rock half the size of a basketball court. Near the middle of the rock were a group of potholes, carved by wind, rain, and ice. All the holes were full of the clear nectar we needed to survive. Taking an empty water bottle from my pack, I filled it, capped it, and was getting on my belly to drink when Lawana came over in a hurry.

"Whoa there, cowboy. You can't drink that without treating it. There are thousands of microbes and bacteria in each of those little holes. You want giardia or dysentery?"

I put my face down closer to the water. The smell of it was overpowering the limbic part of the brain, overriding my good sense. "I have chemicals to treat what's in the bottle. Just let me splash a little on my lips."

She grabbed the back of my shirt and pulled. Surprised, I looked up and again saw a doctor's concern on her lean face.

"We're moving slowly enough as it is without you getting diarrhea. Get up, treat the bottle, and let's go."

As much as I wanted to drink—as much as my body told me I *needed* to drink—I listened to her. The way she said it left no room for arguing. So I stood, found the survival kit in my bag, and used the iodine in it to kill the nasties in the water.

Thirty minutes later, during which we climbed down the mesa and covered another mile, we deemed the water safe to drink and each took a long swallow. Lawana actually smiled.

"Nectar of the gods," I said cheerfully. "So where to?"

She pointed off in the distance, across a tumble of rocks. "It won't be much longer now."

The direction she was pointing in didn't make sense. There was a large swath of brushy flat land that seemed to offer a more direct route. "We should just keep hiking in that direction, shouldn't we?" I said, pointing. "Straight through that sage."

"Can't," she said, shaking her head. "That's the old Gilsonite mining area. One wrong step and we'd be stuck or dead in an old mine."

I'd been through plenty of old mining sites and couldn't imagine missing the opening to a mine shaft and falling in. Especially during the day. I told her as much.

"They mined horizontally. Dug deep trenches a few feet wide that are miles long. Some of them you can see, and maybe jump over; others are covered in rotting timber and a thin layer of dirt."

"The perfect trap."

She nodded. "There are warning signs all over the place. Some people don't read them, and then I end up working on a body that took the whole sheriff's team to pull out. All the kids in town know not to go out here, but it still doesn't stop them from exploring."

"Speaking of the sheriff," I said, "you should try using your phone again. Better service closer to the ranch."

"Already tried," she said in an exhausted voice. "While you were trailing behind, I dialed the Roosevelt sheriff's office. I've also dialed Taylor, the hospital, and a friend who lives in town, Ginny Littlebear. I'm not getting *any* signal. It's usually not this bad."

Those words probably should have worried me. But in the past twenty-four hours I'd gotten into three brutal brawls and trudged up and down two mesas and over five miles of desert. I'd had virtually nothing to eat and had slept only fitfully for a few hours. On top of that, it was barely early morning and the temperature was climbing into the nineties.

So I nodded stupidly and said, "Well, to the ranch then."

CHAPTER TWENTY-FOUR

The air was blast-furnace hot by the time we made it to the ranch.

For a while there I wasn't sure I was going to make it. I had never been so happy to see barbed wire and barns. Lawana still had enough energy to speed up when she saw the house. I didn't. Just kept plodding, trying not to fall on my face.

I was heading to the tack shed to drop like a dead man on my bed when I saw Lawana come out of the main house. "I tried plugging my cell into the charger, but there's still no service. And Taylor's not here," she said, a bit frantically. "He left a note, though."

With difficulty I kept my eyes open long enough to glance at the paper she handed me. On it was what looked like typical teenager handwriting:

Mom: Colorow said not to worry about you and that I should stay at Renee's place for a while. I'll be there. C. didn't say much about what happened last night. I really hope you and Clyde are okay. Love, Taylor.

"Who's Renee?" I asked.

"Renee Serawop. An older woman who's friendly with my father. She owns a spread down by the river," Lawana said, pointing slightly west. She was wobbling on her feet as she waved her arm. I could tell she was close to passing out.

"Listen to me," I said. "We're both hitting the wall here. We need to catch some sleep, shower, then eat something. Can you make it to the house?"

She gave a lazy nod.

"Great. Let's crash for a couple hours, then we'll scope out the situation, okay?"

"But Taylor will be worried."

"The kid probably hasn't made it out of bed yet. No teenager gets up before noon. And you should see yourself. You look like you belong in one of those zombie shows. A couple hours, okay?"

Reluctantly, she nodded.

TWO and a HaLF HOURS later, I was rudely jolted awake by a splash of cold water. I jerked up from the mattress to see Lawana all cleaned up and standing over me. "I'm giving you twenty minutes to shower, Clyde. I'll bring some food for you to eat in the car. We're going to get Taylor." The way she said it could be roughly translated as *Don't even argue*.

From my sitting position, I saluted. I remained that way as Lawana strode to the door, and then, once she was gone, I collapsed back onto my bed. It took five of my allotted twenty minutes to pull my stiff carcass off the bed and bring myself to a standing position. I heard my back popping and cracking all the way up.

As I stood under the outdoor faucet out back, which was

obscured by a plywood privacy screen, I tried to think of what Lawana and I would do after we checked on Taylor. Could we find a phone that worked? How could we learn what trouble the bikers had stirred up after Colorow and the others had taken the girls back and we'd set the Reapers' camp on fire? And how could we protect ourselves if the bikers were in a frenzy to recover the truck and came looking for us? Weirdly, amid these consequential questions were less consequential ones, such as: What more needed to be done on the ranch before Bud was released from the hospital? How many sections of fence still needed mending? How many horses still needed to be shod?

I felt especially guilty about the hay that was probably ruined in the field because I hadn't cut it before the storm.

The irony made me grin. When had Clyde the hunter become Clyde the rancher? Maybe I was kidding myself, trying subconsciously to become Lawana's ideal man. Problem was, I wasn't sure her ideal man was a rancher.

I'd just pulled on my boots, a clean set of jeans, and a Western-style shirt when Lawana appeared at the door to the tack shed, carrying her shotgun. "I'm still not getting any cell service," she said, "and I have a bad feeling about Taylor. Are you coming?"

"You said you'd give me breakfast," I reminded her.

She nodded. "In the car."

Thankfully, she was behind the wheel as we pulled out, allowing me to wolf down a fried chicken leg, a banana, two carrots, a handful of almonds, and a lemon Pop-Tart. I washed it all down with a liter of water. It was simultaneously the weirdest and most satisfying breakfast I'd ever eaten.

"Thanks for the chow," I said, grabbing one of the dainty napkins she'd provided and wiping my mouth.

"That *could* be the world's record for most food eaten in three minutes," she said drily.

"Well, it wasn't as delicious as a Baby Ruth bar, but it'll do," I kidded.

Once we got to the main road, Lawana turned away from town and headed toward the river. About a mile farther, on the right in a dense tangle of cottonwoods and olives, sat a small clapboard house. Around it were the usual corrals and sheds, though all looked to be in disrepair.

"That's the Serawops' place," said Lawana. "Renee, her daughter, and her granddaughter don't have much, but they're some of the nicest people you'll ever meet. Renee really stepped into the gap when my mom died. Dad never forgot it, and she's become like a grandmother to Taylor."

We pulled up the drive, steering around recently fallen tree limbs and branches. In the softer, sandier spots I noticed something wrong. I didn't mention it to Lawana, but I did reach over and grab her shotgun. "Let me take this," I said. "You don't want it to get in the way of your socializing."

"Fine," said Lawana, stopping the car. She got out quickly, strode to the front door, and knocked.

No answer.

She motioned me out of the car, and I shuffled over, shotgun in hand, still feeling less than ambulatory from the previous day's adventures. "This isn't right," said Lawana. "Renee never leaves the house, hasn't in years because of a bad car accident in Price that ruined her hips. Now she stays home and watches her granddaughter while her daughter works at the grocery store. What do we do?"

"We go in," I said, and tried the knob. It turned easily and I pushed the door open. "Hello?" I said.

"Renee?" Lawana shouted, moving past me into the house.

No one answered. Lawana ran into the kitchen, and I kept both hands on the shotgun, ready to bring it up and fire. The only sounds were the creaking of floorboards and the chirping of birds outside the thin walls.

Lawana came back to the door looking pale. "No sign of Renee or her granddaughter, and no sign of Taylor. I tried a cell phone that was left on the table. No service, just like ours. What in God's name is going on?" She put her head in her hands and squeezed.

"It's bad," I said. I pointed out the door. "I saw tracks when we drove in. Motorcycle tracks."

She ran her hands up her face and into her hair, tugging hard at the black strands. "They took them, didn't they? The Reapers. They have Taylor?"

The last part wasn't a question. She'd come to the same conclusion I had.

"We have to call someone, get some help," she said, her face as terrified as I'd ever seen it.

I agreed. We ran back to the car, and this time I took the wheel as Lawana directed me farther away from town, across the river. "We'll get service by the border," she said, meaning the state border with Colorado. "There's a cell tower there, one of the only ones around."

"And if we don't?" I asked. "Do we risk going into town, try the pay phone?"

"I don't think so. We keep driving, down to Price or Green River. Or head into Colorado."

But we never made it to any of those places. After we once again found that neither of our phones was getting service, we pulled over by a lone, rocky hill near the border. I had to get out and stretch, to keep from falling asleep. When I eased the car back onto the road, I noticed movement by the highway, far off in the shimmering distance to the south. Already suspicious that our phone problems were Reaper related, I got out of the car, grabbed my binoculars, and took a better look. Lawana followed me out.

As the binoculars' lenses slowly came into focus, I saw three bikers standing by two bikes in the middle of the asphalt.

"Damn it," I said. "There's a roadblock."

"Let me see," Lawana said, grabbing for the binoculars.

I pulled them away. "I don't think you should—"

"Give them to me."

Reluctantly, I surrendered them.

"Oh my God, Clyde," said Lawana, "what is *that*?"

She'd seen what I'd seen: three men standing by two bikes, and on the side of the road a solitary tree. On the tree limbs something was hanging. Or rather, some *things*.

I cleared my throat. "Looks like those guys cut off six dogs' heads and tied them to the tree branches. A Reaper mobile, you might say."

"How can you be so calm?" she asked.

"Because I've seen things like this before," I said sadly.

"You think they've spotted us?"

"I doubt it. Anyway, the dogs' heads are there to scare people off, get them to turn around. And folks are going to do exactly that. My guess is that there's a roadblock on every exit out of town. The Reapers are going to make us play their game."

"Game?" Lawana said. "This isn't a *game*, Clyde." Her voice sounded shrill now. "We need to get back in the car and figure this out."

No argument on that.

We piled back into our respective seats and I began tapping on the steering wheel, thinking. Lawana didn't say anything for a minute, then turned to me.

"You said you'd seen things like this before. *What* things? Where?"

I closed my eyes for a second. "I've seen worse. Parts of people—whole people. In Africa."

Even for someone as tough as Lawana, it was all too much. I saw the tears begin to spill down her face and it made me want to reach out to comfort her. I touched her shoulder gently and she didn't pull it away.

"Oh, God, Clyde," she said, unable to stop the tears from flowing. "I don't know what to do."

"It's okay," I said softly. "We'll head back to the ranch and think of something."

She didn't answer, just continued to sob.

I'd turned around and covered about a hundred yards when Lawana rubbed her nose and wiped the tears from her eyes. "What if those guys follow?" she said, gesturing behind her.

"Then we'll deal with them at your place."

I drove slowly and easily to avoid dust, and crossed my fingers. If these roadblock teams were under orders to stay put, we wouldn't have anything to worry about. *If* they followed orders. But some of these creeps hadn't been doing a very good job of that lately, and it worried the hell out of me. So I kept one eye on the road and the other on the mirrors. To my relief, no bikers followed.

WE'D BEEN BACK AT THE main ranch house for about an hour, discussing options, when we both became aware of an approaching sound. It started as a subconscious rumble that grew into the faintest buzz of a motor. I waited a few more seconds to try to determine the kind of vehicle, then grabbed Lawana's shotgun. "Small engine," I said.

Lawana calmly walked over to a gun cabinet in the corner of the living room, withdrew a Winchester .30-06 rifle, jacked a round into it, and nodded. We moved to the windows on either side of the front door and waited. "If it's them," I said, "take the rifle to the roof. I left a ladder up against the back, just in case."

"I'm glad you did. Listen," she said. She pointed out the window to the low hills to the east, not the driveway to the west. "It's not coming up the road."

She was right, of course. I listened as the little engine on the off-road vehicle rose and fell as it maneuvered up, down, and through the clay badlands in that direction. Dust appeared behind one of the lower hills and the whining intensified. "Go ahead and get on the roof," I said, "just in case."

"Ninety-five percent it's someone from the tribe. No one from out of town would know those trails."

"Then give me the rifle, and I'll do it."

"Just wait."

Again, no room for argument, so I waited. A few minutes later something appeared, bursting out of a cloud of loose gray dirt. It wasn't a four-wheeler. But it *was* an ATV of sorts, just one I hadn't seen before. It looked like a miniature jeep, with front and back seats and room for three more people in addition to the large one in the driver's seat. The contraption had a little steering wheel, little knobby tires, and a big roll cage. Similar to side-by-sides I'd seen other places, but much fancier. I raised the shotgun, keeping the sights on the driver, until it became clear that it was indeed one of the good guys.

Colorow piloted the toy into the courtyard and slid to a stop.

"Told you," Lawana said as she slung the rifle over her back and stepped outside.

Colorow climbed out of the vehicle and the thing rocked in relief on its shocks. "I told them you guys would be here," he said triumphantly. "They didn't believe me. Everyone else thinks you're dead, but that might be a good thing."

He ran over and gave Lawana a hug. Her look told me it was something he'd never done before.

She pushed him gently away and asked, "Taylor?"

Colorow took a step back. "That's why I came. He's in trouble. So is the rest of the town. Big trouble."

CHAPTER TWENTY-FIVE

"**W**here's my *son*?" Lawana asked, her eyes wide with fear.

"They have him," Colorow said. "They have almost everyone."

Lawana looked from him to me, unslung her rifle. "We have to go get Taylor."

I hefted the shotgun in my hand. I was about to agree when Colorow spoke up. "We can't. That's why I came. It's bigger now, and if we just storm in there and try to get Taylor out, we might *all* get killed."

Before Lawana could ask, I did. "Bigger how?"

Colorow swiveled his head around as if checking for threats. He was obviously jumpy. "Makes me nervous, standing out here. Let's go inside. Lots to talk about."

ONCE WE'D SETTLED INTO SOFT chairs in Lawana's living room, I asked Colorow to walk us through everything that had happened since we'd gotten separated the night before.

The big Ute ran his hands through his thick hair. "After we got the girls away, we took them to Linda's, in town. Then the bikers came." He stopped, coughed, coughed again. The frog in his throat wasn't from sickness, but emotion.

I prodded him along. "What happened in town?"

"The bikers roared in. One group went straight into the clinic and shot Fred. Three times in the head. So much blood. Another group came in, and they argued a bunch, then they all got yelled at by that little white guy, Orval or whatever his name is. He made a phone call, and then both groups rounded up at gunpoint anyone walking or driving the streets and put them in Fred's station and locked them up. Taylor wasn't there at that point."

"So how did he get there?" I asked.

"Not sure," Colorow said, eyeing both of us. "Rob Goff, myself, and Joe Buffalo—another guy who was with us last night—got away, and we warned a neighbor of ours named Cordell, who lives just outside of town." Lawana nodded, obviously knowing all these men, so Colorow continued. "The four of us agreed to meet up this morning at my hunting camp. When we did, Buffalo told us that he'd snuck into town earlier and saw a bunch of people from nearby ranches being herded down the street. Taylor was among them."

"So where is he *now*?" Lawana asked, on the edge of freaking out.

Colorow held up his hand. "Just let me finish. There were a couple of foreign guys in town, too—one was dressed in nice clothes and holding a bullhorn. He made a speech in some kind of accent—I couldn't make it out—to anybody who might still be hiding in a building. 'Rats hiding in the rat's nest,' he called them. He said the town is sealed off. The fiber to the cell tower and the trunk cable for the landlines have been cut. Other measures have been taken. He said he wants his stolen merchandise—'merchandise,' that was the word he used. He also said that he'll kill a hostage every hour until he gets answers." He coughed again, and hesitated a moment. "Renee's dead," he blurted out. "Buffalo saw it happen. He said they dragged her into the middle of the street and shot her in the head in front of everyone. Damned seventy-year-old woman. That was probably ninety minutes ago."

I performed the grim calculation. "Which means someone *else* is probably dead."

"Mother of God," Lawana said. "What are we going to do?"

"Kill them all," Colorow said. His eyes were full of menace.

Lawana grabbed my arm, locked eyes. "Clyde, we have to tell them where the trailer is."

"Wait a sec," Colorow said. "What trailer?"

I briefly summarized how we'd come to be in possession of air force "merchandise" the night before. I didn't tell him where Lawana and I had parked the trailer, though.

For once, Colorow wasn't full-speed-ahead. He paused to wrestle with it. "That's a lot to take in. You think these foreigners already have a drone target picked out?"

I shrugged. "I don't think they'd be so desperate to get that hardware if they weren't planning to use it right away. From how riled up the government seems to be, we could be talking about a lot of people getting killed."

Lawana slammed her fist on the coffee table. "We're *already* talking about a lot of people getting killed. My people. My son. I won't let that happen."

The three of us looked at each other. I was trying to work all the angles in my head. How permeable was the net the bikers had thrown over the area? Could someone get out? How long would it take to summon the authorities? How many hostages would be killed in the meantime? Would one of them be Taylor? *God, is Taylor still alive?* I shook my head. I wouldn't allow myself to think that he'd been the next Ute marked for death.

Other questions plagued me. What were the odds that these madmen would let the captured townspeople live even if we gave them their precious trailer? Once released, couldn't the Utes just disperse in a hundred different directions to warn the authorities? No improvised containment net was *that* foolproof. Something told me that everyone in Wakara was *already* dead unless we could bring the fight to the enemy right now. In this case, the enemy was the bikers, that little guy Orval, and whoever these ultimatum-spouting foreigners were.

I laid out to Colorow and Lawana how I was seeing things.

Lawana was dubious. "You don't think all of these killers wouldn't clear out of town the moment we told them where the trailer is?"

Colorow pointed out the obvious before I had a chance to. "They're not going to just let you 'tell' them where the trailer is. After all, you could lie. They're going to make you *show* them. And once they have it, you're dead."

Lawana's face fell.

"I'm afraid Colorow's right," I said. "I'm also not optimistic about these guys leaving a lot of witnesses to their homicides today. I think we have to get those captured people out of harm's way—and it might involve killing the people who are threatening us."

"Damned straight," Colorow said, standing up. "And we need to do it fast."

CHAPTER TWENTY-SIX

Both the sun and the flies were starting to become a nuisance when we finally buzzed into Colorow's hunting camp. Lawana was a wreck. She nervously worked her strained hands on her rifle, so much so I was worried she was going to rub the bluing off. I tried to put myself in her shoes, but couldn't. Even though I'd lost my mother when I was young, I couldn't imagine losing a child. Still, I'd grown really fond of Taylor. This had become *personal*.

The camp sat on a middle bluff, about halfway between Lawana's ranch and the town. Two red four-man tents were set up next to a fire ring that still puffed a thin line of smoke. Just below the camp an earthen dam had been built years ago by some unknown rancher to catch the runoff from the hill, providing a week or two of water for the sheep or cattle after a rain. It was full, and above it I could see a massive black cloud of biting flies and mosquitoes.

Colorow took the keys from his machine and followed us into what looked like an abandoned camp. "It's me," he shouted. The sound echoed off the rocks and steep clay hillside, and when it drifted away, two people emerged from behind a boulder. Each carried a hunting rifle. I recognized them as the two Utes, Goff and Buffalo.

"It's a relief to see you guys," Goff said, smiling broadly. "Buff and I were ready to go back into town, see if maybe we could pick off a couple of those assholes."

"Where's Cordell?" Colorow asked.

The Ute named Buffalo, a thickset type, rolled his eyes. "We couldn't keep him here. Said he was going to go back to his place. Said any of those bikers who tried to mess with him would get some lead in the face."

Colorow stubbed his foot into the dirt. "That's Cordell."

Observing Lawana's increasing agitation, I decided to interrupt this impromptu coffeepot palaver. I quickly filled in Goff and Buffalo on enough info to make them aware what was at stake and why we had to make an immediate attempt to change the situation in town. Fortunately, I wasn't hearing any resistance.

Colorow waited till I finished and said, "So it's settled. Let's stop at Cordell's on the way and hope those murdering bastards haven't killed a third person."

Which, of course, made me think again about who the *second* victim may have been once that hour mark had ticked by.

TWELVE MINUTES LATER WE WERE paying Cordell a visit, Colorow, Lawana, and me in the ATV and Goff and Buffalo in a pickup. I was told that the man we were trying to recruit for this mission was a white guy, a Brit expat geologist who'd fallen in love with the rocks on the rez, and then with a Ute woman from Wakara. He'd retired and set himself up on a small plot of land on the edge of town, wanting to be left alone. Sounded like my kind of guy.

As we drew up to Cordell's shiny Airstream trailer, I noticed right next to it two large tents.

"Are those tepees?" I asked, to no one in particular.

"Don't," Lawana said.

"Don't what?"

"Don't say something insensitive. I know you want to."

I didn't. What I wanted to say was how much I loved them, how they were the best-designed tents in the world. With their liners and their smoke flaps, they made a natural chimney for a central inside fire, and they stayed warm during all but the coldest nights.

Dogs greeted us when we pulled up next to the pickup parked by the camper. The truck looked like it was from a *Mad Max* movie, and the dogs looked more like wolves, with huge yellow fangs dripping slobber. They weren't friendly, and none of us got out of the vehicle until a tall, thin man came out of the trailer carrying a shotgun. He had it pointed at us, and yelled at the barking and slobbering mutts, telling them to get their asses back. They did, most with their tails between their legs.

"Us again," Colorow called out. "We got the doctor and Barr with us. Things are looking worse since our last conversation. You want to go to war with us?"

The Brit slowly lowered his gun to his feet and withdrew from his pocket what looked like a can of chewing tobacco. He took some chew out of the can and stuffed it into his upper lip. "You got an army I'm not seeing, boy?"

"Not exactly an army," Colorow said, "but—"

Lawana hurriedly explained about the roadblocks and what

the request for the "merchandise" was all about. Cordell had already been told that morning about the ultimatum and that people were getting killed.

"So are you in?" Colorow asked.

"You want me to join a suicide mission?" Cordell asked.

"We can take these guys if we're smart about it," Colorow said with his usual bluster.

"Smart?" asked Cordell incredulously. "As in six of us driving into town in broad daylight and taking on twenty-five killers? My wife is with her sister in Colorado Springs, but if she were here she wouldn't like those odds."

Goff called out from the driver's-side window of the pickup. "So what are you going to do, old man? Just let people die?"

"Suit yourselves," Cordell said airily. "Drive into town and catch some lead. If it was me, I'd wait till dark. Surprise 'em."

"And let them kill how many more people?" Lawana said from the backseat of the ATV. "They have my son. He may not be *alive* tonight."

No one wanted to finish her thought. *He might not be alive now.* For a while, we all stared at each other, reconsidering. Cordell had sown doubt in the Utes about the likelihood of success. Heck, he'd even given me food for thought. And yet Lawana was as determined as ever. She reached forward and gripped my shoulder, looked at me with that stare that said, *Do something.*

I cleared my throat. "Okay, I have a plan. Cordell's right. It's smart to wait for dark to stage a rescue. If the six of us go in loud, we'll hit whatever tripwire they've set up and they'll unload on us. I think you guys should hang back until it gets dark, while Lawana and I creep into town and size up the situation. Buffalo did it this morning. They can't be guarding every alley. And anyway, Lawana and I have something to bargain with if we get jammed up. Not that we're going to tell them anything. But we can let them *think* we're going to tell them something—if we get caught."

Colorow rubbed his chin. "I don't like it. Your plan splits us up. If you do get grabbed—or *worse*—there's only four of us to take them on. Plus, I want a piece of these bastards right now."

I shook my head. "Take it from someone who's been in a lot of firefights," I said. "Good intel accounts for most of the success of a mission. Let Lawana and me scope out where they've put their men and what the best access routes are to the hostages, then we can work out a plan that makes sense."

Silence. Then Goff said, "He's right, C. Let's hang here for a while, give 'em a few hours to nose around and see where the bikers' positions are."

Colorow said, "A few hours? That's three or four more people dead. And if we wait till dark, that's what—*eight* hours? Eight *more* people dead?"

Everyone looked at each other. We couldn't seem to make a decision.

"Anybody here ever been to Africa?" I asked after a few moments of silence. Everyone shook their head. "South America? Mexico?" More head shakes. "I spent sixteen years in those places. Got into a lot of wars like this one. Saw things I wish I could forget." I looked around, made sure I held everyone's gaze. "My guess? This 'kill someone every hour' threat burns itself out. Guys like this don't have the patience for that. They'll want to go to plan B pretty damn quick."

"What's plan B?" Goff asked.

"I'm not sure," I answered, "but when Lawana and I get to

town, we'll see if we can figure it out. If you *don't* hear back from us, you go into town tonight with all guns blazing. You know the layout. They don't."

"We *won't* get killed," Lawana assured them. I wished I had her confidence.

"Wait," Cordell said, holding up his hand. He fairly sprang into his trailer. "You'll need these," he shouted from inside. We waited. When he returned he handed us a walkie-talkie, a pistol, and a rifle—a large one. "It's a .470 Purdey Express," he said, almost lovingly. "My dad's elephant gun. Cost a fortune to ship over, and it kicks like a Clydesdale, but it's handy."

CHAPTER TWENTY-SEVEN

As we drove the ATV away from Cordell's Airstream, Lawana told me of a small trail that led into a drainage near the tribal housing. Not many people knew about it, so she was pretty sure it wouldn't be blocked. As we rattled over the brush that grew in the middle of the two tracks, I asked, "So what percentage of people in town you think they actually rounded up?"

"Hard to say," she said, yawning. Both of us were still pretty sleep-deprived. "Depends on how organized the Reapers were. And whether it was a surprise move. If any of my people *are* hiding under a bed, or in a wood bin or barrel, they're likely not going to make a move until dark."

We dropped through a cut in the rocks that rimmed the bluff, sped down a steep draw, and then slowly followed another wash to town. As we bounced along the bottom, through a cloud of rabbit brush and sage seeds, I glanced over at Lawana. She'd fallen silent and was staring out over the ATV's hood. Her eyes were red, her hands balled tight into rock-hard fists.

"You okay?" I asked, but I knew the answer. I just wanted to get her talking again.

"No," she said, "I'm not. If they hurt Taylor . . ."

"He's tough," I said. "Tougher than he looks, and smart. He knows enough to keep a low profile, not be the guy they pick to make a point." Of course, sometimes these things are a matter of sheer luck, but reminding her of that wouldn't be comforting.

"You think?" She managed to look at me, her eyes glazed and her mouth pinched tight.

"I do. He reminds me of myself."

This brought a slight smile from Lawana. "Really," she said. "How so?"

The wash started to widen, and we almost ran right into a wall. Debris that had been washed down in the last storm clogged the gully from one side to the other and all the way to the top. Rocks, tree limbs, and trunks, which meant that we weren't driving any farther.

I turned off the ignition, pocketed the keys, then reached behind me and grabbed my pack and the .470 Purdey. Lawana decided to trade her Winchester for the pistol. We started climbing out of the gully.

"You asked why Taylor reminds me of myself," I said in a low voice. "Well, I was raised by a single mom. Until she was murdered. My sisters and I had to grow up fast. Taylor has had to deal with some of the same stuff. He's more of a man now than most of the grown-ups I've seen in cities."

She smiled again, but there was no happiness behind it. "He is. But I would have coddled him if I could have."

"Then he would have resented it. Maybe even rebelled. Right now, he adores you. He brags about you, you know."

"He does?" she asked, smiling again. This time her face glowed.

"Absolutely. And I agree with him. You're a good person, Lawana."

She blushed slightly and looked away. We were on the flats now, heading toward town. We walked for another hundred feet, then Lawana wiped the sweat off her forehead and frowned. "If they see us, we're dead."

"We won't let them see us."

"This is insane. We won't even be able to get close to Orval."

"Oh ye of little faith. Just hold up a minute." I stopped, gently set my rifle against a large rock, and shrugged my pack off. I dug into it and pulled out Jury's vest. Or *cut*, as he would have called it. Then I pulled off my shirt and slipped into the leather.

"What the hell are you doing?" Lawana said.

I smiled. "It's called blending in with your environment. The first rule of camouflage is to not stick out like a sore thumb."

"And what am I supposed to be, your biker chick?" Lawana asked. "I didn't notice any women traveling with them. Your trick isn't going to work anyway when we get close enough for them to see our faces."

"So, no plan is perfect," I said, slipping my pack back on and grabbing the .470. "For now, let's just pretend I'm a Reaper on patrol and you're coming with me as if I've ordered you. Stay ahead of me a bit so it looks as though I'm telling you where to go. And keep that pistol out of sight."

Lawana rolled her eyes. If the situation didn't feel so desperate and we weren't both so tense with worry, she probably would have made a smart remark, but she saw the wisdom of what I was saying. With a sigh, she quickened her pace to stay ahead of me, and slowly we both made our way closer to town.

From here on out Lawana and I would be making it up on the fly. I figured it would be only a matter of minutes before some of the bikers showed themselves.

CHAPTER TWENTY-EIGHT

Lawana and I walked in silence, kicking rocks and gravel, and a few minutes later we slipped into town. Or what was left of it. I noticed that a lot of damage had been done: busted car windshields, splintered picnic tables, signs torn down over business establishments. The place looked like it had been hit by a Reaper hurricane. The croaking of ravens was the only sound other than that of our boots crunching gravel, and the silence bothered me.

We hurried down the side of Main Street, our heads constantly turning, looking for leather-vested men with guns. We hadn't seen any by the time we got close to the tribal police station. No bikers were visible, just their rides, but as a precaution we turned onto the only side street available and stayed on it until we were on the opposite side of town. We didn't see another living soul or moving vehicle. As we started to swing around to find a building that we could climb up on to watch from, I wondered why, over the years, I kept living this nightmare—why I was always three steps away from a whole lot of bloodshed.

As usual, I didn't have a good answer.

On impulse, I walked behind the general store, which looked as if it had been set on fire. The cinder-block walls and metal roof were still whole, but the insides were black ash and melted lumps of plastic. I was *really* starting to hate these guys.

"You coming?" Lawana whispered.

Her voice wasn't beside me, and it took me a second to realize she'd already climbed to the flat roof of the boarded-up building next to the store and was waiting for me. I pulled myself onto the plywood that covered a window, then reached up and gripped the roof's edge. I pulled myself up and felt every muscle in my upper body tell my brain that I was pushing myself too hard. After making a mental note of that and deciding there was nothing to be done about it, I rolled onto the roof. Then I found the binoculars in my pack and handed them to Lawana.

She scanned the front of the police station. "No one is outside. How do we know that Taylor and the rest of the people they rounded up are in there?"

"We don't."

"What if they're holding them somewhere else?"

"Let's wait for a while. We just got in position here. Patience."

So we waited. Ten minutes, then twenty, then a half hour. All the while, I listened intently for voices, disturbances— anything. It was eerily silent.

Finally, I broke the silence. "I think I'm going to have to go down there to take a peek."

She looked at me, terrified, then bit her lip and nodded. I handed her Cordell's rifle and radio and took the pistol from her. Slowly, I moved to the edge.

"Please be careful," she said, and gripped the rifle tight.

"Always," I lied, and climbed down.

As I brushed off the dust and ash from my new vest, I noticed that I'd gashed my elbow as I climbed down. *Sonofabitch*. I pondered how I would sneak up to what was likely a heavily guarded building in the middle of the day without getting noticed and shot. I considered creating some sort of distraction but ruled it out. Orval seemed smart, and his men would be wary of anything out of the ordinary. With the vest and my tattoos, beard, and scars, I *looked* like a biker, which had probably served me well so far. But now I was close enough that anyone who spotted me would instantly shoot, which meant that what I was about to do—just go for it—didn't stand much chance of working.

I moved around the edge of the building, peered into the street, and, not seeing anyone, sprinted across into the clump of dying elms surrounding a condemned house. Once there, I dove into the fallen leaves and crawled to the edge of the crumbling building. On the way, I crawled over a couple of jagged beer cans. Not fun. I craned my neck to look around the corner, and saw nothing again. I was starting to worry that no one was left in town.

Maybe those crazy Reapers had killed everyone they were holding and moved on. The thought of not ever seeing Taylor again was creating a horrible feeling in the pit of my stomach when I saw Orval walk out into the street.

Two burly bikers escorted him, carrying what looked like belt-fed machine guns. I hadn't seen weapons like that since South America, and the sight was more than worrisome. It meant that whoever Orval was teamed up with was a big-timer. I didn't have to wait long before two new guys came out and joined the street party. Neither of the men seemed like he belonged—not just because they were dark-skinned and wearing what looked like tailored clothes, but also because they stood too tall and walked too fluidly. Like the world was their property. Instantly, I disliked them.

The five men meandered away from my hiding spot, moving up Main Street toward the opposite end of town. Once they were almost out of sight, I stood and ran to the tribal housing buildings, using trees and abandoned pickup trucks as cover. I couldn't see the men, but they must have turned back toward the station because the sound of their voices was getting stronger. As I listened to the new guys speak in a language that might be Arabic, I looked for a place to hide—one where I could still have a line of sight to the station. Didn't see one. So I jumped a chain-link fence and crept through the overgrown grass until I came to another fence. Then I went to my belly and pushed the grass to the side until I could just make out the men as they walked past the station and turned to go down the street that would lead to the tribal housing area.

Damn it. I'd wanted to sneak up on them in the station, not hide from them as they walked past me. I watched through the grass as the five men marched down the road. They'd been joined by three others: a young girl; an older, fat man; and yes, *Taylor.* At first, I just felt relief, but then I saw that the three had been trussed with duct tape and were being pushed down the road by the muzzles of the men's guns.

I rolled to my side, pulled the pistol, and chambered a round. Made sure the safety was off. Over the pounding of blood in my ears, I heard a different thumping. I looked up at the small, decrepit pressboard house next to me and saw two older Ute women staring at me with wide eyes. One woman had turquoise earrings the size of half-dollars. The other wore a loose-fitting red blouse. The thumping came from the floorboards, and soon a third woman appeared in the window, holding a young child wrapped in a Pendleton blanket. As soon as she saw the clothes I was wearing she disappeared from the window.

The other two ladies didn't. The one in the red blouse handed Ms. Earrings a shotgun. Half of my brain frantically tried to figure out a way to keep them from shooting, and the other half wondered how many more people were hiding in their houses. Neither half came up with a quick answer. The lady with earrings opened the window, and I put the pistol down. Raised my hands and whispered, "Ma'am, I'm working with Lawana Nicholas, at her ranch. I'm not with *them*." I motioned at the bikers marching down the road.

It took her only a second to decide. She raised the gun to her shoulder and waved the barrel at me, then at the house. "Get inside."

I didn't argue. I grabbed the pistol and crawled through the grass, over a broken bicycle, and pulled my way into the window. My arms were getting ridiculously tired of pulling the rest of my body around, and they almost gave out. The woman in the red blouse grabbed my arm and, with surprising strength, dragged me inside. With not a lot of grace, I settled on a wooden chair next to a box full of beads and string.

"That's Lawana's son out there," the lady with the shotgun said, watching from the front window as the bikers and their bosses marched their captives past.

"What are they doing?" I asked, afraid to hear the answer.

"They've killed three people so far, besides Fred. Two

women 'bout my age, and a young fellow, our school principal. They've been leaving the bodies in the street by the school."

As if to answer the question I was going to ask next, the two new, well-dressed men walking beside Orval stopped the procession. One grabbed a bullhorn from Orval and started speaking. "People of Wakara: You will continue losing your friends and loved ones if you do not give us the information we seek. I will give you another chance to tell me who has my merchandise. We do not wish to harm anyone else. We simply wish to know who has our missing trailer."

I watched both of the women sit down on the couch, trembling. The one with the earrings said in a voice that was a half moan, "Why are they doing this?"

"Money," I said, watching the two Middle Eastern–looking men walk in circles around their captives. "And maybe something else." As much killing as they'd done so far in this town, I was pretty sure they had in mind something far worse for people who *didn't* live there.

The more I thought about it, the more I figured that this whole spectacle was about a group of people deciding that another group of people needed to be removed from the earth. Not just killed in battle, but wiped clean. A century and a half ago, many white people had thought the same about the ancestors of the women who were sheltering me. It was a horrible cycle that I'd seen all over the world and had read about in every history book I'd ever picked up. When would it end?

Not today, apparently.

I moved closer to the window and watched one of the new men—tall with longish hair—grab the bullhorn again. "Last chance," he yelled, his voice barely controlled.

No one came out of their house. The dry, dust-gray air was still and the only sounds were those of the magpies cawing on the now useless phone line spanning the street. I kept a good grip on the pistol, but I didn't raise it. I tried to imagine what would happen if I took a shot. The ringleaders weren't more than eighty feet away, so even with the less accurate pistol I might have a chance of hitting them before the street exploded. But when that happened the bikers would mow down half the people hiding in the thin-walled houses, and they'd certainly mow down the prisoners. One of those prisoners was Taylor.

So I kept the gun low and watched as the long-haired man shoved the bullhorn at Orval and took his rifle. Orval stared at the ground like an ashamed dog. The long-haired man moved to the prisoners, who shook like wilted leaves in the heat. He looked over at his partner, a more closely cropped man squinting in the sunlight, and nodded. Squinty grabbed the bullhorn from beaten-looking Orval and continued the speech. "Last chance. Someone will die in one minute if no one comes forward."

The man with the rifle shoved past the fat Ute and the young girl, straight to Taylor. The man put the rifle against the side of the boy's head. Taylor stood tall, pushed his chin up, and tried to stop trembling in the hundred-degree heat. No one else moved. The two foreigners shared a look, and the one with the rifle focused back on the boy.

No.

I had to do something.

Before I could, the third woman in the house appeared from a back bedroom. She didn't have the baby. "It's *him* they want," she said, pointing at me. "Him and Lawana. They were with the people who got those girls back. We have to turn him in—now." She started walking to the front door. For a second, I was distracted by the woman's words, and then I heard the crack of a rifle.

Without looking outside, I shoved the woman away from the door, flung it open, and ran into the street.

Taylor was still standing.

Long Hair was not.

That's all I needed to know, and then I realized how exposed I was, coming out of the building into a street full of armed men. Two things saved me. One was the confusion caused by the rifle shot, the other the confusion caused by my clothing. I also knew—after looking at the dead man on the ground—who'd taken the shot, and why. That gave me a little bit of a chance.

And I took it.

CHAPTER TWENTY-NINE

I jerked the pistol up, took quick aim, and fired two fast shots. The biggest bikers with the biggest guns twisted and stumbled. I sprinted toward the group before they could think of a proper response.

As I pumped my arms and pushed hard, lungs working like a mule, I kept my gaze on Orval and the other new leader, the squinty-eyed one. Both were looking over toward where I'd left Lawana. The captives milled, unsure what to do or where to go. I helped them with that. Once I burst into the group I grabbed Taylor in a half tackle and dragged him with me as I kept running across the street, heading to an unused carport attached to a not-much-bigger house.

I saw over my shoulder that the two biggest bikers were down and bleeding. Not dead, but worthless for the fight. Orval's new friend Squinty had his gun out. As soon as I tossed Taylor under the rusty awning of the carport, another shot rang out. A distant boom, meaning it didn't come from the street.

I shoved Taylor down next to the concrete steps by the house's door, then turned my attention back to the other two captives. They were both on the ground, trying their best to become small. The big man was having a hard time doing that. I worried that Orval and his boss would turn and end them.

I shouldn't have worried, because suddenly both found their feet and bolted. Orval and the squinty-eyed man seemed heedless of them, tracking the rooftops for the sniper. They'd soon be getting a fix on Lawana's position.

"You okay?" I asked Taylor. He looked up at me with a face much younger than the one he'd presented to his captors. He didn't say anything, just nodded. I noticed the duct tape around his wrists and reached down to grab the big Green River knife from my belt. With a couple of strokes, I slashed the tape off and then I pounded on the little house's door. No one answered, of course, so I kicked it in. I helped Taylor up and ushered him inside, keeping my pistol up as I did, just in case this house, too, was full of shotgun-wielding women. It wasn't.

Instead, we found a skinny, leathery old man sitting in a leather recliner. He was sucking on a can of beer and watching television on a huge screen mounted on a badly painted wall. The TV made no sound. Dressed only in his boxers and compression socks, the man croaked out what sounded like a question. When I told him I needed a place for the kid to stay, he pointed at his ears. He repeated the question and pointed again, and I told Taylor to stay with the guy and explain. Then I ran back outside.

My eyes swept for any sign of Orval or his dark-skinned partner, or even the bikers I'd bloodied, but everyone seemed to have cleared out. *Good.* Or maybe not so good. I had to find Lawana. I sprinted down the street and made it back near the store in under a minute.

Which is when I saw Lawana running to the house I'd just come from. Also, four more bikers exiting the police station, as angry and agitated as kicked-hive bees. I spun and took off after Lawana, a smile forming under my beard. I almost laughed. Not because it was funny—it *wasn't*—but because sometimes circumstances slap you with such absurdity that your only choice is whether to chuckle or cry.

I ran toward Lawana, awkwardly, because my head was turned, watching the Reapers mount their bikes—doubled up two to a bike—and begin to head in our direction. One dreadlock-wearing biker riding on the back of a Harley put a rifle to his shoulder. I threw a round his way, knowing it had a snowflake's chance in the Sahara of hitting, but wanting to give him something to think about. Surprisingly, the bullet grazed the shoulder of the biker riding the *other* bike, and he almost spun out before recovering.

I saw Lawana disappear inside the carport and I followed. She went into the house, but I didn't want to disturb the deaf old man, so I stayed outside. I also thought it would be a good idea if someone watched out for the four armed men bearing down on us.

I could hear the throaty growls of the Reapers' bikes getting closer. We had to *move*. I was about to go inside and grab Taylor and Lawana when I heard a sound I hadn't heard in quite some time.

Somewhere between us and the police station, an ear-drum-shattering firefight had erupted. Full-auto fire mixed with high-powered rifles. The air ripped with booms and cracks, rattles and echoes. I hadn't heard that many shots in such a short amount of time since before landing in prison. It sounded like someone had lit up a fireworks stand. I could only assume that at least ten well-armed people were trying to kill each other.

I leaned out into the street to see the battle. But I couldn't get eyes on it. I yelled, "We gotta go," and pounded on the thin wall. Lawana appeared, Cordell's rifle slung on her back, pulling her son along by the hand—the way she might have done when he was little and they were about to cross a busy street. "I know," she said. "We need a car."

I made a quick inventory of the vehicles parked randomly around the tiny houses: mostly older Broncos, Suburbans, and pickups. Any one would do—*if* we could get it to start. I was trying to remember how long it had been since I'd hotwired a truck when Lawana ripped open the door of the nearest Chevy pickup. She hopped into the driver's seat and told her son to sit in the passenger side. I waited to see if she could start the vehicle, and was surprised when she had it going in less than a second.

I jumped in the back and stole a look at the ignition, wondering what kind of magic she'd employed. It was simpler than that. The owner had left his keys in the truck. Again, I'd forgotten where I was—forgotten that in a community this tight, in a town this small, why *wouldn't* a pickup owner leave his keys in ready mode? Who was going to make off with the vehicle?

Us, apparently. Lawana jammed the selector into reverse and we tore off, heading away from the sounds of gunfire.

I pounded on the back window and Taylor slid the small middle window open. "Circle back around. We need to come in from the opposite end of the police station."

Lawana shook her head. The bright light shining on her hair had turned it a dark purple. "I need to get Taylor away from here."

"The fighting—it's Colorow, Buff, and the Englishman, right?" I asked. "You called them in early?"

"They were going to kill my son."

"I get it," I said. "But we can't let Colorow and the others fight alone."

"They can handle themselves. They said so, on the radio."

"We're in this *together*," I insisted. "What about the rest of the people locked in the station, and in town?"

Taylor shouted over the engine noise, "He's right, Mom, we can't just leave them. The other two they dragged out into the street with me—one of them was Pepper. And her hands are still duct-taped and she's alone, probably back at the school. We have to help her."

From some offhand comments Taylor had made two days before, when we were doing chores together, I'd gathered that Pepper was his sort-of girlfriend. They were in the early stages.

Lawana was having none of it. She was like a mother bear protecting her cub. Gunning the engine, she swerved off the partly paved road and rattled onto a dirt trail that led south, away from town. It was hard to hear what she said next. "You can stay if you want, Clyde, but I *have* to get my son out of here."

"But Mom—" Taylor said.

"No buts," Lawana said with unexpectedly fierce intensity. "I'm not losing you, too."

If I'd learned anything in my years of wandering, it was that you *never, ever* fight with a determined mother. Animal or human. "Stop," I yelled into the cab, "and I'll bail."

CHAPTER THIRTY

The gunfire had dwindled to the occasional shot every other minute by the time I hauled my beaten carcass back into Wakara. Out of breath, legs shaking, I tried to come up with another plan. If I could get my hands on another rifle, maybe I could help with a tactical retreat. Perhaps even take out the other new guy and Orval both. That might end it. As I walked past the torn-up buildings on Main Street, I mentally shuffled through firefights I'd been in before and the books I'd read, trying to piece together a strategy.

When I made it back to the general store, all my plans went out the window.

From a semi-hidden vantage point behind the corner of the store, I could see the police station. And two bloated figures lying facedown in the street. I saw the rest of the bikers milling around their dead brothers, occasionally shooting out at the surrounding hills, but I couldn't see Cordell's truck.

They were gone, pulled out.

I slumped down with my back against the cinder-block wall and pulled on my beard.

I was alone.

Absently, I ran a hand through the grainy sand I was sitting in and brooded on what my next move should be. I grabbed a handful of almonds from my pack—all that I had left from my breakfast—and looked out at the surrounding hills, mesas, and cliffs, which from my sitting position seemed as formidable as prison walls. Funny how something so permanent could be so relative. A few weeks ago, those hills had been my home. They were comforting, offering food, shelter, and warmth. Now, they seemed like a giant palisade, keeping me trapped.

I sat there for a long time, pondering. After the losses Orval's people had just taken, would the killing of Ute towns-people continue? Were there any able-bodied men hiding in these homes who I could turn into allies? How many bikers were left to support Orval and the stranger who now seemed to be calling the shots, the squinty-eyed dark-skinned guy? It felt as if the situation might pivot. Orval and the others had to realize they couldn't hold this position much longer. That sense of narrowing options was likely to make them desperate.

I figured I'd wait till dark and then creep up next to the police station and see if I could overhear anything or glean what Orval and the others were intending. Until then, there were still things I could do to help. I stood, press-checked my pistol, and readjusted my pack, then shuffled across the street to the school.

Like the store, this building had been torched. Smoke had curled out the windows and left wavy black marks on the once brown brick. It was the largest building in town, taking up most of the small block. A brightly colored playground sat empty and still just inside the fence. I crackled through the broken glass doors and into the dark halls.

"Pepper?" I called out as quietly as I could. As the only sound, the question enlarged and filled the empty place. The question was soon accompanied by my boots clomping down the old tile. "Pepper?"

The adrenaline and other survival hormones had worn off, leaving me with another headache, but my ears were still in hunting mode. I took another step toward the devastated office and heard something.

A shushing, then movement.

"I'm on your side," I said, slowly moving toward the sound. "I'm the guy who grabbed Taylor and shot the bikers."

The movement and rustling stopped.

"Is Taylor okay?" a small, unsteady voice asked from somewhere inside the office.

"He is. He's with his mom and they've left town."

"Good," said a man's voice. I assumed it was the other hostage—the fat man.

"I've got a first aid kit," I said. They clattered through the rubble and moved out of the shadows.

The big man's name was Mateo. He introduced himself after they came out, shaking my hand with duct tape still dangling from his wrist. He was a tribal council member, he said. He couldn't believe what had happened to his town in such a small amount of time. He shuffled over to a nearby staircase and settled his massive bulk on the bottom step, while Pepper stayed and stared up at me.

She was short, barely five feet, and wore dirty jeans and a university T-shirt. Her black hair was pulled back in a messy bun, exposing an angular face beneath thin, dark eyebrows. The high school war paint that she called makeup had run down her face, making her look even sadder than she was.

Behind the sadness, though, was determination. It was the same look I'd seen on most members of the tribe.

What had Taylor said about warrior spirit?

I dropped my pack, knelt by it, and found the first aid kit. I wished Lawana were here, with her big bag of medicine and doctor skills. They'd have to settle for my cruder ways. After I'd cleaned up both of them and patched their various abrasions and cuts, Pepper asked, "Where did they go?"

"Lawana and Taylor?"

She nodded.

"Don't know," I said. "I doubt back to the ranch, since the bikers may come looking for her there. Any ideas?"

She shook her head.

"Before all this trouble started, back at the ranch, Taylor mentioned you," I said. "Sounded as if you guys are pretty good friends. Maybe even *more* than friends?"

Pepper blushed. "Maybe," she said. "I guess, I mean, yeah."

Funny how kids are: embarrassed to admit they like each other. It made me think of this girlfriend I'd had when I was just a little older than Pepper—Maria. I'd done her a favor by leaving town after high school. It allowed her to have a calm life, free from the trouble I tended to get into—trouble like what we were experiencing now.

"You got any family nearby?" I asked Pepper.

She looked sad, almost teary-eyed. "I'm not sure where my mom and older brother are. We live just outside of town. I was in town when all this happened. My mom is probably crazy worried."

I nodded and slowly rubbed my beard, thinking through the possibilities.

"Well, I suggest we all relax, maybe even catch a little

sleep," I said, looking at both Pepper and Mateo. "Nothing to be done until dark. Pepper, when we move out, it's probably best if you come with me. Mateo, I need you to go around town, find who's left in their homes, especially those with guns who are willing to fight, and assemble back here at the school. Can you do that?"

It was clear that Mateo wasn't used to having people believe he could effect change. His chest swelled up slightly and he said, "You got it. You can depend on me."

I nodded. Now the question was whether I could depend on *me*.

CHAPTER THIRTY-ONE

A few hours later, I was driving with the lights off as quietly as I could over to the isolated parking lot by the arena that the Utes had used for the dance. Once darkness had set in—there were almost no lights on in town and the moon hadn't fully risen—Mateo had led me over to the housing area, where he handed me the keys to his truck. Pepper had settled into the passenger seat, and I'd given Mateo a short wave as I drove off. Now I stopped, killed the engine, and considered what I was about to do.

"Why are we stopping?" said Pepper anxiously.

I gave her a reassuring smile. "I'll tell you in a second. I just need to go over again what you told me earlier."

"Okay."

It was then that I noticed the wind gusting. It was blowing almost as hard as during the previous storm. Garbage cans rolled past the parked truck; tree branches flew and fell around us. This wind didn't foretell another storm, though. It was just the pressure change following the last one.

"So," I said, "how many people you figure are still in the police station?"

"I told you back at the school," she said. "There were maybe ten people in the cell with me, and I could see through an opening into another room, and it was full of people."

"All right," I said, "how large was that room? Like classroom-size?"

She nodded.

"And it was *full*? Not a lot of room to move?"

Another nod.

"So maybe another thirty people there. And as far as you know, no members of your tribe on the upper floor?"

Pepper wrinkled her forehead. "There could have been. One of the bikers they called Ace, a skinny guy with a weird droopy mustache—he was complaining, saying he had to bring a 'shit pot' upstairs." She looked embarrassed. "They made some of the people go to the bathroom in trash cans."

I didn't like what I was hearing. It sounded as if Orval and the Middle Eastern guy had north of forty people under guard in the station and conditions were deteriorating. The big question was, how badly was I outnumbered? I thought about it. Watching that many people would require four bikers, minimum. I counted in my head. So far, I guessed that in the last twenty-four hours, at least eight of the Reapers had been taken out of action, which left how many?

I recollected how many bikers I'd seen the night before when Lawana and I had fired down on the camp. It might have been forty. Which meant thirty-two left, four of whom were bogged down guarding the locked-up Utes. And Orval or whoever was calling the shots had dispatched sentry bikers to the main roads out of town. That move might be tying up another eight or ten. Best case, I had only eighteen bikers to deal with. *Only.*

I stared out the window at the dust whipping across the empty parade grounds. "Okay, that's good information. I think I know what I have to do, and I *know* what you have to do."

"What do you mean?" Her eyes widened.

"We're splitting up. You can drive this truck, right?" She nodded. In this part of the country, even fifteen-year-olds were pretty familiar with driving. "Well, I want you to head on out of here. Stay away from the main roads. They have roadblocks set up on them. Men with guns. Do you know enough of the back roads?"

She rolled her eyes. "Of course. Where do you think we party?" She paused a moment, then gave me a worried look. "But where should I go?"

"You've got two choices," I said. "Find a way back to your place, or maybe go look for Lawana and Taylor. You must have a couple notions of where they might go."

The implications of what I was asking her to do were beginning to set in. I could see the fear surging. "I don't think that's a good idea," she said. "I think I should stay with you."

"Trust me," I said, "you don't want to do that. From here on out, I'm moving toward danger, not away from it."

She still seemed hugely reluctant.

Time for some amateur psychology. "Taylor's been telling me that a lot of people in your tribe have a warrior spirit. I see that. When things get tough, your people get tough. Can I count on you to get tough?"

She thought about it a moment, then seemed to make up her mind. "All right, I'll try."

We both got out of the truck and she slipped into the driver's seat. I waited while she turned the key in the ignition and threw on the lights.

"Hey," she called out as I was walking away. "What's your name, anyway?"

I smiled. "Clyde . . . Clyde Barr. If you see Lawana or Taylor, tell them I'm trying to end this thing."

I pulled the pistol and ran to a tree. Watched the truck to see if anyone, or any bikes, followed. None did. I continued watching the red taillights as they moved to the south and disappeared. Quietly, I wished Pepper luck, then I turned toward the police station.

CHAPTER THIRTY-TWO

The wind huffed and puffed, showering the narrow side street with dry leaves, grass, trash, and dust as I ran. Normally I hated the wind. I couldn't see how anyone other than sailors and kite lovers might enjoy it. It caused headaches, sinus issues, depression, property damage, and wrecks, and was just generally annoying. But tonight, the wind hid the sounds of my jogging and my ragged breath, and the dust clouds and fluttering debris offered good concealment. After a few minutes of fighting the gusts, I made it to the back of the station.

The place was long and narrow, had the fabricated look of a manufactured home, and was two stories high. It was solid, made out of the same cinder blocks as the store, but had recently been painted white. There were no windows, and the doors were steel. A veritable fortress. I slowed and shifted instinctively into stalking mode, making sure to place my feet carefully even though the howling of the wind made it impossible to hear any missteps.

As I moved from tree to tree, my hands felt sweaty on the pistol. The wind was growing worse and getting on my nerves.

But it wasn't just the wind. Something was wrong. Or more wrong than anything had been to date. My hands shook, and I felt the hair on the back of my neck go rigid. A primitive response to danger. Some of the guys I'd fought with called it "Spidey sense"—that feeling you're being watched, or that something is about to go bad.

The feeling grew overpowering as I moved closer to the station. It got harder and harder to breathe, like someone was sitting on my chest. I wished like hell I had a Kevlar vest.

I pushed the feeling deep down inside, where all the old memories and emotions fermented, and made it to the back door. Which was locked. The feeling came back, stronger this time, and I whirled.

Nothing. Just the wind and the leaves and the dust. I couldn't shake the primitive alarms that were going off, so I made a quick patrol around the whole building, hiding in the trees and the dust clouds in case someone was watching. Nothing. No shots, no guards, no bikes. Nothing was parked at the station.

What the hell is going on?

I went back around to the rear door, just in case someone happened to pass by on the road. I swung my pack off and pulled out my lock tools. It was a loose doorknob lock, so I figured it would open with just a bump key. The dead bolt above it would be harder, but if I had the time I could probably get it open with a better tension wrench and by pushing up each tumbler pin individually.

I slid the bump key into the bottom lock, and felt cold steel touch the back of my neck.

I started to whirl, amped and ready to smash whoever was holding the gun, and got hit by lightning.

Or at least that's what it felt like when the Taser fired. I flopped and seized on the ground, then the world went black.

I came to tied to a chair. Someone had relieved me of the vest I'd taken off of Jury. In its place was an old T-shirt. My hands were duct-taped behind me, my ankles were taped, and a twenty-foot rope had been wound around my chest and the chair's back. I couldn't move. I wasn't sure that I could have even if I *hadn't* been trussed up. Every muscle ached. My skull felt too big for my scalp. My eyelids refused to open, and my teeth throbbed. It was a horrible and new feeling. Not the being-tied-up part—that had happened a few times before—but the being-hit-with-electricity part.

When I finally was able to open my eyes, and when my muscles finally started listening to my brain, I surveyed the room. White cinder block, no outside window, metal cot with blanket, steel sliding doors with Plexiglas viewing panes. My stomach sank, my bowels tightened, and the pain in my head doubled.

I was in a cell. Again.

It was the kind of place I'd vowed never to return to. I struggled against the rope and tape, but they were tight and held. I tried to hop in the chair, but I only succeeded in almost tipping myself over, which wouldn't do anyone any good. So I stopped.

A part of me knew that my predicament couldn't be more dangerous, that I was probably just a few minutes from death. But I'd been a few minutes from death several times in the past. It always helped to not get ahead of oneself, to just focus on the next step.

So what *was* the next step? I told myself to appear confident when someone showed up, act like I had something to bargain with. It might make them think twice about putting a bullet in my head.

In minutes, someone did appear in front of the glass. He was small in stature, and wearing a short-sleeved dress shirt and slacks. His bespectacled eyes were focused on a small flat square of plastic in his hands. The plastic had a screen that was flickering something blue. He pushed at the screen with his thin, manicured fingers, and the door slid open. My good friend Orval was paying me a visit.

Behind the little man, half-hidden by shadows and still standing in the hall, was an immensely wide-shouldered and tattooed Reaper waving a Taser at me. He smiled and pushed the button on the stun gun, arcing a blue light that lit his face. This was probably the guy who'd jolted me into unconsciousness. "Play nice," the Reaper said in a gravelly voice, and immediately I recognized him as Jury's second-in-command. It was the same voice Lawana and I had heard coming out of the tent when we eavesdropped on the Reapers' camp. Taser Man smiled and walked down the hall.

"Orval," I said.

He looked up from the device and smiled. "You should have forgotten my name."

The open door helped ease my anxiety. I made my best effort to smile, but it came out like the grimace of a constipated man.

"Where is my trailer, Barr? As you surely know, I have a friend in town, and he very much wants its contents."

I shook my head. Silence was the way to go with someone who enjoyed talking. It drove them crazy.

"What was that? I couldn't hear you tell me what I want to know."

I shook my head again.

"This isn't a game. And it isn't funny. You're only alive because we haven't been able to find the woman you were with. We will, though, in time, and then I'll have Boom shoot you in the face. Where is it?"

"My face?" I said. "It's just north of my neck."

He flushed red and looked back to his screen. "My friend, he doesn't like jokes. He likes killing people. Now that we've coaxed you to this cozy little station house, we've been able to let those smelly Indians go. No need to hold on to the bait once the mouse has been caught. But we *can* have every one of those citizens rounded up again in thirty minutes, and shoot them all at once. Would you like that?"

My instincts told me to keep him talking. "Help me understand something, Orval. You seem like a pretty smart guy. The American education system has apparently done right by you. So why do you want to throw in with terrorists?"

Orval *tsk-tsk*ed, as if I were a mental midget. "Well, I haven't been dreaming of jihad, if that's your question. You see, I like money. And the business I'm transacting here is going to earn me a lot of it."

"Is it enough to buy your dream car?"

Orval sighed. "You're endlessly amusing, Barr. No, you need to think on a much larger scale. Imagine enough money to buy a small country."

I whistled. "That much? So I guess that justifies whatever annihilation that psychopath boss of yours wants to create with his drones."

"I'm really quite indifferent to what Mr. Omani wants to do with his merchandise."

Keep him talking, Clyde. "And your leather-vested enforcers? Not a patriot in the bunch?"

Orval smiled. "Only Jury knows what's actually in the trailer, and he shares my affection for obscene wealth."

I noted that Orval had referred to Jury in the present tense. Did he not know that I'd left him for dead on the road? Unless . . .

I persisted with my questioning. "One more thing—"

"No more questions!" Orval interrupted. "I will ask the questions. And the only question that matters is, where is our trailer?"

I thought for a moment. "What are you going to give me for telling you? I mean, you're not giving me much incentive to talk. I talk, I die. I don't talk, I die."

Orval pulled up a stool at the corner of the room and sat on it. He looked at me intently. It was kind of unnerving. "I know what you're all about, Barr. I ran some computer checks on you when you hit town. At first, I thought that just knowing the bare bones about you was enough. But then, when you became a giant thorn in my side, I accessed some more obscure databases. You seem to have a bit of a knight-in-shining-armor complex, and a lot of people you've gone to war with and for have paid the price, even some fair maidens. Those sluts probably regret ever getting involved with you—the ones still alive, that is."

Button pushed. I tried to bolt out of my chair, wanting with all of my being to close my hands around his throat, but of course the coiled rope and duct tape held me in place.

Orval laughed. "It seems as if I've touched a nerve, Sir Knight. Anyway . . . I know that your partner in crime in the trailer theft was the lady doctor. You asked me to give you an incentive to talk. How about this? If you talk, I have my men stop searching for the doc. We just let bygones be bygones.

But if you *don't* talk, we find her, make her tell us everything we want to know, and then we make sure she dies as slowly and painfully as possible."

I still needed to stall. "The military is looking for that trailer, too. They'll find it first."

Orval *tsk-tsk*ed again. "Barr, you insist on underestimating me. I built into the planning of this project a clever feint. I'm afraid the military is off following red herrings. They won't be wandering into this area for a couple days at least, and by the time they do, we will have offloaded Mr. Omani's merchandise onto another vehicle that won't look like a vehicle at all—in fact, just the opposite."

The little man was talking in riddles now. He looked down at his screen, then punched at it furiously, as if it were a keyboard. A few moments later he looked up. "Last chance, Barr. Where is my trailer?"

"I don't think you're nearly as smart as you think you are," I said.

His face flushed again and for a moment it looked as if he was going to smash the device he was holding onto my head. Then he calmed himself and said, "Have it your way, Barr. I will send in Boom. He won't be as professional as I've been."

CHAPTER THIRTY-THREE

They made me wait. Part of Orval's plan, I'd guess. Not a bad one, either. Waiting to get tortured is sometimes worse than the torture itself, if you have any kind of imagination. Your mind will run through every possible scenario, trying to brace for whatever is coming. You imagine rusty, dull knives; red-hot pokers; heavy-duty wire cutters. Anticipation can be hell.

I tried to imagine myself camped on a green hillside, next to a crystal-clear pool of water, under leafy foliage, watching robins flit through the trees. It was calming.

Until the sliding doors clanged open, and the wide-shouldered biker who'd Tasered me walked in.

He might have been an inch taller than me, making him at least six foot three or four. He had a salt-and-pepper beard, long curly hair cut in a mullet, and green ink all over his neck and up to his ears. From my vantage point only a few feet away, I noticed that he wore a white T-shirt under his vest that hadn't been washed in weeks. The guy smelled like a hog farm.

"Where is it?" Boom said as he came into the room.

"Bring your Taser?" I asked.

"No need." He took one step forward and rocked me with

a backhand to the face. Cheek bruised against bone, and I felt blood leak out of the corner of my mouth. "Where's the trailer?" He went for the backhand with the opposite hand, to let the sting wear off in the first hand. This time I was ready, and rolled my head with the smack. It still hurt like hell, but not as bad as the first. The first one rattled teeth. This one didn't.

"Okay, wait, hold on," I said. He stood, expectant, rubbing the back of his hand. There were a few options here. I could tell them where the trailer was located and save Lawana, or I could hold out and take another beating, which I wasn't sure my battered body could handle. I decided to go in a completely different direction. "Okay, don't hit me again," I said.

He smiled, showing a gap in his yellow teeth. "You gonna talk?"

I nodded, trying to look sad and defeated. Like he'd already broken me. Like I hadn't been to prison or locked up at borders before. "I'll talk. But you need to promise that the woman and her son won't get hurt."

He smiled again, and lied. "Yeah, no problem. You talk, I'll have my boss call the Persian and tell him to lay off."

The Persian? Was Omani Iranian? Maybe that had been Farsi, not Arabic, that the squinty-eyed man and his now dead partner had been speaking earlier.

"How can I trust you?" I said, because of course anyone would doubt this creature's assurance. I had to sell this confession with every ounce of acting skill I possessed.

Boom suddenly turned into a man of vast uprightness. "My brothers aren't into hurting women, despite what you might think," he said. "Even last night, we weren't going to hurt those girls. We were just having fun. My club's Nomads were in the wrong, and were dealt with. It won't happen again. Just tell us what we want to know and we're out of this town. None of us want to spend another minute in this shithole if we can help it."

I was actually impressed that he could put that many words together. Of course, he'd neatly sailed over the fact that earlier in the day his crew had ended the lives of two innocent Ute women. I mulled over his logic as if weighing a car salesman's best price.

"Okay," I said finally, scrunching my features into a look of meek surrender. "That woman and I, we got scared. I was the one driving. I kept the pedal to the metal and didn't look back. We went all the way to Vernal, about twenty miles west of the Colorado border, before our nerves settled down. We parked the trailer in the back lot of a truck stop, got a couple sodas, and headed back. On the way back, Jury tried to run us off the road, but he can't drive and ended up crashing his rig into a wash during that last storm. Then we walked back into town, and here we are."

"So it's in a truck stop? In town?"

"In Vernal, yeah."

"You're lying." He leaned forward, only inches from my face, and made sure I was looking back at him. I could smell his breath, and it was worse than the hog farm smell of his clothes. It smelled like sewage ponds in the summer in a town where everyone only eats junk food.

"I don't want to die," I said, "so why would I lie to you? It's there, you can go see."

"We will. And if we don't find it, I'll shoot you in the eye."

I nodded. So much for those upright qualities he'd been putting on display a minute ago. If nothing else, I figured I'd bought myself some time. Now I just had to figure out how to escape. Boom, or whatever his name was, left and the doors clanked shut. Now it was a waiting game—except I didn't have long to wait.

Five minutes later, Orval and Boom both came back. Boom moved past his boss and punched me hard in the face. I wasn't ready, and barely twisted enough to avoid a broken nose. It still smarted, though, and my left eye started to swell. So did my upper gums. I spit blood at Boom's feet and waited for whatever was next.

Orval pushed past the biker and leaned down. "You wouldn't lie to me, would you?"

I looked from him to the big man and tried to appear all played out. *No, not Boom. Anything but Boom*—that's what I was trying to convey with my *don't hit me* cringe. Come to think of it, maybe I wasn't acting.

"Good," said Orval. To the big Reaper he said, "Move him to the basement, where it will be easier to clean up."

This is my chance, I thought. *When they untie me, I'll rain hell down on them.*

I didn't get the chance. Orval reached into his front pocket, where he kept his pens, and pulled out a syringe.

I tested the ropes again, struggling to break free. They held. Orval pushed on the syringe, squirting clear liquid out of the long, thick needle. His hand remained steady as he leaned in and put it to my neck. I tried to bite him, twisting and chomping. Couldn't reach him, so I spit in his face. He issued a stream of profanity, wiped his face, then plunged the needle into my neck.

The world went blurry, then dark.

CHAPTER THIRTY-FOUR

I woke up in a small room that smelled like dirt. No way to tell how much time had passed. This time there were no rope bindings. I was slumped against the cinder-block wall, this one unpainted gray. The room was twenty feet by ten, with a twelve-foot-high ceiling. A long fluorescent light flickered high above me, but produced almost no light. My hands were handcuffed behind me, but my feet were free. So when the headache abated and whatever Orval had given me had worn off, I pushed up to my feet and inspected the room.

High on one wall hung one of those monstrous flat TVs that people watched sports on in noisy bars. The screen was black. On another wall was a metal round-rung ladder that led up to a trapdoor. That, combined with the smell of earth, told me I was underground—in a basement of some kind. It reminded me of 1950s bomb shelters. In the center of the clean concrete floor was a drain grate, and there was a faint trace of bleach in the air.

What the hell else had happened here?

I stopped inspecting the place and collected my thoughts. It wouldn't take the Reapers longer than thirty minutes to see that their trailer wasn't in the lot—maybe an hour tops, factoring in the darkness—and then Boom would come down the ladder and try to beat the information out of me again. I needed to come up with a plan and move. Fast.

I squatted down and shoved my hands under my ass, hooking the handcuffs under my knees. Then I rolled to my back, pretzeled myself into a crazy yoga position, and snaked a foot through and under the handcuff chain. I rolled and grunted and squirmed until I got the other foot through. Finally, breathing and swearing heavily, I had my hands free in front.

Moving to the ladder, I climbed up awkwardly, stepping off each rung and reaching up to catch the next with my shackled hands. At the top, I steadied my feet on a rung, let go of the ladder, and pushed on the trapdoor. It didn't budge. Locked from the outside. Of course. I started falling, but I grabbed the top rung before gravity won. I'd just have to wait until Boom came back.

He did, about ten minutes later. By the time the lock clanged and the door started to move, my legs were shaking and my hands were beginning to cramp. If I'd had to wait any longer, I probably would have slipped and fallen, cracking my back and skull on the hard concrete below. Instead, I used the little strength I had left to swing to one side of the ladder and try to make myself look small.

Boom wasn't a complete idiot. He opened the door with a flourish and poked a flashlight through the little square. He was on one knee, and I watched his ugly face behind the light search for signs of movement, looking for me. He found me and started to say something, but I let go and grabbed the arm above the flashlight with both hands, then let my feet slip off the ladder. Time for gravity to do its job.

As he fell through the hole, I pulled up on his arm and rolled on top of him. He flailed and twisted as we started falling, but by then I was pulling and repositioning myself. I felt one of the rungs rip up my forearm as I wrestled the bigger man underneath me. The floor flew up to meet us, and the sound of his body hitting it was sickening.

I bounced off the pigsty in skin and crashed into a wall. The flashlight clattered against a different wall. I looked over at the burly biker and saw his limp form shake, starting to seize. Black fluid leaked out of a most likely broken skull. I stood, waiting a second to make sure that nothing in my body was ruined, then went and picked up the light. Orval could be coming next, at any time, so I had to hurry.

I checked Boom's pulse. Nothing. So I went through his pockets. No pistol or Taser, just some lint and a set of keys, only the ring didn't have the little key that I was looking for—the one for the handcuffs. But I'd had to improvise before, so I took the keys off the ring, then bent an end of the spiral wire ring out straight, then back at one end, making a little hook. I snaked the hook into the keyhole on the cuff and twisted. With practice, you can open a pair of cuffs in seconds. It took me most of a minute.

When I had a hand free, I let the other end dangle—it would take too much time—and bent and grabbed the knife from Boom's belt. They'd taken mine, along with my pistol, after they'd Tasered me. One always finds a need for a knife. I put the knife and flashlight under my belt at my back and went to the ladder. Above, I heard footsteps approaching.

I started up the ladder, feeling weirdly somber. Not because I'd killed the biker, because he would have done the same to me, but because the world kept producing people like him. Also people like Orval, who I hoped was the man I was going to meet in a few moments. Everywhere I'd wandered, I'd found people like the Reapers. Every. Single. Place. As I climbed, I wondered whether there'd ever come a day when such people didn't exist. Then I chided myself for the thought. The answer was, *of course not*.

I pushed out of the hole, crouched beside it, and pulled the knife, ready for whatever was up there. If it was Orval, he'd probably be surprised that I was free, and maybe I'd have a second or two's advantage. If it was someone else, hopefully I'd get lucky.

I got lucky.

The footstep sounds came from a young, skinny biker sporting a Prospect badge who barely looked old enough to drive. He carried a brand-new AR-15 in a fancy sling, and when he tried to raise it to his shoulder, the sling caught on the ball-peen hammer that he'd slung on his hip. As he struggled to free it, I popped up and flung the knife. I watched it spin end over end, hoping that the distance was right.

It wasn't.

When you throw knives, you need to know exactly how far away from the target to stand to get the knife to stick. You also need to know the weight of your knife, and how it flies, neither of which I knew then. It's not like the movies, where the hero throws from anywhere and sticks a knife in the villain's throat. In the case of my throw, the knife wobbled and smacked the kid in the eye with the butt of the handle.

He bent over, gave up on his rifle, and put both hands to his face.

I threw the flashlight at him next as I closed the gap quickly, put both of my hands on his head, and brought up my knee. I felt the nose break on my kneecap. Then I threw a quick palm into the back of his head and shoved him into the wall. When he stumbled and crashed to the floor, I untangled the rifle for him and took it. I looked up and down the hall and didn't see anyone else.

Maybe I had a chance.

I wanted to take out the kid permanently, or at least tie him up so I wouldn't have to deal with him again, but I knew there might not be time. And I was trying not to add to the nightmares. So I left him in a room full of desks and computers and then headed out into the narrow, faux-wood-paneled hallway. The length and the smell of the hallway reminded me of my childhood trailer, and I couldn't wait to get out of there.

Before I left the building, though, I ran to the other end of the long hall and checked the door. Locked. I took a quick peek through the small window and saw a cell, and past that, a large room, its door flung open. A few items of clothing lay on the floor. Had the hostages been there only a couple of hours earlier and been released? It looked as if Orval's story about letting the Utes go had been the truth.

The halls felt like they were closing in when I finally made it to the main office area—the last place I'd seen the tribal cop alive.

Instead of Fred, behind the desk in the only big office, was Orval.

He was staring at a computer, completely engrossed, and typing faster than anyone I'd ever seen. Before I could decide whether to run out or stay and pound the runt into the floor, he saw me. His hands leaped from the keyboard to a handheld radio next to it. I raised the AR-15 and pointed it at his head, but he ignored me and keyed the mike.

"Everyone back to the station," he said, almost screaming. "Now!"

"Put it down," I said, waving the rifle at him.

He did, slowly. I walked into the room. Kept the rifle steady and pointed it at his sweaty face. The radio crackled three times, each with a different response.

"On the way, boss," said one deep voice. "Couldn't find the trailer. Dude must have lied."

"Am returning now," said another, his accent placing him as Middle Eastern. "There was some trouble, but we'll soon have the information we need—from one or the other."

And a third voice came on immediately after. "Bringing the bitch now." There was laughter in the background, and I lost my temper. They had Lawana. And probably Taylor.

I let the rifle fall away in its sling, took a step forward, and swung the handcuff at Orval's head.

He screamed and fell out of his chair, then I shoved the computers and screens off the desk. They crashed in a pile of broken glass and cracked plastic.

Orval screamed louder. I bent down next to him and grabbed his collar. Jerked him up and tossed him against the wall. Pictures fell and crashed, showering Orval with glass as they shattered. He kept screaming.

"Shut up," I said, and pulled him to his feet again. I jerked him over to the radio, pointed at it and said, "Tell them to let her go."

His screams faded, and a small smirk appeared on his face. "Why would I do that?" he said. "You obviously haven't been truthful with us. Now we get to convince someone who is less mule-headed."

Less mule-headed? He didn't know Lawana.

"Do it," I said, reaching down to grab the radio.

He shook his head. "I will not."

I twisted my new rifle up to my shoulder. Pointed the barrel at Orval's face. "Do it. Or you die."

He tried to laugh, but it came out squeaky, like a dog's chew toy, and his face turned the color of a baboon's ass. Sweat started to gather under his thinning bangs. Then a smile formed beneath his mustache. "I think *you* will die first," he said. I followed his gaze to the door behind me and saw the Reaper.

He was wearing what I'd come to recognize as the typical Reaper uniform—vest, jeans, and T-shirt—and was raising a gigantic .50 caliber revolver when I finally made a move. I grabbed Orval again, tossed him in front of me, and put the rifle to his head. All in one swift movement; one I'd unfortunately had to execute before.

The Reaper didn't stop raising the pistol. I positioned Orval to cut away the biker's angle to my head. It didn't get the guy to back off, though. I could barely make out the beginnings of the revolver's cylinder start to spin.

"No, wait, don't shoot!" Orval said, squirming in my arms. I tightened my grip.

"There's only one play," the biker said. His voice sounded robotic. I got the feeling this Reaper was like a machine calculating probabilities. He didn't give a rat's ass about Orval, who was clearly not one of his biker brothers. "I gotta kill this dude."

"And shoot through me?" Orval asked, squirming.

Dimly, Robot Reaper seemed to be weighing whether there might be consequences if he offed the man who'd been calling the shots for most of this mission—before the arrival of the Persian.

The biker shrugged. "Don't matter to me."

"It will," the little man in my arms said, "when you don't get paid."

I peeked again and saw the biker lower the pistol slightly. "Huh?" he said.

"The deal with Omani, you idiot," Orval said. "The money is being routed through *my* accounts."

I had no idea whether Orval was telling the truth or bluffing like a champ. But it didn't matter. What he'd said had distracted the biker, so I shoved Orval aside, whipped my rifle around, and took a shot.

The Reaper jerked, pulled the revolver's trigger, and then slumped against the door frame. A gigantic bullet ripped past us and tore into the wall behind me as I put two more rounds into the slumping man. He slid to the ground, blood leaking out of his chest.

Time to move. I put the radio in my back pocket, then slung the rifle out of the way, pulled Orval close, and slapped the open handcuff on his wrist. Why marry us up like that? I had to find Lawana, and I needed Orval to communicate with his men to do it. That, and he'd proven that he could come in handy when people were shooting at me.

CHAPTER THIRTY-FIVE

As we emerged from the station, I tried to gauge the time. It wasn't light yet, but I had a feeling the sun would dawn soon. And then the town would turn blast-furnace hot again. *Where to now?* I considered going to the school. Would Mateo have rallied his fellow Utes and brought the armed ones there to help out? I wasn't sure, especially since all of the Ute hostages seemed to have been freed. I also wasn't sure whether a full-out war would get Lawana back. This was a situation that required finesse.

I looked at my new safety buddy, Orval, who was cuffed to my wrist and cursing. "All right, boss man," I said, "where should we go to parlay with your fearless leader, or business partner, or whatever you call him?"

Orval scowled. "And I want to help you *why?*"

"Simple. You don't want to stay handcuffed to me any longer than necessary."

Orval didn't reply at first. I could see his wheels turning. Finally, he spoke. "The plan, once they found the woman, was to take her to the store. Omani had something in mind. I'm not sure what."

"I think you're lying to me," I said.

"In most cases you'd be right," Orval said, smiling. "But I really do want to rid myself of your odious presence as soon as possible, and going to the store will hasten a meetup with my partner."

What he said made sense. He had no reason in this situation to take me on a wild goose chase. "Lead on, then," I said, "I'll be just a quarter step behind."

With that, Orval turned toward the store and I shuffled along with him, our handcuffed wrists making it seem like we were holding hands.

I WAS HALF EXPECTING LEAD to start flying at the sound of the door cracking. That's why I shoved Orval in front of me as soon as the door flew open. But no one shot. In fact, the store seemed empty.

One way to find out. I put the rifle on Orval's squirming shoulder and pulled the trigger. Orval probably screamed, but in the enclosed space a rifle is deafening, and I wouldn't know. What I did know was that no one came running, and neither of us had gotten shot or blown up.

I debated where to position myself in the store. It made sense to be by the windows so we could have advance warning of Omani's arrival. But I was dog tired and not anxious to remain standing with my new buddy for ten minutes. I thought about trying to grab chairs from the bar area but remembered they'd all been burned in the fire.

Orval seemed to sense my exhaustion and began smiling. "How many hours of sleep you get in the last two days, Barr? You're not going to pass out on me, are you?"

I smiled back. "Not a chance. Not with a conversationalist like you to keep me company." I watched out the window, looking in the pale light of a just risen sun for a glint of motorcycle chrome or the telltale dust cloud of a car making its way in our direction.

"I'm curious," Orval said. "Just how do you think you're going to get your girlfriend back?"

Girlfriend? The word caught me by surprise, but I could see why he chose it. "Lawana Nicholas *is* a friend of mine," I said, "and I'm going to do what I can to help her." I shoved Orval against the wall so that he wouldn't have the same ability to look out the window that I had.

"Goddamn it," said Orval, "that hurt."

I just continued staring out the window.

"Hey, Barr," Orval said after a minute. "Do you usually run and fight with a man handcuffed to your wrist? Why not give us both a break and open these cuffs?"

I didn't reply.

"C'mon, you've got the gun. I'm not going anywhere as long as you've got it pointed at me."

I knew he was a scheming little bastard, but having him hanging on me *would* limit my mobility. The immediate challenge was to pick the lock, because I didn't have the key. I looked around and spotted what I needed among the blackened and broken Sheetrock, scattered screwdrivers, and melted plastic that once contained pills and chips: a roll of rebar tie wire. I lowered the rifle and jerked Orval over, listening as we waded through the burned debris for any outside noise. Nothing so far.

It didn't take long. A few minutes later I had the cuffs off, and Orval was my new not-so-secret admirer. "That's pretty impressive lock picking, Barr. You're a regular Houdini. Maybe if we kiss and make up you can teach me how you do your magic."

I kicked the cuffs into the corner. "Don't hold your breath," I said.

"You never know, I'll bet—"

Orval suddenly pointed at the wall nearest us, close to the worst of the burned and ruined beams. "What's that sound?"

Maybe that rifle shot I'd fired into the store had more effect on my eardrums than I thought. I wasn't hearing anything. I pushed away from Orval, swung up the rifle, and slowly stepped toward the wall. My ears strained for any sound other than my blood rushing through them. *Nothing.*

"Right there," I heard Orval say over my shoulder. He was still pointing at the dark and blackened spot on the wall.

I was leaning toward it, concentrating hard, when Orval shoved me violently with both hands, using all his strength. He succeeded in pushing me headfirst into the wall. I hit hard, and as I did both the wall and the ceiling above gave way. A chunk of beam landed hard between my shoulder blades, knocking the breath out of me and sending a ragged jolt of pain up and down my spine. As I went to the ground, I realized too late that I'd underestimated the little weasel. He'd obviously analyzed the structural integrity of the building, figured out the weakest point, and turned me into a human wrecking ball.

I caught a brief glimpse of him running away, and then the darkness descended. Again.

CHAPTER THIRTY-SIX

I lay under the pile of broken wood and Sheetrock for God knows how long. Consciousness came and went, like sunlight on a cloudy summer day. I didn't remember anything hitting my head, but if something had—hard enough—I might very well not recall it. It didn't matter. In fact, right then, nothing much did. I was finally ready to give up.

I didn't want to think about Lawana and Taylor. I feared the worst, and contemplating my probable blame in exposing them to all this danger was too painful.

For a couple of minutes there, lying under the wood, thinking about all the people I'd teamed up with in the past and how few of them had made it, I wondered where I'd gone wrong. What had been the moment, the fork in the road where I should have turned right but turned left? And how many more wrong turns had I taken since?

Yes, you could say that I was holding a pity party for myself. But then I heard the roar of Harleys outside, and that almost extinguished fire inside me blazed back to life. *Time to get moving.*

Once I'd pushed away the blackened mess, I gingerly got

to my feet. I found the rifle in a pile of burned books and newspapers, grabbed it, and headed to the window. Outside, a row of bikes was filing into town, two abreast, rolling down Main Street. Maybe fifteen bikers, and behind them a black SUV. I pulled the magazine from the rifle, checked it. Half-full, somewhere close to fifteen rounds. If this became a firefight, I'd have to make every shot count.

But it would be better if that never happened. I was about to turn and look for the back exit when the SUV stopped right in front of the store. The bikes roared around the vehicle, settling into protective positions, and I watched as Omani exited the rear passenger seat, pulling someone with him and slapping him hard on the back of the head. My heart sank again, almost back to the point of hopelessness it had occupied a few minutes earlier.

Taylor.

Omani had Taylor.

I looked across the street and saw someone I should have expected to see, but the sight still caught me by surprise. It was Orval, emerging from a nearby building and walking with a sprightly gait to the group in the center of the street.

"I killed Barr for you," he proudly told Omani. "He got the drop on Boom and took me hostage, but I outfoxed him in the store over there and sent a pile of timbers crashing on top of him." Everyone looked over at the blackened building and I moved away from the window for a second so as not to be seen. When I returned to the window, Orval was only a couple of paces away from Omani and Taylor.

"That is most unfortunate," Omani said, obviously seething.

Orval's face fell. "I don't understand . . ."

"You idiot," Omani thundered. "I told you to hire good

people. Instead, you hired these uncontrollable Nomad characters. That crazy biker Gunner beat the woman into unconsciousness. The stupid ass called me on the radio and asked what he should do. When we arrived at his location, we found him and three others sprawled across the rocks, dead. The boy was hiding in a ditch and the woman was missing. Some of the locals—the ones who killed your men—must have hauled her away. With Barr dead, that means we have no way of locating the trailer, unless the woman said something to the boy."

Everyone looked at Taylor.

I could see where this was heading. I'd never seen a human being look so forlorn as Taylor did right then. He'd lost almost everything, and now he might lose his life as well.

For me, it was another right turn/left turn moment, and I needed to choose correctly. My first instinct was always to fight, but my gut told me that wouldn't end well. It was time to finish it. Too many people had died for this damned trailer. I'd surely be signing my own death warrant by offering to guide Omani and the Reapers to it, in exchange for their letting Taylor go, but it seemed like the only way to save the boy. He deserved a chance to grow up.

I dropped the rifle and headed out the front door of the store into the blazing morning sun. My hands were held high and I was smiling.

"Clyde!" Taylor shouted, happiness filling his face.

It took only a moment for the men centered in the street to all raise their guns and point them at me. Orval looked like he was seeing a ghost. I must have been quite a sight, limping slightly and covered in soot.

"Howdy, boys," I said, drawing up to Orval and Omani.

Orval seemed to be in a full panic. "I thought for *sure* he was dead," the little man said to the Persian. "When I left him he was buried. Look at him—with that black soot all over him. I thought his head was caved in."

Omani fixed Orval with an icy stare. "Lucky for you that you're hopeless at getting rid of irritants." The dark-skinned man motioned to a long-bearded biker with purple tattoos flowing down both arms, and the biker stood directly in front of me and pointed an AK-47 at my forehead.

"Hot out," I said, making sure everyone could see my empty hands.

"On your knees," the biker said, pushing the end of his gun barrel into my chest.

"Nah," I said. If I was going to die, I'd die on my feet.

"That's all right, Riley," Omani said. "Let him be for now." The squinty-eyed Iranian, if that's what he was, hadn't stopped clutching Taylor for even a second.

I looked at the boy. "Pepper's okay," I said. "I want you to hang tough, all right?"

Taylor nodded, tried to keep the tears out of his eyes.

"You will address your remarks to me," said Omani. "Tell me *now*, Barr. Where is it?" His English was flawless, but there was still the slight accent that I assumed was Farsi.

"First let the boy go," I said, "and I'll tell you everything."

"No," Orval said, interjecting himself into the conversation. "That's not how this works. You tell us, and *maybe*, just *maybe*, we let you both live."

I looked at the little man as if he were an insect that had just flown into my soup. "Haven't we had this conversation before, Orval? You're not giving me much incentive," I said. "If I don't know that either of us will live whether I tell you or not, why would I? You have me, and I have what you want. Let the boy go."

Four of the bikers dismounted and walked over to join Riley in flanking the two bosses. One carried a sawed-off shotgun, two sported pistols, and one held a shiny ax handle. These, combined with Riley's AK-47, should have made me feel a little uncomfortable. But I was already *very* uncomfortable, just trying hard not to show it, so I stood my ground and tried to look thoroughly bored, as if I were in line at the DMV.

Orval balled his fists and thrust out his jaw. "You will do what you're told, or you will *die*."

Before I could reply, Omani curtly said, "I don't care about any of you. I want my merchandise. Tell me now, or I will kill the boy."

I looked at Taylor, who was beginning to tear up and shake. Without saying a word, he pleaded for help, looking every bit the kid that he was. In response, I put my chin up, the way I'd seen him do before, to try to give him a little reassurance.

Omani had noticed our exchange. "He is something to you, isn't he?"

I didn't answer, looking instead at the men stoically standing beside him holding instruments of death.

"If so, tell me now, and he lives," Omani said. With those words he brought a small-caliber pistol to Taylor's temple.

I just stared at him and the boy, trying to seem unmoved.

Omani screwed the pistol tighter against Taylor's temple, and I could see the flesh under the muzzle wrinkle and turn pale. My head started pounding, my heart raced, and my stomach felt as if it were in a runaway elevator. But I tried not to show it.

"You have two seconds," Omani said. "I am getting angry."

"Me too," Orval said. His voice was too high, and he was starting to sound less confident, less in control.

"One," Omani said. He stared at me with no expression on his dark face. I tried to return the stare, using all the facial skills I'd acquired in prison, but I wasn't sure I was succeeding.

"You don't believe me?" Omani asked. "You don't believe I am serious?" Taylor was weeping now.

I was going to tell Omani yes, I believed him. I'd heard about the three Utes who were executed in the street. I'd seen the devastation inflicted on the town. I knew that, for this man, what was happening in Wakara was only a side drama. He was playing a bigger game, planning devastation on an unimaginable scale. Before I could tell him, though, he pulled the pistol away from Taylor and popped three quick rounds into Orval's head. The little man dropped into the dust, small red holes leaking into the already red sand.

The bikers nearby all wore the same expression that I did: one of complete disbelief. If this man was willing to kill the person who'd set up this whole heist, then he was desperate and ruthless enough to do anything. There was no getting away from him.

Omani put his pistol back against Taylor's head, turned to me, and said, "Shall I continue counting?"

I didn't get a chance to answer that question, either.

Before I could, the man closest to Omani dropped to the ground, grabbing and clawing at his chest. His grunts and gurgles were drowned out by the report of a hunting rifle. A .30-06, if I had to guess. Lawana's rifle.

The bikers ducked but stared at the buildings along the street, unsure what to do. Omani dropped and rolled, pulling Taylor with him, and shouted something in Farsi.

The Reapers surprised me, abandoning their bikes and their posts, hurrying to find cover behind buildings and parked vehicles. Like experienced fighters. Omani called out again, this time in English, "Return fire, and advance, one at a time." A few of the bikers did just that, pouring rounds into the nearby buildings.

A fusillade of single shots responded, ringing out from nearby, and I dropped to the ground, rolling against the curb. I kept an eye on Omani and Taylor. The Persian had Taylor by the collar and was on the pavement in front of me, trying to crawl backward to his SUV.

Another round of rifle shots sounded, and I felt more than saw that they were coming from atop the nearby school. With the bikers occupied with returning fire, I rolled over the broken glass in the gutter and scrambled into the small crease between the store and the boarded-up house next to it. I watched Omani pull himself up and drag Taylor at full speed over to the SUV. Once there, he hurled the boy inside, and with his gun trained on him, put the car in drive and peeled out. A few bullets hit the rear fender but failed to puncture a tire.

Three bikers emerged from behind their individual choices of cover, hopped on their Harleys, and roared off toward the SUV, following Omani. Cracks of rifles followed their retreat.

I used the disarray and the screaming sounds of wounded men as a distraction and ran, or shuffled, across the street, looking up at the walls of the broken schoolhouse, shimmering in the heat.

On the edge of the roof, standing up against the skyline, were four figures I recognized. Each held a rifle, and each waved at me. As I neared the broken doors and the sounds of gunfire faded away, I heard someone far behind me, calling out.

I was confused at first. *What the . . . ?* I turned.

It was Omani, at least eighty yards away. He'd stepped out from behind a stone wall for a second to deliver a message.

"One hour," he yelled. "At the station. If I don't have what is mine, the boy dies."

The next moment he was gone, and all that was left was the faint sound of an SUV engine fading into the distance.

CHAPTER THIRTY-SEVEN

The broken doors of the school had been barricaded, and I had to wait for Buffalo and Goff to move the desks and chairs out of the way before I could enter. Shattered glass crunched under my boots as I followed them deep inside the old building, eventually coming to a stop at the gym. A rumbling cacophony of voices drifted out the door.

As we walked in, the two other figures that I'd seen on the roof greeted us.

"Aye, mate," Cordell said, nodding in my direction. "Surprised to see you again. Glad you made it."

Colorow came over, carrying an extra rifle. "He wouldn't have, if it weren't for us. Here," he said, shoving the recently cleaned rifle into my hands. Then he slapped me on the shoulder. "Kidding, man. We're glad you got away."

I stared at the rifle, pulled the bolt, and checked the magazine. Full of long shiny brass, which was the best thing I'd seen all day. It took a moment for my eyes to adjust to the dimmer light, but when they did I looked up and saw the cots, sleeping bags, and blankets arranged inside the three-point lines. In the center of the court were tables set up with makeshift food stations. It looked like an indoor refugee camp, or a hurricane shelter. There must have been close to a hundred and fifty people cloistered inside the big space.

A young woman came over and handed me a damp cloth to wipe my sooty face. I pressed the cloth to my forehead, then brought it down slowly to my chin. Finally—with the part that wasn't already black—I wiped my soot- and dust-caked hands. Man, that felt good. I set the cloth down on a cardboard box and turned back to Colorow.

"Everyone here?" I asked.

An extremely large figure shuffled over from a table covered in canned goods to answer. His shoes squeaked on the rubber floor. "Most people, yes," Mateo said. "Some old people—you can't move 'em. Set in their ways. I did like you said, worked most of the night to get them here. The fire only affected the outside classrooms and office. Most of the tribe, including the hostages who were freed, are in the gymnasium, but a few people set up in the classrooms, especially those with infants. Also," he said, scratching his large belly, "I had those who have guns bring them along. They're guarding the school's entrances, and as you noticed, several of them helped lay down fire a few minutes ago."

"We're ready to go to war, dude," Colorow said with his usual bravado.

Mateo shook his head. "My people are not trained fighters. Their great-grandfathers were warriors, but they are tradesmen or ranchers, or work on the rigs. Anyone wants to enter the school without permission, my guys will cut them down. They don't lack courage. But it would be a mistake to get overconfident against the remaining bikers. We have a couple guys who are ex-army and can help take the fight to them, but I think most of us should continue in our defensive position."

"Makes sense," I said. But my mood darkened as I thought about Lawana. "I've got to know. Is Lawana . . . did she . . . ?"

I couldn't say the words.

Goff cleared his throat as the others shot glances among themselves. "She's here, Barr. But . . ."

"But what?" I asked frantically, looking around.

Colorow pointed to the far corner of the large room, underneath a basketball net, where three women hunched over one cot in particular.

I started to rush over, but Cordell grabbed my elbow. "She's not good, Barr. Buff and I killed the bastards who had her, but she went through some nasty stuff before we got there."

I nodded, kept walking. Buffalo followed. "You saved her?" I asked as I stomped across the gym.

"Yeah," he said. "It was four guys with Nomad patches who beat her. We heard screams, but it took us a while to get there. It ain't pretty."

When I looked down at the figure on the cot, my guts seized and bile started climbing up my throat. One of the women in the circle—the lady with the shotgun whom I'd met the day before when Taylor, Pepper, and Mateo were marched down the street—said, "She needs a doctor bad, but she'll be okay."

I stared and knew she was trying to be optimistic. Lawana was stretched out in a mummy bag, underneath two Pendleton blankets, her arms hanging straight on either side of the cot. Her face was bloated and blue-black, and her breathing came in raspy, short gasps.

Without thinking, I reached for her hand, pulled it up,

and held it to my cheek. Then I kissed it. "What were the bikers doing when you got there?" I asked over my shoulder, massaging Lawana's limp hand. I remembered when it had felt so strong.

Buffalo coughed, which echoed in the large room. "Probably not what you're thinking. She had her clothes on. But they were punching and kicking her, saying no squaw was going to keep them from getting paid. They were pretty excited, until Cordell and I blew their brains out."

"Glad you did," I said. I squeezed Lawana's hand harder, and she responded with a weak countergrip. She rocked slightly back and forth on the cot and let out a small moan.

"Clyde?" she croaked.

"I'm here," I said, choking up but trying to hide it from the people watching us.

"I didn't tell them," she said. Her lips barely moved, and there was no way her eyes could open. Her face was too swollen. But I knew what she was talking about.

"What happened to 'protect your own'?" I said, trying to make it sound gentle. "You should have just told them."

She moaned something but I could barely hear it. I leaned my ear to her mouth and said, "What?"

"*Wujakiyu.*"

Huh? I couldn't make it out so I leaned even closer. "What did you say?" I said, squeezing her hand.

Her lips parted. "They would have killed you . . . if I talked. *Was* protecting my own." With that, she seemed to fade back into semi-consciousness, and I felt the tears falling down my face. Not just a few. A river of tears. I didn't make any effort to hide them.

I'm not sure I'd ever felt this way before, part of a loving family where everyone is looking out for each other. Staring at Lawana in that puffed-up state, her raspy breath coming in fits and starts, I made myself a promise. Somehow I'd get Taylor back. And somehow I'd kill the man who was responsible for all this.

CHAPTER THIRTY-EIGHT

Over by the gym's double doors, eight of us gathered—Colorow, Goff, Cordell, Buff, Mateo, myself, and two other Utes who'd each done a tour in Afghanistan. I'd come up with a plan, and wanted to run it by everyone, make sure we were on the same page. As I choked down a cup of black coffee to keep myself awake, I made a quick inspection of the new guys. Both were muscled and in their early thirties, with the hard stares of men who'd seen some of the same things I had. I decided they'd do. An important question was, how many bikers did we have to defeat? It seemed to depend on whether Omani had finally pulled in his sentries from the main exit roads, but I figured it could be as few as twelve or as many as twenty. Not great odds, but we'd find a way.

"First things first," I said. "I need one volunteer to recruit a few people from the tribe—I don't care if they're men or women. We need Utes who aren't afraid to fire a gun, even if they're not particularly good at it. Whichever of you raises your hand will be the mission leader. Your job is to grab a truck, load Dr. Nicholas into it, and try blowing through the roadblock to the north, then head into Vernal. Once there, you need to get her to a hospital and contact law enforcement. Let them know what's going on here and have them call the military. Tell them we found the drones that they lost."

There were surprised murmurs from Mateo and the new guys. "Yeah, that's what Lawana and I found and hid from the bikers," I said. "I have no idea what they intend to do with those things, but the guy in charge—his name is Omani—strikes me as a dude with an itchy trigger finger, and I'm guessing that, with the special ordnance we saw in that trailer, he can light up part of the state. It might even be worse—he may be going for something that would have a multiplier effect, a nuclear storage facility or something."

Goff was the first to speak. "Clyde, what if there are a couple Reapers at that roadblock, and they've got one of those belt-fed machine guns they hauled out yesterday?"

I eyed the group, took a moment to choose my words. "Look, I don't have a crystal ball. There are no guarantees, but I think Omani probably pulled in his sentries. A lot of blood has been spilled in the past twenty-four hours. He's lost several men. He'll want safety in numbers and he'll be counting on us to assume he still has the area sealed off tight as a drum."

Everyone nodded.

"So who's my volunteer?" I asked.

Heads swiveled around, looking at each other, then one of the new recruits, the taller one, stepped forward.

"Why you, David?" asked Mateo.

The Ute shrugged. "Doctor Nicholas saved my mom last winter when we all thought she wasn't going to make it. The doc stayed up three nights with her, giving her meds. If she hadn't been there . . ."

Goff leaned over and squeezed David's shoulder.

"We're all counting on you, David," I said, meaning it. "Get the right folks to help you and *please* head out as soon as you can."

He nodded, turned, and waded into a group at the opposite end of the gym, making a pitch for people to accompany him.

"Maybe I should go with him," said Cordell, hefting an impossibly big rifle. Did this guy own nothing but elephant guns?

I shook my head. "No, I'm going to need your firepower." I turned to the others. "Some of you heard Omani issue that ultimatum out there in the street. Taylor Nicholas will be dead in less than an hour if we don't intervene. And my guess is, Omani will go on a punishing rampage if he doesn't get his way." I let that sink in, then looked at Mateo. "You should stay here, big man, make sure the women and kids are defended." I eyed the others. "It's up to the rest of us to make a run at the station."

Buff was the first to ask the question I'd been dreading. "How exactly are we going to do that?"

I paused, waited a beat, then: "We go straight at them. Two groups, one that'll do a drive-by hit and run, hopefully provoking some Reapers into following them, and the other slipping inside. We'll need some luck. I'm betting that Omani will wait till the last moment before actually harming Taylor. Right now, the kid is the only bargaining chip he has, and this guy seems obsessed with getting his hands on those drones."

"So, that's it then? The big plan?" Cordell asked, the sarcasm apparent even through his thick accent. "Like stealing candy from a baby?"

"It sounds like we could all easily end up dead," said Colorow. "Taylor too."

"We don't have a lot of options here," I pointed out. "No one is coming in the next thirty minutes to save this town. And I don't think any of us want Taylor's death on our conscience." I looked around, made sure to lock eyes with each of them, including the somewhat short, thick-chested new guy, who was dressed in camo pants. They called him Mingan. "The kid used to tell me about you Utes and your warrior spirit. I've seen some of that today, but we can't quit now."

"We Brits have a little of that spirit, too," Cordell said, lifting up his gun, and I smiled.

Colorow seemed persuaded. "Well, let's go kick some Reaper ass, then."

CHAPTER THIRTY-NINE

Standing in the back of an F-150 pickup driven by Colorow, we heard the Chevy Tahoe driven by David and carrying Lawana speed down Main Street and, at the first intersection, take a screechy turn. We waited another minute and then pulled out. "Take the back streets, through the housing area," I yelled into the cab. Colorow nodded, easing the rusty vehicle out of the parking lot.

"Who's with who?" Buff asked, crouching next to me in the back of the truck.

"You and I are going in," I said. "Mingan, too, if he's up for it," I added. I looked over at the short, beefy Ute and he gave me the thumbs-up. "We'll have Colorow drive the hit-and-run, and Cordell ride shotgun. And Goff here"—I nodded at him—"can stay in the back of the truck and lay down covering fire. That okay with you, G?" I asked.

Goff gave a slight nod. "I guess that works. I hope those guys are lousy shots, because they'll be tearing after us once we shoot up the front of the station."

I smiled. "A man on a motorcycle isn't much good at aiming," I said. "That's your advantage."

No one disagreed with the plan. It took only a few agonizing minutes to reach the housing area, and the lull gave me a chance to think of how Taylor must be feeling right now, and how I'd feel if I let Lawana down and didn't save him. I scolded myself. *Failure is not an option.*

I banged on the cab's window when we were three blocks from the police station. Still no sign of riders, and I hoped David in the Tahoe hadn't seen any on his way out of town, either. At a shabby gray house close to where the deaf old man lived, I had Colorow stop the truck. When he did, my senses came alive. I noticed the beautiful mural painted on the side of one house, half-hidden by a dead elm tree. It depicted a lone woman, her hair full of flowers, looking up at the sky and smiling. I also sniffed the sharp smells of dust, exhaust, and Russian olives. I heard the birds chirping and the far-off sound of motors. I felt charged and ready—like I'd felt in Monrovia ten years before, right before I marched with twenty teenage boys into a raging battle with government troops. All but three of us died that day.

Not this time, I told myself.

Buff and Mingan jumped out of the truck, rifles at the ready. I hopped over the edge and ran to the driver's door, where Colorow sat sweating. "Still want to do this?" I asked. "They'll likely have a few guys posted in front of the station. You can expect to take fire right away."

In the truck bed, Goff rested his elbows on the roof of the cab, lined up his rifle, and prepared to pull back the trigger. "I'll give 'em something to think about, C," he called down.

Colorow gripped the steering wheel in the ten-and-two position and looked determined. "I figure I'll drive right at them, make them think my bumper is going to turn them to pulp."

"How about you, Cordell?" I asked the gray-haired Brit sitting in the passenger seat. "You ready to mix it up?" The Englishman didn't say anything for a moment, just looked past me at the brown and red hills around us. "I've done this before, mate," he said, "in a place like this—all sand and heat. Sixteenth Air Assault, Pathfinder Platoon."

"Then it'll come back to you," I said confidently. "Like riding a bicycle."

I thumped the door and wished them luck. As I took a step back, Colorow said, "Hey, where do we meet if a lot of them are left alive and somehow we live through this?"

It was a good question. I didn't want to draw the Reapers over to the school. There were too many people there who could get hurt. I suggested the only other place I knew well. "Bud's ranch," I said. "Find a way to get there. We'll assess when we meet up."

"All right," Colorow said. "Hope I see you there and not in hell." He stomped on the gas and took off, spraying gravel five feet in the air.

I rechecked my new rifle and noted for the first time that it was a .300 Winchester Mag. Great sniper rifle, but not great for the kind of assault we were planning. I said as much to the new guy, Mingan, who seemed oddly composed.

He nodded. "Glad I brought my AR," he said. "I should have brought the rest of my armory."

"Armory?"

"Yeah," he said. "I like my guns. ARs, AKs, Mini-14s, FNs, H&Ks, I got 'em all. Here," he said, switching his rifle to his off hand and swinging his hunting pack off. He reached into a holster between his pants and his back and pulled out a shiny black pistol. "Take my Glock. It's a twenty-three, my favorite carry. It'll help. And I still got this," he said, bending over and pulling up his pant leg. Strapped in an ankle holster was another, smaller pistol. "Ruger LCP. Six plus one, weighs almost nothing."

"Much obliged for the Glock," I said. I stuck the pistol in my right rear waistband. Obviously this guy had never met a gun he didn't like. My kind of person. How had we found him in a school gym? I felt a little more confident about this mission, knowing that Buff and I were going to have Mingan for company.

Apparently the man's talent for destruction wasn't unknown to Buff, who said, "He's going to come in handy, Clyde. Mingy here likes seeing the bullets fly."

CHAPTER FORTY

By the time we rounded the corner of the alley that led to the back of the station, we could hear the shooting letting up. Men were running out of the doors, jumping on bikes—those that weren't shredded with bullet holes—and ripping out onto Main Street. As the sound of Colorow's F-150 diminished, I noticed two bikers lying dead in the street, one missing most of his head. That forfeiture of above-the-neck flesh looked like it might have been Cordell's handiwork.

Buff raised his rifle and I grabbed his arm. "Wait," I said, shaking my head. "Let them follow Colorow."

He kept his rifle up but didn't shoot. Meanwhile, Mingan, on my other side, seemed calm as a cucumber. We all edged behind a large metal Dumpster and waited, listening as three, four, five motorcycles roared away. "Five less," I whispered.

"What now?" Mingan said. "Breach the place?"

I duck-walked away from the Dumpster and checked the station again through the scope, repeating my reconnaissance of the night before. No external air-conditioner, gas meter, or generators. No windows. No way to cause a major distraction. Unless . . . I looked at the overhead power lines, saw the line that dropped into the ground nearest the station. I put the crosshairs on the transformer that connected to the line, calculated how far away we were. A few seconds later I was back by the Dumpster.

"Listen to me," I said, making sure Buff and Mingan were paying attention. "When we get close, I'll shoot the station's transformer. It might get us a second or two of confusion. We'll use it to shoot at the door and try to disable the lock—if the station even *is* locked. They may have a welcoming party right behind the door, ready to surprise us. My thinking is, let's not take chances. Go in with guns blazing. Just make sure you keep an eye out for Taylor. You okay with that?"

In every battle there is a moment that is a leap into the void, an act of faith. It helps to tell yourself that it is the *other* guy who is going to pay, that you're invincible. Crazy confidence keeps you loose. Fear makes you tight. I knew that. Mingan apparently knew that. Buff was learning that.

"I'm in," said Mingan.

"Let's do it," said Buff.

"Okay, then," I said. "On three."

I put the transformer in the crosshairs. Squeezed the trigger. The rifle shoved my shoulder and I started running, my ears ringing. I didn't look up to see what damage I'd done, just swung the scope to the door and began firing. Buff was already running and shooting, three-round bursts every few strides. Mingan was shredding the door with his AR.

As I came up on the door, I aimed at what looked like a dead bolt. I had to stop to sight it, and to calm my breathing. While Buff and Mingan kept running to my right, I steadied the rifle to a slight sway, took a couple of slow breaths, and squeezed off another shot. I kept the scope relatively steady and saw the hole in the door where the upper lock's bolt would be. I hoped it was enough and ran to catch up with the others, who were still blistering the back of the station with bullets.

Frantically, I signaled Buff and Mingan. "Wait, back me up," I shouted. "I'm trying the door."

I'd just stepped gingerly to the side of the door and reached for the knob, which our combined fire had done a great job of surrounding with holes, when the door blew open and a tall Reaper ran out, holding a belt-fed PKM under his shoulder and spraying a steady stream of lead.

CHAPTER FORTY-ONE

I grabbed the door and held it, while Buff put three rounds into the biker. The tall man dropped, crashing into the loose gray gravel. Mingan yelled over the ringing in our ears, "I got right," and swung inside. I followed, going left. Buff trailed behind us.

I pulled my rifle up and cleared my corner—meaning that I swept the muzzle through my nearest corner and checked for targets—while my eyes tried to adjust to the red of the emergency lighting. I hurried along my wall, keeping an eye on the room until I got close to the corner. Then I turned and swept the rifle through the place until I saw Mingan on the opposite side doing the same thing. I couldn't see anything besides desks and computers and cubicle walls. Staying to the right, Mingan gave me a thumbs-up and called out, "Watch the desks. I'm moving."

He headed to the doorway that opened into the middle of the station. From there we could go into the front offices, or left to the locked hall that held the cells. Right would lead us to more offices and storage units, if I remembered correctly. I covered Mingan as he moved, occasionally checking the room we were in. Behind us, Buff kept his rifle sighted, ready to fire.

Nothing moved but Mingan, who was slowly pushing out of the room.

He stopped short of the next door, which was open, and leaned against the wall. He kept his rifle pointed at the entry. "Scout and snake," he said. I made my way beside him, almost hip to hip.

"Hallway next," I said.

"Watch the funnel," he said, pointing at the opening. "I'll go right first, you sweep left and keep the center clear."

I understood half of what he said, having never used the terminology before. I'd just done it on instinct with others—usually young villagers—and had apparently gotten very lucky. I hoped that would continue. Very quickly, I threw a glance over my shoulder and confirmed that Buff was still trailing us. That's when I heard something. I put up a fist to signal Mingan to stop.

All three of us froze. The sounds of feet were shuffling toward us.

Mingan and I both went to the wall on either side of the entryway. Buff ducked into an alcove. Mingan then crept farther down the wall, halfway into the room, to change our fields of fire so we wouldn't shoot each other. When the two Reapers edged into our room, both holding AKs like they knew what they were doing, we cut them down.

Four quick shots, and both men crumpled. One skidded into a chair, his head clanking into the metal leg. The other biker wobbled on weak knees, then fell on top of a desk. A phone and keyboard went flying. "I'm watching the door," Mingan said. "Get one of their AKs."

Another great idea. I slung the hunting rifle across my back, then hurried over and relieved one of the corpses of his firearm. I'd just dropped and checked the mag when my ringing ears heard commands, but they weren't coming from either of my guys.

"On me," I heard someone shouting from the other room. "Thumper, watch the front." I hurried back to the corner closest to the entryway, charged the AK, and waited. I kept the front sight trained on the open door.

That's when I saw a grenade fly into the room.

Instinct made me duck under the closest messy desk. I covered both of my ears, closed my eyes, and opened my mouth to equalize the pressure that comes with a shock wave. Just in time. The tube banged, and I opened my eyes and smelled smoke. I couldn't see well, because even with my eyes closed the light from the stun grenade had been horribly bright. And the sound of the bang had still managed to ring already ringing ears, along with making me slightly wobbly. I recovered as best I could and rose up over the desk, AK ready.

A bullet ripped through the desk, just to my right. I watched the drawer explode maybe a foot away, then focused on the room. Two bikers were in, already shooting.

Another shot had ripped into the wall behind me by the time I pulled the trigger and took a chunk out of the closest biker's shoulder. He dropped his rifle and fell hard into the wall. When he did, I pushed him against it harder by putting three more shots into his chest. Then I swung the muzzle, searching for the other biker, and saw him on a knee, grabbing at his throat. Buff had shot him before I could, and he fell over, his throat pulsing blood onto the carpeted floor.

Where the hell is Mingan? That's when I saw the body of the Ute sprawled on the carpet. Something had scraped away his forehead. *Damn*. His death was a huge loss, but right now there was no time to process it.

When the second biker fell, I noticed the card hanging on his chest. A key card. "Moving," I yelled. I went around the desk to the dead man and ripped the card off the green cord that hung from his bleeding neck. Buff covered the door, and I ran back to the corner by the door. "Go," I said, and peeked around the corner, searching over the front sight for any movement.

I heard Buff's boots stomp next to me, then felt him squeeze my shoulder. He put his hand on my back and we started moving out through the door. Once through, I went left and he went right, clearing as Mingan had done. I looked down the locked side hall that led to the cells and saw movement. I heard Buff say, "Clear," and I replied with, "Bastard's down the hall. Behind that locked door." I pointed at the thick door between us and the cells.

"I see 'im," he said, and I was starting to follow when shots broke out from another direction.

Thumper. Probably all alone now and worried. "Let's get him," Buff said. We moved fast into the waiting room area, both of us covering our respective sides of the room. But Buff didn't see the biker fast enough.

I heard the shot before I got my muzzle to the chair that Thumper was hiding behind. I pulled the trigger until the AK clicked, then scanned the room as I dropped the AK and swung the hunting rifle around. No other threats. "Clear," I said, but there was no reply.

I looked over and saw Buff slumped against the wall.

"I've been hit," he said, and pointed to his leg. The lower half of his left pant leg was covered in blood, soaking his jeans.

On instinct I went to take off my pack, then remembered I didn't have one. So, while watching both the front door and the door that led to the hall, I ran to Buff and helped him take off his T-shirt. I turned it inside out and shoved it against the hole in his leg. Then I eased his belt off and ran it around his thigh, but I didn't pull it tight. Not yet.

"It isn't that bad," I said, which was mostly true. The bullet had gone straight through the large calf muscle, barely missing the shin. "If it bleeds through, use your belt as a tourniquet." I stood and started for the door.

"Where you going?" he asked, his voice weaker than before. With Mingan dead and me about to leave, he'd be all alone.

"I'm going to get Taylor," I said. "Remember to pull the belt tight if the shirt starts to soak through. And stay here, no matter what you hear." I was already thinking about what waited for me down the locked hall. It wasn't going to be good.

"I ain't moving nowhere," Buff said. "Bastard nicked me good." I nodded and started moving.

"Clyde?" he said. I turned and saw his thumbs-up. "Good luck."

I thanked him and took off, knowing I was going to need it.

CHAPTER FORTY-TWO

As I moved, I checked the hunting rifle. Loaded. I also felt the reassuring pressure of the Glock in my right rear waistband. Once in the hall I went low, under the viewing window's line of sight. At the door, I grabbed the key card. I hoped to hell it opened this door and wasn't for something else. As I crouched by the door, I noticed how badly my hands were shaking.

This had to end. Even through my adrenaline I could feel immense exhaustion. I couldn't go on much longer. Couldn't keep fighting. My body and brain were both at the point of shutting down, and the thought of a long nap was increasingly taking up space in my mind. Squatting there, I willed myself to think of Taylor—of how much he reminded me of *me* when I was a kid. Without a dad around to offer protection.

It was enough to get me going. Enough to make me look up and find the little black box next to the door. I ran the key over it, and when the light went from red to green I pulled on the door handle. It opened.

I swung inside the door, my rifle tight to my shoulder, and felt sick again.

Jury and Omani stood in the inner hall, both with pistols, both pointed into an open cell door.

Jury! How had he made it back?

This was over. But not the way I'd hoped.

"Great seeing you again," Jury said. If I hadn't been so close to him so many times, I wouldn't have recognized him. He wore a new vest, this one without the patches, and his head was covered in blisters and bruises. Around his throat was a nasty rope burn. His left hand held the pistol and his right was pressed to his side, as if he'd popped his liver. I was having trouble believing it was him. Like a dark pursuer from a sweaty nightmare, he just stood there, a smile on his swollen face.

"Drop the weapon," Omani said, squinting at me. "Unless you want this boy to die." His left arm shook slightly, and his right hung limply at his side. It was wrapped with medical tape around an area where he'd been nicked, but the wound looked to have stopped bleeding.

I didn't move at first. I was tempted to take a shot—kill Omani and save Taylor. Except I assumed Jury had his gun pointed at the boy, too. And I was worried about Jury's mind right then. To punish me, he'd clearly do anything. Slowly, I lowered the rifle.

"Long walk back?" I asked Jury as I set the rifle on the tile floor.

He didn't answer, just kept smiling and kept his weapon trained into the cell.

Omani said, "Good. Now kick it away."

I did, hearing it clatter against the tile. I was still very tempted to pull the pistol that was riding against my back and take a couple of shots. Just to end this nightmare. But again, I had to think about Taylor. So I put my hands up and said, "I want this over. I'll take you to the trailer."

Omani smiled and said, "Of course you will. Jury, please secure Mr. Barr, then get the vehicle ready to go."

Jury moved from the door, his grin that of a hungry man who is about to eat a hearty meal. "I've been looking forward to this for a long time. That whole walk back, in fact." He grabbed my shirt and shoved me hard against the wall. After I bounced off, he caught me and spun me around, then pushed me forward until my face was against the cold, rough wall. If I hadn't turned my head, I would have broken my nose. Instead, I took the brunt of the force with my chin.

"What's this?" Jury said as he pulled the pistol from my waist. "Use it to kill one of my brothers?" He smashed the gun hard against the side of my head.

Which hurt like hell, and I went to my knees, the world going gray during the time it took Jury to wrap my wrists in duct tape.

When I recovered, Jury was gone and Omani was pointing his large pistol at me. I was still on my knees, jammed into the corner near the open door. My head pulsed and pounded as if it were full of tiny, thundering elephants on the march.

"I said I'll take you," I told Omani when the pain subsided enough to talk again, "but you have to let Taylor go."

"No," he said. "I do not. *You* do not get to make demands. *You* will do what I say, and then I will turn you over to Jury, who will get revenge for his fallen brothers."

"The kid had nothing to do with any of this," I said. "Let him go."

He laughed. "I think not. The boy will come with us. That way you won't try anything out of the ordinary. I'll let him go as soon as the trailer is located. For you, though, there'll be no freedom."

I wasn't too worried about me. I was too tired and worn out. But the thought of Taylor with us as we drove into the desert scared the hell out of me. There was no way to keep him safe, and no way to tell if Omani would keep his promise. I strongly feared he wouldn't. I turned my head around to see if I could peer into the cell. Why hadn't Taylor called out? Why couldn't I see him?

The ultimate irony would be if he'd never been there to begin with. Maybe Omani had gotten impatient and killed him before I'd even arrived.

Jury came over to stand guard by me, and Omani walked back toward the cells. I saw him disappear into the first one and, a few moments later, emerge, pulling Taylor by the hair. The boy's wrists were duct-taped like mine and his mouth was also taped. His eyes were wide with fear. Omani ripped the tape off his mouth. "Say hello to your annoying uncle Barr," the Persian said almost gleefully.

"Clyde?"

Taylor said my name in a way that broke my heart. It was uttered as a question that contained at least four different questions, such as: *Is this the end? Is there any hope for us? Am I going to die? Will I ever see my mom again?*

"Your mom's going to be okay," I said. "I saw her. I made her a promise and I intend to keep it." I gave him a long, lingering look that said, *We'll figure something out.*

CHAPTER FORTY-THREE

I was pushed by the busted semblance of Jury to an old crew-cab truck in the rear parking lot. The damage to Omani's SUV must have been more severe than I thought. This older truck had come off the assembly line maybe twenty years before. Omani was in front of us, dragging Taylor, and he never looked back. He just jammed the boy into the truck's passenger seat, kept a pistol pointed at his head while he made his way around to the other side, then placed himself behind the wheel like a guy about to make the drive home from work. The pistol was in his weaker right hand now, but even with a damaged arm it was still ready to be pointed at Taylor's head in an instant.

When I got to the truck, Jury slammed me into the side and got close to my ear. "I'd hoped it would be your lady friend we picked up. Kinda need a doc's expertise right now. But you'll do. I owe you something." He patted the pistol in his hand. "Try anything, and the kid gets a hole in his head. Then I'll give you one to match—*if* you're lucky."

Idly, I wondered what delicious plan Jury had for drawing out my death. If I possibly could, I'd deny him the pleasure of prolonging things.

"Hop on in," Jury said as he opened the back door of the truck on the driver's side. As I lowered myself to scoot in, he violently jabbed his foot into my side, as if compressing the trash in a trash can. If I weren't so tired, I would have been white hot with rage. Instead, I looked at him with a bland expression as if I'd barely noticed.

I leaned back into the rear upholstery directly behind Omani and closed my eyes for a second. Jury walked around the truck's hood, jerked open the opposite back door, and jostled in next to me. He kept his pistol trained on me, leering and looking like he was ready to spit in my face. I thought about returning the hard look but was too tired and broken. I felt like a toy in a landfill, used and abused and finally tossed away.

Omani started the truck and said over his shoulder, "Now you'll take us to the trailer. I have a promise to keep."

Hmm. That was interesting. He had a promise to keep, too. To whom, I wondered.

As we drove slowly back toward Main Street, Jury's sunburned face turned sour when we passed the fallen bodies of his brothers lying by the station's front door. He waved the pistol at Taylor and locked eyes with me. "You get my man to the trailer," he said, "and the kid lives. But *you?*" He moved the gun to point between my eyes. "Me and you gonna have a talk. A long, nasty talk."

"Spent a lot of time in the sun, huh?" I asked. "What happened? Stuck your thumb out but were too ugly to get a ride?"

Jury swung the pistol backhanded, and I dodged away. I smacked my head against the glass, which caused me to glance out the front window and see something move near the front of the police station. I couldn't be sure, but it looked like a man in jeans, hopping on one leg.

Omani sped up and Jury took another swing. This time I was distracted, and he caught me square on the nose. Something cracked and blood poured out.

Omani jammed the accelerator and the truck leaped forward. It was then that I heard Taylor in the front seat, softly crying. I watched through my own tears as we left the station behind and began heading out of town.

"Shut up, boy," Omani said. "And you two in the back—" He'd turned his head slightly when his side-view mirror exploded.

Glass and chrome fell off the side of Omani's door, and the dark-skinned man looked genuinely stunned as he focused his attention on driving. Jury rolled down his window and stuck his bulky upper body far out, firing in the direction the shot had come from. I stopped pinching my nose and considered making a move. It was the only time, I thought. Jury busy, Omani driving. If I could kill them both, somehow, quickly, without Taylor getting hurt, the whole mess would be over. That was a pretty immense challenge, though, given that my wrists were still duct-taped.

What the hell. I lurched toward Jury, intent on pushing him out the window.

"No, Barr," Omani said. His voice caught me in mid-lurch. I looked at the sleek man in the driver's seat and saw the pistol again. One hand was on the wheel, but the other held the big black gun across the console, pointed at Taylor's temple. "You move one more inch in Jury's direction and I swear I'll kill the boy."

I grunted and sat back in the seat. As Omani pushed the truck up past highway speed, I thought about putting on my seat belt, but with the duct tape that wasn't happening. Taylor didn't have his belt on, either, I realized. Oh well, getting into a fender-bender was the least of our worries right now.

Jury fired the last round in his pistol and pulled himself back into the truck. He withdrew a spare magazine from his pants pocket and swapped it with the spent one, staring at me with cold fury.

"I think I got the son of a bitch," he said, smiling broadly.

I doubted it, because shooting a pistol from a moving vehicle at a target more than a hundred feet away was next to impossible. But I knew why he'd said it. To rattle me, and show me how dangerous he was. I smiled back, like a dog showing his teeth to another in a dog park, and ignored him. I had other, more important things to think about.

Omani lowered the pistol and rested his hand on the console. The barrel, however, was still pointed at Taylor. "Where to?" he asked.

I told him to head on the main road toward the gas field. Then I sat back and looked out my window and tried to think of a new plan. There was time, since the side road that led to the trailer was still miles away. We sped through the town, then through the narrow valley, and with most of my attention focused on a means of escape, I barely registered the tall red walls of rock whizzing by.

Having been in a situation or two like this before, where I was outnumbered and outgunned, I remembered that it always helped to get into the enemy's head, figure out where they were coming from. Sometimes it created an opening.

"I have to admit, Omani," I said, forcing myself to sound a tad awestruck. "You've been pretty much unstoppable throughout this whole thing. I don't often see that type of commitment in people. This promise must be a sacred thing to you."

No answer. The Persian kept driving. Time to work further on his ego, make him play the role of wise teacher instructing me, the dim-witted student.

"The thing I can't figure is, how are you going to lug those drones over hill and dale, given how much heat is already on you?"

Omani kept his eyes on the highway and his foot on the gas pedal, so I had a hard time seeing his face, but I imagined that there was a sneer on it. "You can't 'figure' it, Barr, because you have no imagination. You observe, but you don't see."

"See what?" I said, continuing to play the dunce. "You're going to have to offload those drones to another vehicle, aren't you?"

"Come now, Barr," said Omani. "Surely you're brighter than that. Drones fly, do they not? As soon as we arrive at the trailer, they will be in flight within minutes and my promise will be kept."

I thought about it. He must have brought with him some launch mechanism, or maybe a code sequence—something that perhaps even Orval didn't know about—that could put the drones on a certain trajectory. "So," I said, "an eye for an eye, that's what you're cooking up?" I watched the highway asphalt roll beneath the truck and felt the sweat trickling down my shirt.

"Try a *million* eyes" was all Omani said.

I thought of what that might mean, and for the first time, I didn't regret hiding the trailer. The resulting standoff had gotten a lot of people killed, to be sure, but if I *hadn't* stolen it . . . The implications were too horrible to contemplate. Trouble was, if I didn't come up with a final stunt to undermine Omani's scheme, it was going to succeed anyway.

"You think you're brave?" Taylor piped up. "My father was brave. Clyde is brave. You're like every other terrorist who kills innocent people without looking them in the eye."

Uh-oh. I braced myself for Omani to lose his composure, but instead, he did something I didn't expect. He laughed and said, "So the boy has some fight in him after all." The Persian raised his pistol and pointed it inches from Taylor's face. "Let me tell you, boy, you have no idea what bravery is. My father and three brothers would be alive right now if they hadn't had the courage to rise up against those oppressing them."

"How about you, Jury?" I asked, wanting to take the focus off Taylor, "you sign up for jihad, too?"

The big man stuck his gun in my eyelid and pressed hard. For a second I worried that he was going to crush my eyeball. "I'm a simple guy, bumpkin. I like money. *Lots* of it. And I love stomping on people who don't mind their own business."

CHAPTER FORTY-FOUR

A minute later, I got a major morale boost. As we came up to a small ridge that ran perpendicular to the road, I saw the bodies.

Omani slowed to a stop. He pointed at the dead bikers lying next to bikes that were still propped up by their kickstands. He stared at Jury and asked, "Is this why your men didn't answer the radio? Your men who you promised would keep the locals secure *inside* the valley?"

Inwardly, I let out a whoop. David and Lawana must have gotten through. I'd apologize later for predicting that they wouldn't meet any resistance.

Jury stared, stunned. For less than a second. Then he looked at me. "More to pay for, bumpkin." He launched a straight right at me again, and in the confines of the truck, the most I could do was take it and roll with the punch. My head made contact with the window, but just barely.

"Doesn't matter now," Omani was saying. "We have Barr, and we have the boy for insurance. Soon the birds will be in flight, and I will be wiring you the rest of your money."

The rest? Maybe when Jury had wandered back from being

left for dead, he'd demanded an early installment? I just needed to find a way to keep him from ever getting the chance to spend it.

Jury spit something obscene under his breath but didn't hit me again. Instead, he decided to play with me as the truck started rolling forward. "Hey, bumpkin, you know what a Reaper does to someone who really pisses him off?"

I smiled and said, "I bet you're going to tell me."

"Ball stomping is what," he said through clenched teeth. "We toss the maggot to the pavement and take turns crushing boot heels into his softest parts. After that, well, we usually set the maggot on fire."

"So you don't let 'em off with a warning?" I said, pleased with my reply. I was still pleased even after he smashed his gun onto my knee. I had a lot more hope now, knowing that help might be on the way.

I felt even better a couple of minutes later, as we rolled through the red sand and brush, when Jury jerked his head to the open window. "Brother," he called out to Omani. "We got company."

I looked over his shoulder, following his gaze, and saw the black helicopter. It started as a speck far out in the sage, moving low over the old mining equipment in the distance. It didn't get bigger, so it wasn't headed our way. Instead, it moved south, toward the town. It would be back soon, or others would, and they'd spot us.

"I see it," Omani said. He pushed the pedal to the floor and put his pistol in his lap. He held tight to the wheel with both hands. When he turned his face to the right at one point, I noticed that he'd become quite anxious. "Tell me where to turn, Barr."

"You can't outrun a chopper," I said. "He might be gone for now. But there'll be others."

"You hid the trailer from us, so they won't find it, either. Not for a while. By then I will have fulfilled my promise." He turned and shot a quick glance at me. "But I've grown impatient. I've just decided that the boy has two minutes to live if I don't see my trailer in the distance." He grabbed the gun from his lap and pointed it at Taylor, touching the muzzle to his forehead.

It hit me then, looking at the helicopter and where it had just come from. A plan. Of sorts. The usual Clyde Barr plan, one that had more chance of going wrong than right.

"Perfect timing," I said. "Slow down. Up ahead a hundred yards is a real tall sagebrush. Take a right there."

He nodded, his neck still and his face pained.

Jury said, "Better be telling the truth, asshole, or I'll splatter the kid."

I looked up front at Taylor. Sitting diagonal to him, I could just see part of his face. The boy had flinched at the words, but he was looking better. There was more color in his cheeks.

"I am," I said, trying to remember exactly where I'd seen the old, overgrown two-track that led out to the defunct Gilsonite operation.

Omani touched the brakes and I said, "There, turn on those tracks."

He did, just as another helicopter appeared on the western horizon. This one was moving west to east, and if it kept its current path, it might fly close enough to see us. If it didn't, then the next one would. The searchers were tightening their grid.

"Now where?" Omani said. He put the pistol down and

fought the truck's wheel as it tried to kick back due to the red rocks and spindly brush that littered the little road.

"Out by that equipment. We parked it by an old derrick and some wrecked cars. You'll see them." It was a lie, but if you lie with specificity, then you're twice as likely to be believed. It was also a way to try to get Taylor on board with my plan. "Hey, kid," I said. "Good spot to hide it, right? Out by that old mine?"

Jury smacked me in the back of the head, openhanded, to shut me up, but when Taylor looked back at me I noticed his change of expression. He *knew*. As I caught sight of him bracing himself and tucking his chin in a bit, I wished like hell that both of our hands weren't duct-taped. We hadn't been able to put on our seat belts.

Of course, far as I could tell, neither had Omani or Jury. And thank the Lord for old pickups—there hadn't been any warning beeps to remind Omani and Jury to strap themselves in.

I glanced out the window again and noticed a couple of lone horses and an antelope grazing in a dry pond. Then I saw a helicopter beating its way in our direction. Neither of the assholes had seen it yet. I pointed.

"Another one, brother," Jury said. Omani didn't answer, just responded by slamming the gas pedal down, pushing the truck much too fast for the terrain. Rocks thudded and thunked under the wheel wells and greasewood scraped against the paint. I took a deep breath, savoring the smells of the dry dusty earth, the bitter brush, and the hot air that floated over the cactus and locoweed. I caught the briefest musky aroma of antelope. It might be the last time I ever smelled anything that pure, and I savored it.

"The boy has a minute left, Barr," Omani threatened.

"You'd better hurry up, then," I countered.

He tried. The truck bounced and hopped over the rough spots, the shocks and struts creaking and squeaking every time we almost left the ground.

"It's just over the next ridge," I lied. "Cut left off the road, through that big flat of grass." He turned, his desperation stopping him from second-guessing me. We flew across the relative flat of the dead cheat grass.

"I don't like this," Jury said. "You can't trust this guy."

Omani jerked the wheel to maneuver around an old, abandoned coil of steel wire. His hands were white and tight on the wheel. "What choice do we have?"

"Kill 'em both and walk away. Money's always good, but breathing is better. Those choppers are getting too close."

Omani worked the truck past an old cabin, its roof caved in and one wall slumped into the brush growing around it. He didn't say anything.

I looked at Taylor, who'd turned his head slightly to observe Omani's increasing anxiety. The expression on the boy's face—one that all warriors wear right before battle—made me proud. His chin had gone slightly lower into his chest, and his shoulders had rolled slightly forward. I couldn't see his feet but was sure he had them firmly planted. Omani was too preoccupied with the rough terrain under his wheels to notice.

He had no idea what was coming.

CHAPTER FORTY-FIVE

I started to worry that the surprise I was anticipating wouldn't happen before the clock on Taylor's life ran out. Heck, it had already been at *least* two minutes since Omani's threat. Time for a distraction. Anything to get Omani's mind off the narrowing funnel of escape into which he was driving.

"This whole area looks a lot like the Kalahari," I said. "When I was there about twelve years back, I ran into a bunch of assholes like you two." Jury and Omani were still ignoring me, but I continued. Taylor kept his chin tucked in and his body braced. "Actually, some were worse," I said. "Way outside of Xaxa, in the game reserve, I stayed with a group of San. A young man named Gai had brought me in when he found out I was a hunter, and he wanted to swap techniques. They taught me how to track and use poison, and I showed them how to shoot."

Omani looked back at me briefly with an expression that said he thought I was out of my mind. "Anyway, it didn't last long. A month after I first met them, a group of us were out hunting. They had their little bows, and I'd left my rifle at camp so I could learn firsthand how they hunted. Mistake.

A helicopter found us, and a door gunner lit us up. Gai and I survived by running and hiding in a small cave. His uncles and father were killed. I found out later, when I got out of Botswana, that the government was doing that a lot. They called the bushmen poachers. But the government boys really were just pissed off that the bushmen weren't assimilating and were trying to live off the land. Which in turn pissed me off."

I paused as we passed old, rusty trucks, chipped-metal push carts, and even more cable, meaning we were off the reservation and in the mining area. My plan should have come to fruition by now, but still nothing.

Until it did.

Everything happened so fast that I barely remember the sequence. Suddenly the front end of the truck dropped. We slammed to a stop. All of us flew forward, then the rear of the truck rose and pointed to the sky and the whole truck flipped upside down. Metal crashed and clanged, and I turned to the side as the roof caved in. I snaked my duct-taped wrists forward, managed to grab Taylor's shirt, and pulled him toward me. Glass tinkled and fell around us like green snow. I blacked out for a bit, then kept still until the vehicle settled. A moment later, I slowly looked around.

Omani had disappeared. Taylor was huddled on the ceiling of the upside-down truck, still inside the cab but unmoving and bloody. Jury was also unmoving. *Got to get this damn tape off my wrists*, I told myself. I looked around and saw a razor-sharp part of the twisted door protruding from the metal below the window. Awkwardly, I brought my wrists around and used the metal as a saw. Back and forth, back and forth. A couple of times I slipped and drew blood. If I wasn't careful I'd slit my own wrists. I'd just sliced through the last gummy strand of tape when something smacked the side of my head. It hurt, almost worse than anything had up to that point, and I turned to see Jury shaking his head and pulling his arm back for another blow.

I'd made the mistake of assuming he'd stay unconscious. Big error. I'd thought he'd sustained a knockout blow, but apparently he was back in the fight. He looked terrible, worse than before, and I knew he was weak. *Time to end this*, I thought.

When Jury threw another punch, I slipped inside of it and grabbed him, then jammed a hand in his face. I tried to get a finger or two in his eyes, but he turned his head away. Which worked well for me, because I leaned in and snaked my other arm around his neck, then stuck two fingers in his mouth. He wriggled and growled and tried to push me off, but I was too close and the truck was too small.

I curled my fingers in his mouth and pulled back, wrenching his neck with the fishhook. Then I got a hold of his throat with the other hand and squeezed. Hard. As hard as my shaking and aching muscles would allow. I felt his windpipe crack under the pressure, then felt something slice through my ear. I couldn't let go, even though Jury's flailing arm had found a piece of broken truck that he was slashing with. I felt the metal bite deep under my beard, sensed the blood welling up and rolling down my cheek.

But I didn't let go. I squeezed harder. I pushed against the bucking and thrashing of a dying man, felt another slash on my shoulder, kept squeezing, until the big biker finally slumped in the wreckage and lay still. That was it. No final words, no pleas, nothing. Just another life gone. I shoved the beginnings of rationalization out of my mind and tried to feel for Jury's pulse, just in case. But my arms were shaking too bad, and both of my hands were cramped into curls, so I gave up and pushed off the dead man. That's when the exhaustion and the pain really started to kick in.

"Hey, kid," I muttered, trying to move. Unfortunately, my body wasn't responding. I was almost too worn out to curl my toes. My eyes started to lower, and the thoughts of both sleep and death were looking better.

"Hang on, Clyde," a voice said weakly. Taylor's voice, but it seemed miles away. "I'll get us out," he said. I heard what I thought was the sound of his duct-taped hands working at the door release, and then, finally, the creak of the mangled door opening. I caught a glimpse of the boy wriggling out, and then lost sight of him. About two minutes later he appeared on my side of the overturned truck and began awkwardly pulling at my door. I looked up and saw blood streaming down his face from a nasty scalp wound.

"Stay awake, Clyde," he called in through the shattered window. "We're going to make it."

The concern and care in his voice made me rally. I shook my head, forced my eyes to stay open, and tried to focus on the door. The impact seemed to have crumpled its release mechanism, effectively jamming it. The window was crumpled, too, making it too narrow to escape through, even if I punched out the remaining glass. And I couldn't follow the route out that Taylor had taken. There was a whole section of roof that had punched into the cab compartment, effectively cutting off the back section from the front. I thought about whether I could maneuver around it and escape through the same door Taylor had.

Only problem there was the position of the truck. When we'd flipped, the back end of the truck had landed on the ground. The front end, however, bridged the chasm of the horizontal shaft. Looking out, all I could see was darkness. I had no idea how deep the thing was, but I knew I didn't have the strength to go out the door and crawl up and over the hood and tires.

"Gotta admit, kid," I said weakly, "I'm fresh out of ideas on how to get out of here."

"Thank God," Taylor said. "You're back. Just sit tight, I'll find a way." I heard him scurrying around and beneath the upside-down truck bed. What was he doing?

Suddenly, I heard the sound of violent kicking.

Of course. Good idea. I hadn't thought about it before because the mangled seats were in the way, but most crew-cab pickups have a sliding glass section in the rear window. With my head turned to avoid flying pieces of glass punched in by Taylor's feet, I shoved broken parts of the seats aside and tore away at the other debris until I found what remained of the little sliding window. Somehow I had to wedge my body through the tiny aperture.

"You have to crawl out, Clyde," I heard Taylor say. "My wrists are still taped. I can't pull you."

I had trouble summoning the energy at first. Until I heard the boy scream.

CHAPTER FORTY-SIX

I used mostly my legs to push my way out of the cab, then pulled with my cramped hands and arms and crawled into the light.

The sun hit my tired eyes harder than any Kalahari glare ever had. It almost blinded me. I shaded my face with my hand.

That's when I saw Taylor rolling on the ground, through the clumps of cactus, wrestling with someone.

Omani.

Seeing him was enough to get me to my feet. I forgot about my lacerated hands, my bruised ribs, my ripped cheek, and every other damned pain that was plaguing my skin sack. I moved with the determination of a wounded bull elephant.

Omani had Taylor's hair wrapped in both hands and was struggling to roll on top of him. Taylor's wrists were still duct-taped, but he was using his hands as a club, trying to bludgeon Omani's face while simultaneously wrapping a leg around the older man's back. I couldn't tell who was hurt worse, since both were moving too fast, and since both their clothes were ripped and torn and blood-soaked.

By the time I made it over to where the grappling was

taking place, Omani had pulled Taylor in front of him and was lying on his side. Taylor had stopped moving, but I couldn't tell why until I got closer. It was because of the small knife pushed hard against his throat.

"Stop right there, Barr," Omani said.

I did. I studied both boy and man. Taylor's face was covered in cuts and cactus spines, and his bloody scalp was caked with sand, but he still looked determined, red with blood and anger. Omani, however, shouldn't have been alive.

When he had been ejected from the truck he must have bounced and skidded across the desert, because a foot-long stob of greasewood protruded from his chest. Half his hair was missing, and I could see places on his bare scalp where the bright white of his skull was showing. His face looked like someone had raked grooves into it, but none of that stopped him from holding tight to Taylor and pushing the knife harder into his neck, drawing blood.

I couldn't get any closer. Omani would slash Taylor's throat before I reached the kid. My only hope was that the bastard would die before he cut further, but that wasn't likely, either. It was much more likely he'd kill the boy out of spite as a final act, and there wasn't a damned thing I could do about it.

Which brought me to my knees. Literally. I fell, thinking that after all this, the psycho had still won—that all of my fighting had been for nothing. Dimly, I thought I heard a vehicle behind me, but I knew it didn't matter. If someone showed up, they wouldn't have any more options than I had.

I was wrong.

I heard the gunshot before I saw what it did. The shot partly cleared my stupor, and when I focused I saw Omani's head fly back. Saw the red and the gray splatter the sand.

Then Taylor was rolling away and to his feet. His legs didn't hold and he fell, then crawled over to where I was kneeling. Blood covered his face and neck and chest, and I couldn't tell if it was his or the psycho's.

I grabbed Taylor in a hug and looked to where the shot had come from. On the other side of the mangled crew cab sat Colorow, cross-legged, with his rifle in his hands and his elbows on his knees. Classic shooting position. Cordell stood about ten feet farther away, his rifle on the F-150's hood. Goff was positioned just to his right, carrying a pistol. I waved at them and took in more of the scene.

The crew cab was a wreck and stretched across a deep cut that seemed to go on for miles in either direction. I could see a faint blood trail across the undercarriage where Omani had dragged himself or crawled to get to the boy. Taylor and I both limped and hobbled back to Colorow's truck along the same route, taking extra care across the upside-down truck. Colorow and Cordell both gave us a hand and helped swing us to the safe side of the cut. Goff took Taylor to an open door of the F-150 and pulled out a first aid kit. I limped over to Colorow and Cordell.

"Just in time," I said, shaking their hands. "How'd you find us?"

"Luck," said Colorow. "We shot up the station, like we planned, and got five of the bastards to follow us. We pulled down a lease road and stopped, let them come to us. Cordell, Goff, and I each got one of them, and the other two turned tail and started running away toward Vernal. We started chasing them, but saw a truck crashing through the brush and went after it instead. Good thing we did."

"You have no idea," I said.

"The kid going to be okay?" Cordell asked, looking over at Taylor.

I followed his gaze. "I expect so." Taylor looked like hell, but he was standing. Ten minutes ago I'd thought he was dead, so the fact that he was up and talking seemed nothing short of a miracle. His mom was going to be pleased.

Which reminded me. "Lawana made it," I said.

Colorow nodded. "We saw the roadblock, or what was left of it. David and his people did good."

"Damned right," Cordell said, smiling. "After all these years, the Utes were due for a victory."

The three of us started walking to the truck. Taylor had crawled into the back and was lying on a blanket. Goff came over with the first aid kit, and Cordell insisted I bandage my still bleeding cheek. Colorow stood alongside watching the patch-up job and commented, "The kid's covered in blood and still looks better than you."

"Well, that was true *before* we got into this fracas," I said, smiling.

All of us piled into the truck, but before we even started the engine we saw dust roll up in the air to the east. We sat and watched a flying beast rise up from behind a small hill and head our way. The machine made it over the nearby derricks before we heard the thumping of its blades.

"We have to get out," I said. "Out of the truck."

No one moved. Everyone was too transfixed at seeing a chopper where it didn't seem to belong. It isn't every day you see a military aircraft flying over an abandoned mine, bearing down on civilians. The problem was that the people in that machine didn't know we were civilians. Or that we were the good guys.

"Move," I said, knowing all too well what could happen. "Everyone out and on our knees, hands in the air, or they'll cut us down."

That did it. Four doors squeaked open and Taylor hustled out of the truck bed. We went to our knees and laced our hands behind our necks, just in time.

The helicopter bounced to the ground, its big blades swirling dust and thistles and sticks high into the air. Five men in combat fatigues burst out, crouching at first, then running full speed to stand and point nasty-looking weapons at us.

I took a deep breath and prepared for the worst.

CHAPTER FORTY-SEVEN

Four Months Later

The little scraggly-antlered buck walked broadside into my sights as the first snowflakes started to fall. I put my finger on the trigger, breathed out slowly, then took the finger away and lowered the rifle. There'd been too much killing. I let the little animal move away, then turned and started heading back.

There was no real reason to hunt, but I did it out of habit, and to clear my head. Every day since the army investigators had released me I got up at dawn, found tracks, and followed. Every day I thought about pulling the trigger, but didn't. The concentration of the hunt helped to erase thoughts of all the people who'd been killed in such a short span of time. It helped to dull the memory of all those hours locked in an interrogation room, getting grilled by men in fatigues. I repeated the same story over and over, telling the truth, leaving nothing out. Colorow, Cordell, Goff, and Buff all did the same. When the trailer was recovered intact, and our stories all checked out, we were released, freeing us to go back to our normal lives.

But they'd never be normal again. Not after everything

that had happened. I shook my head to clear it and watched the snow settle on the sage as I tromped back to the ranch. I remembered the week after being released, when I'd spent night and day at the hospital. I'd wandered with Taylor from room to room, checking on Lawana, and her father, and even Buff, who was hurt worse than I'd thought. Eventually everyone was released, but the worry during that week had almost broken me.

Now I was back to a routine, in a good place. As I walked across the dead grass and through the log fence, Lawana and Taylor rode past on dark bay horses. Lawana smiled, and Taylor waved, but they kept moving. There were fences to check and horses to wrangle. No time for pleasantries.

The old man, Bud, had plenty of time, however. He lifted himself off his rocker on the porch as I walked up, and hobbled over to talk.

"Nothing again, eh? You ain't the Great White Hunter you think you are, huh?"

"You aren't supposed to be walking around, old man. Get back in the chair and I'll make sandwiches."

He grumbled and limped back over to the porch. I went inside, put the rifle on the rack, and opened the fridge. I pulled out last night's beef roast, cut a couple of slices, and put them on bread. Added mayo, horseradish, some lettuce, and called it good. It was simple, but I liked simple. So did the old man.

We ate in silence on the porch, both of us staring out at the trees and the snow and the far-off mountains.

"You gonna stay the winter?" the old man asked, wiping mayo from his pockmarked face.

I shrugged.

"Hope so," he said. "Appreciate the help. You're a hell of a hand, know horses pretty well, and the boy likes having you around. My daughter, too."

I nodded. I'd stayed at first because of my injuries. Which were myriad, but which Lawana had no problem looking after as she mended her own. I'd worried that, after all that had happened, she'd want me gone and as far away as possible. But it turned out that the opposite was true. She'd hugged me in the hospital, thanked me for helping her son. And that hug had led to more intimate touches once she was released.

By the time we'd both healed I'd fallen into a pretty good spot. Taylor had become almost a son to me, showing his toughness again and again when the work on the place got hard. Not once did he break down and cry when he talked about what had happened. I was proud of him. Lawana was, too. Not that she saw him much lately. She worked on the ranch when she could, like today, but she spent most of her time in town, helping Colorow and the rest of the Utes rebuild. I would have, too, but she didn't let me. She said that I wasn't one of them, and that someone needed to watch over the old man. Keep him from breaking his ticker again.

"Only thing you ain't good at is making a sandwich," Bud said, putting his plate on the wood planks by his feet. He burped, then rubbed his belly.

I grunted. I finished my own sandwich and watched the fog off the river drift through the falling flakes.

"Your stories ain't too bad, though," he said. "You got a few good ones, but mine are better, of course."

"Of course," I said.

"Hear you're starting to fit in in town, too," he said. He pulled a pipe from his jacket and started packing it with tobacco, then he handed me a flask from his other pocket.

I took a sip of the strong bourbon and nodded. "So they say."

It wasn't true. They might like me in town because of how I'd helped, but no matter how hard I tried, or what I did, I'd still never belong. I wasn't Ute. I didn't have the culture in me. I respected and loved the people. I understood their constant fight to find a voice and a place in a country where they were often forgotten. But they'd always see me as an outsider.

It had dawned on me recently that, eventually, I'd have to saddle up and ride away. And not just because I didn't belong. There was more to it. It had to do with the life itself—the way one day on a ranch resembled the next, the demands it put on a person to be patient, to work out problems in a subtle way. It just wasn't me.

I never felt so alive as when everything was teetering on the edge of chaos, and one person was depending on me to act quickly—and yes, riskily—to make it right. That was what I missed. That was what I couldn't get out of my system.

I handed the flask back to Bud, and he took another sip. "Did I mention Lawana doesn't mind having you around?" he said.

"Might have," I said, smiling.

The old man hadn't objected when Lawana and I spent our evenings on that same porch, holding hands and watching sunsets. Or when we both slipped off to the tack shed after dark. He'd simply smile and laugh and hobble back to his own room, saying someone needed to keep an eye on the boy. He was obviously rooting for the two of us to deepen our affection.

Unfortunately, lately we'd been drifting apart. We still spent many nights together—upstairs now, in the main house—but it was mostly for companionship. Neither of us wanted to be alone, especially in the dark, after all we'd been through. But that wasn't enough to really bring us together.

The snow started coming down harder, obscuring the view of the mountains and stacking up on the dead grass. It meant that the mountains would be out as an option for the winter. It also meant that if I didn't leave soon, I'd be stuck. And I didn't know how well that would work out. Before the snow I could get out, go hunting. In the winter it would just be us, cooped up together in a small house, repeating the same conversations and remembering the same good and bad times.

"Starting to pile up," the old man said, his gnarled hands holding tight to the flask. He stared at the flakes with the same bright-eyed wonder that children have.

"Yup," I said, and let the conversation die.

So we sat and watched the snow accumulate and waited for the riders to return. They were looking for four of the mares, one of which had just recently figured out how to open a gate. Taylor and I had looked all day for them the day before, but Lawana was sure she'd have better luck. That, or she just wanted to spend a little time with her son.

Probably the latter. Everything that had happened reinforced the importance of spending time with the ones you love, before it's too late. That was part of why I felt so torn about the fact that I'd have to leave eventually. I was starting to love being there. We were starting to feel like a family—even though I didn't really belong. The togetherness made me want to see my sisters again, be in a place where even if I wasn't liked, I knew I belonged.

The old man and I passed the flask back and forth until it was empty, then zipped and buttoned our jackets against the cold. I picked up a John D. MacDonald paperback that I'd been reading and continued the adventures of Mr. McGee. Hours later, as the sky dimmed, we finally made out the forms of four horses running, then the silhouettes of two riders who followed and whooped behind the loose beasts.

"Got 'em," Bud said.

I grunted and stood. I went over to help Lawana and Taylor catch the mares and then unsaddle. As I hefted a saddle, I watched the snow fall harder and start clumping in the leafless trees. With each flake, I felt more and more trapped. It was like being locked in a cell of snow. After we finished the chores, we all had a small dinner and retired to warm beds, exhausted and quiet.

That night, I made my decision. Lying next to one of the toughest, smartest, and most beautiful women I'd ever met, I decided to leave. It wasn't easy. Lawana and her family liked me. Maybe even loved me. And I liked the hell out of all of them. But they deserved better. Lawana deserved a man who'd devote his life to her, and to her son. Someone who didn't feel the constant urge to see what was over the next hill, or run headlong into trouble if he was asked to help. Someone other than me.

The next morning I started packing at sunrise. I didn't have much, so it didn't take long to throw on a new pack and sling a new rifle over my shoulder. I strode quickly and quietly out to the corrals and caught my mare.

Lawana walked up behind me as I was trying to catch the mule, Bob. It had stopped snowing sometime during the night, and the sun broke bright into a clean and crisp blue sky.

"You're leaving," she said. It wasn't a question. She stared out at the new fallen snow, shading her eyes from the white glare.

"I was going to say good-bye after I saddled," I said, finally getting a halter on the skittish mule.

"I certainly hope so," she said, forcing a smile. I walked Bob out of the corral and tied him to a post. Lawana came up beside me and put an arm around my waist. "I understand," she said. "You need your family."

I nodded.

"And you need to be out there," she said, pointing toward the far-off desert and mountains.

How could I explain? I locked eyes with her, tried to put what I was feeling into words. "Somewhere along the way, the empty spaces became part of who I am. It's where I'm at my best."

She seemed to waver for a moment, as if trying to think of words that would break the spell I was under, then pulled away. "I'll miss you," she said. "But I understand. And Clyde?"

"Yeah?"

"Thanks. For *everything*."

I nodded. I wanted to tell her that she was the one who needed thanking, that she'd saved me more times than I'd saved her, and that my life would never be the same now that I'd met her, but I didn't. Because it might have made me stay. Or cry. Or both.

I finished saddling the mare and putting panniers on Bob while Lawana watched. I swung into the cold saddle, making the leather squeak, and said, "Tell Taylor—"

"Tell me yourself," he said, having come out of the main house dressed for chores. He stared at the pack and the panniers. "You're leaving? Why?"

"I need to be somewhere else. But I'll make you a deal," I said, walking the mare and mule in small circles, warming them up. Taylor frowned but listened.

"You stay in school, take care of your family, and I'll come back for your graduation," I said, looking to Lawana, who stood stoically in the cold, brisk air. "If that's okay," I added.

She nodded, and I put out my hand. Taylor took it, shaking it with the firm grip of a grown man. "Seriously?"

"Promise," I said, hoping he understood what that word meant to me. Then I kicked the mare into a trot and headed for the road.

ACKNOWLEDGMENTS

Once again I need to thank all of those who made this book possible. Though writing is viewed as a solitary practice, there are many people who contribute along the way, whether or not they know it. This book required a considerable amount of research, and I'd be remiss in not mentioning the folks who helped in that effort. Thanks first to the Kahpeeh Kah-ahn Ute Coffee House, for brewing a great cup of joe and for allowing me to sit and compose notes. Thanks also to the Ute Crossing Grill, which kept me fed while I explored and observed. Thanks, too, to the coordinators of the Fourth of July Pow-wow, who put on a heck of show. Most of all, thanks to all the wonderful people living and working on the Uintah and Ouray reservation. This book was written partly as a testament to your way of life.

As for the historical research aspect, I'd like to first thank the Rio Blanco County Historical Society, which fed my interest in the history of the land on which I grew up and provided much needed information on the Meeker Massacre and the Battle of Milk Creek. A big thanks as well to the Utah State Historical Society for directing me to site-specific information.

Also, to the Ute Indian Museum in Montrose, where I first saw the beautiful handiwork created by past and present Utes.

A novel's villains need to be studied and researched as much as its heroes. Among those who were very helpful in this regard were the owners and employees of the Silver Dollar Saloon in Leadville, Colorado, and the Triple Tree Tavern in Clifton, Colorado, for their acceptance and willingness to put up with my stupid questions and awkwardness. Thanks also to the coordinators and participants of the Laughlin River Run, for immersing me in motorcycle culture and simultaneously scaring and entertaining me. And of course, thanks to all the riders who've taken the time to talk and share their expertise. No names will be mentioned, as agreed, but you know who you are.

I very much need to thank the wonderful bookselling community that championed my first book and gave me the courage to write a second, including specifically Patrick at the Poisoned Pen, Marya at Out West Books, Carole at Book Train, George and company at *Deadly Pleasures*, Doris at the Book Rack, and Mystery Mike at Bouchercon, as well as everyone at the Tattered Cover, Boulder Book Store, Old Firehouse Books, and Murder by the Book. Thanks also to others who rallied behind *Nothing Short of Dying*, specifically Ryan at *The REAL Book Spy*, Sue with the Glenwood Springs Branch Library, Luke at KDNK, Jason with *Westword*, and all the folks who make up or work at Rocky Mountain Fiction Writers, Western Colorado Writers' Forum, and the Mesa County Libraries.

And, of course, the process of creating books has two halves: the writing and the publishing. For the latter, I've counted on my beyond brilliant Scribner editor, Rick Horgan; his wonderful assistant, Sally Howe; talented and hardworking publicists

ACKNOWLEDGMENTS

Jessica Yu and Jeremy Price; and my steadfast production editor, Dan Cuddy; as well as publisher Nan Graham, editor-in-chief Colin Harrison, publicity director Brian Belfiglio, and the great folks in Sales who are too numerous to mention. Art director Jaya Miceli, her assistant Janetta Dancer, and jacket designer Christopher Lin deserve credit for this book's wonderful jacket.

I'd also like to thank the folks at Pocket Books, especially publisher Louise Burke and her hardworking coordinator Irene Lipsky; the folks at S&S UK, including publisher Ian Chapman and editor Carla Josephson; and S&S Australia managing director Dan Ruffino.

My literary agent, Darley Anderson, continues to be a constant advocate for me. Without the work of this wonderful man, none of this would have ever happened. I remain eternally grateful to him and his team, with a special thanks to Mary, Emma, Rosanna, Pippa, and Mr. Fisher.

Lastly, I need to thank the ones who are a constant in my writing life—those who enable me to punch keys, which usually results in their having to work twice as hard. Thank you, Stephanie. Without you and all of your dedication and hard work, I'd probably be examining gutter angles for a living. Thanks to my daughters, for continuing to put up with Dad disappearing into the office. Thanks to my parents, once again. And always.

Lastly, a huge thanks to the readers who keep asking for more. We writers only do it because you ask.

ABOUT THE AUTHOR

Erik Storey is a former ranch hand, wilderness guide, dogsled musher, and hunter. He spent his childhood summers on his great-grandfather's homestead or in a remote cabin in Colorado's Flat Tops Wilderness. He has earned a number of sharpshooter and marksman qualifications. *A Promise to Kill* is his second novel in the Clyde Barr thriller series, after *Nothing Short of Dying*, which hit international bestseller lists and received raves from more than a dozen bestselling American thriller writers.

Turn the page for an extract from Erik Storey's debut novel,
introducing the tortured hero, Clyde Barr:

NOTHING SHORT OF DYING

Available in print and eBook

SIMON &
SCHUSTER

CHAPTER ONE

It started with a phone call in the Utah wilderness, about a week after I'd been released from prison.

I'd been enjoying one of those perfect spring mornings in the mountains. Baby-blue skies, soft breeze out of the northwest, sweet sage dripping with dew, and wildlife that practically ran from the trail into the frying pan. A great morning, I thought, on the way to many more like it in the Yukon, where I planned to live in the peace and cold.

I'd spent the morning tracking and then shooting a young mule deer buck. He led me through creeks swollen with muddy runoff, across hillsides so slick with fallen aspen leaves that I took a few ungraceful dives, and into a meadow of young lupine, where I pulled the trigger on my big African rifle as he turned broadside with his nostrils flaring.

The rest of the day was spent cutting the buck into steaks for dinner and strips to be smoked and air dried for later use. That night I built a small campfire out of wrist-size branches of juniper and sat staring at the flames as I fidgeted with the little hunk of plastic and wires I'd bought to contact my sisters as I passed through.

I'd hoped for a storybook homecoming—me calling them

and telling them I was home and them suggesting I come over straightaway so they could cook for me. In my daydreams we'd have a merry old time catching up and talking like the family we used to be. In reality Deb didn't answer and Angie told me I could go to hell. Jen wasn't in any phone book, so I didn't call her. Odds were good that if I did, she'd tell me something similar, so I put the phone away and set about cooking the steak.

I was sitting in a camp chair, listening to the crickets and the night wind, and had just finished rubbing salt and pepper into the meat, when the damned plastic contraption started chirping in my pocket. The sound was like an Atari video game, and I couldn't push buttons fast enough to make it stop.

"This is Barr," I said.

"Clyde." It was Jen, her voice barely a whisper. "I need you to come get me."

I looked up at the night sky, pulling on my beard. As happy as I was to hear her voice, the tone scared the hell out of me and lured me back to a time of fear. It was the same tone and pleading I'd heard as a child on the bad nights. The nights that Mom and Dad—or Mom and some new guy—were fighting, or when one of those guys, drunk and out of control, chose to hurt us.

Back then Jen would often crawl into my room and wake me with a trembling whisper. Together, we'd push the dresser against the door, huddle in a corner, and ride out the storm.

"Where are you?"

"Clyde, you need to *hurry*. He's going to kill me. After I help him, I'm dead."

"Who's going to kill you? Help who with what?" I had absolutely no idea what she was talking about or where she was.

"Jesus, Clyde." Even though she whispered, I could hear her panic. "After I help him get inside a week from now, I'm no use to him. Please, *please* get me the hell out of here. You owe me."

She was right about the obligation. "Okay. Tell me where you are."

"Promise me. *Promise* you'll come get me."

This part was important, and she knew it. If I gave my word, nothing short of dying would stop me. It hadn't *yet*. I stood and watched the constellations disappear, blanketed by invisible clouds. "I promise," I said. "Now, where the hell are you?"

Suddenly there was a muffled shout and what sounded like a crash. I heard a male voice, then silence.

"Jen?"

There was no reply. I looked at the phone's screen. The call-time numbers were still running. "Jen?" I said, louder.

Nothing.

There was a faint click and the line went dead. I flipped the phone shut and shoved it in my pocket.

As the night wind stirred the trees, I pulled a soft pack of straights from my flannel shirt pocket and shook out one of the last cigarettes. After touching it to a glowing ember from the fire, I stood in the darkness next to a sweet-smelling serviceberry bush.

One of my resolutions had been to quit smoking when I went into the backcountry. It was reassuring knowing there's no better counter to the bad habit than fresh air and open spaces. But this new development put my vow on hold.

As reluctant as I was to delay my journey north, I'd made a promise. And this time it was to my sister—not some vil-lager or desperate campesino in one of the many jungles I'd hacked my way through. My own flesh and blood—whatever the hell that meant.

I limped back to the fire and tossed the butt into the flames. From the valley came the lonely cry of coyotes. The wind rustled up the smells of melting snow and slowly caressed the pines as I looked back up at the stars and wondered what Jen had done this time.

Like me, and unlike our straitlaced sisters, she'd always been a troublemaker. She had a knack for finding the wrong people, the wrong times, and the wrong places. When we were young it had been us against the world. But then I left—left her to fend for herself, because I'd been selfish.

Now I had a chance to make up for it. First though, I needed a direction. A track I could follow. I called Angie again.

No answer, so I called Deb.

I got another one of those mechanical voices telling me to leave a message, so I did. I wasn't sure Deb would call back, so I went ahead and started breaking camp. The tent came down in the same amount of time it takes most people to strip their beds. It and my sleeping bag went in my big bag, a beat-up ruck I'd hauled halfway around the world. I limped over and shoveled dirt on the fire. As the last few embers suffocated under the soil, I silently said good-bye to the oak brush, aspen, and pines that had been my home this last week. I tipped my hat to Mount Lena, who'd let me sleep on her for the last couple of days. It was the closest I'd been to a woman in three years.

The phone rang as I began climbing into the truck. I stepped back out into the cold mountain air and pushed buttons until the ringing stopped.

"Barr," I said.

"This is Nick."

I didn't know any Nicks.

"Deb's husband."

"Oh," I said.

"Stop calling. She doesn't want to talk to you. Ever. Got it?"

I nodded, watched the moon start to peek over the ragged horizon. Nick went on to tell me that I was a worthless bastard who'd abandoned his family. When his rant was over, I informed him what Jen had said. He told me that she was just as bad as I was and that he couldn't care less what happened to her. I eventually prodded him into telling me that he'd seen her in Clifton with "her lowlife friends" and that she was using drugs again.

"Okay, well, thanks for—" He broke off the call before I could finish.

I got back in the truck, threw the phone on the cracked dash, then turned the key in the ignition. Nothing. I got back out, kicked the door, kicked the side panels, then slammed a fist on the hood. Satisfied with my mechanic skills, I got back behind the wheel and tried the ignition again. The dilapidated engine turned over, started, and made unhealthy grinding noises as I headed south.

I drove off the mountain, under a brilliant moon, back toward the country I thought I'd left for good. I smacked my hands against the steering wheel and felt both it and the truck wobble. The grimy wheel was connected by an iffy steering rod to a junk pickup that I'd bought for two hundred bucks from the coyote who'd driven me across the border. Listening to the creaks and moans of the aging steel, I wondered if either of us would survive the trip.

My eyes burned and the road blurred in front of me. I

wanted to stop and crawl into my sleeping bag but decided on a drink instead. I grabbed the paper bag that sat on the passenger seat, pulled the bottle out, put it between my legs, and then took a big, long pull.

After the liquor hit, driving away from my Yukon dreams and back toward the place I'd grown up didn't feel so bad. But deep down I knew I was kidding myself. The truth was, Jen's call had surfaced memories that I'd buried under many years and thousands of miles. With one phone call, she'd made me remember what I wanted to forget.

When our dad left, and our mom died, I did something stupid that almost got me killed. Jen did something worse that saved my life. If anyone ever found out what we'd done, we'd both be serving life sentences. Jen's keeping quiet kept me free. Because of that, and of what we'd endured together, I'd do whatever she asked.

CHAPTER TWO

I awoke in a tangle of sweaty sheets. The screams of women and children and the popping of Kalashnikovs faded slowly back into the realm of dreams as the morning light filtered in through the slightly drawn curtains. Though I'd come to consciousness coiled for action, I relaxed when I spotted a cheap television perched on a nearby entertainment stand.

It was the TV that told me what country I'd woken up in.

The soft bed beneath me was another tip-off. I wasn't surrounded by snoring people wrapped in dirty blankets and crowding all of the available floor space. And there were no chickens or goats. I scratched my flat naked belly, felt the reassuring cold steel of the rifle by my side, and shook my head, amazed by what the developed world takes for granted.

Water heaters, for instance. I loved water heaters. Their existence meant I could take a gloriously long shower without any work. I was absolutely filthy. A week on the mountain swirled around my feet and down the drain in a black slurry. After toweling off, I wiped condensation from the bathroom mirror and used my scissors to trim back my unruly hair and beard. The sight of gray tufts mixed with black should have been depressing, but I had a slightly different thought—how much I'd changed in the years I'd been away. I was staring at a naked ape with wide straight shoulders, hard sinewy limbs, and hairy tanned skin. I actually looked *too* lean. If I didn't get some calories in soon, I'd drop to under two hundred pounds for the first time since high school.

After pulling on a pair of jeans and a denim shirt, I sat down and drew a little notebook out of my pack. I bit the inside of my cheek and flipped through the pages, staring at the phone numbers written inside. *Who do I call first?*

I decided to call Juan. He was my only real friend from Riverside High. While other kids focused on geometry and biology, Juan taught me how to steal cars and pick locks. In return I taught him how to shoot and brawl. I hoped he still had his family connections.

"This is Barr," I said when Juan picked up on the third ring.

"Barr?" There was a brief silence, then hushed Spanish. "*Seriously?*"

"Yeah. I need some help."

"Well, I'm good, thanks for asking."

"Sorry," I said. "How you been?"

"Good, man. It's been a lot of years. Where have you—"

"I'll fill you in later. Right now I need info."

"What kind?" Juan asked warily.

"Jen's in trouble—*again*. Maybe mixed up with somebody very dangerous."

"I'm not sure how much help I can be, now that we're outside of it."

"We?"

"Me and Maria."

I didn't say anything for several moments, tried to ignore the punch to the gut.

"Oh, man ... you didn't know?" Juan said.

"You still live in the same place?" I asked.

"Yeah, but, Clyde ..."

"I'll be there in thirty," I said, and hung up.

TWENTY MINUTES AND A STOP for smokes later, I pulled into Riverside, Colorado, and stopped in the public park. The cottonwoods were finally beginning to leaf out and the grass was short and green. On the far side of the park, protecting the town from the river, was the levee where kids played and rode their bikes on the crest. From behind it wafted the sweet, earthy scent of the mighty Colorado.

The park nearly overflowed with very large families in the middle of various get-togethers, birthday parties, and picnics. I got out, leaned on the hood of my truck, and lit a fresh cigarette. Most of the folks were Hispanic, happy, and boisterous. I could have been standing in a village in any of the Latin countries I'd wandered through, but I wasn't. I was home, staring at the central gazebo that had changed my life. Memories of this place came flooding back, as if the levee had suddenly given way.

Down the street, Juan's house sat next door to the one Maria had grown up in—Maria, the girl I'd dated all through high school, the one who'd taken my virginity with relish and let loose feelings I'd never had before.

Sixteen years ago, I'd sat with Maria under that gazebo, my arms wrapped tight around her thin waist, and told her I was leaving. She didn't cry, just looked into my eyes and nodded. It was inevitable, she'd told me. She said I needed to escape, run away.

Is that what I'd been doing all this time? *Running away?*

I crushed out my cigarette, got in the truck, and drove to Juan's.

I WAS SITTING IN HIS backyard, in a flimsy white plastic chair, my chukkas propped up on a cooler, drinking a Bud Light, and trying to pretend I wasn't uncomfortable as hell.

"So, I can try to help, but like I said, we're out of the life now," Juan said.

I took a sip of beer. "About this *we*—"

"Sorry you didn't know. We would have invited you, but no one knew where you were."

I looked at the ground.

"Really," he said. "You can't be that mad, right? I mean, you've been gone for almost ... When *did* you leave?"

"A year after high school," I said.

Juan shook his head. "Sixteen years, then. So, you gonna hit me or just drink all my beer?"

"You happy? Is *she* happy?" I asked.

"Of course, man. Especially now. Two little ones running around, her finally finishing nursing school. I just got a raise at the shop."

"Then that's all that matters." I reached into the cooler for another beer, popped the tab on another can of Bud. "I thought you guys only drank Coronas?"

"That horse piss? You probably assume we eat burritos three times a day, too."

"You mean you *don't*?" I said.

Juan laughed. "Well, that's what we're having tonight."

Maria came out then carrying paper plates loaded with food that smelled of cumin and pepper. Flies flitted around the burritos. I couldn't meet her gaze, stared at the top of my beer can instead. She and Juan exchanged love sonnets in a fast Spanglish that I had a hard time following. I told her thanks, but she ignored me and walked back inside. My eyes followed her soft retreat, imagining a past that could have been. I took one bite, then finished the burrito in three more.

"I'll call my cousins," Juan said. "My brothers, too. They still got a hand in all that. See what they can find out."

I nodded, not really paying attention. The house, the kids, the jobs. They were living the American dream, one I could have had if I'd stayed.

"So I'll call you," Juan said.

"Sure," I said, draining the dregs of my beer.

When I finished, I crushed the can, tossed it into a steel drum set out for that purpose, and stood. "Thanks, man. And, uh … tell Maria she's beautiful, okay?"

CHAPTER THREE

The sun finally gave up for the day as I cruised down the interstate toward Clifton. In the rearview mirror I could see the tired old ball of atoms settle down in its bed of rocks and sand, pulling its pink-and-red blankets over its head, then finally turning off the light. It would be a while until the moon arrived to take its place. Both windows were down and I could feel the temperature drop immediately, as it always does in the desert. In the cool air I smelled the faint river scents start to push away the god-awful gasoline smog that had been plaguing my nose all day.

The lights of the city were glowing now, overpowering the stars and making the world look upside down. The truck rattled and squeaked off I-70, and together we stopped at the first motel we came to. It was one of those leftovers from an era when car travel was exciting. It even had one of those names: Travel Lodge. All dark brown wood with a small faded sign that showed they had all the modern conveniences, like air-conditioning and color TVs. My kind of place.

Juan called after I'd checked in and unloaded my bags.

"I asked around," he said. "Found out some things. They reminded me why I decided to get out of this shit. My oldest brother, Alejandro, remember him? He's still running a crew in Clifton. Mostly sells pot and a little crank. He used to sell it out of a place on F and Susan called the Cellar. Know it?

Anyway, about a year ago a new guy came to town, some white dude with a lot of muscle, and he ran Alejandro out."

"What's this got to do with Jen?" I asked with a sinking feeling. Getting involved in stuff like this was the reason I'd wound up in prison.

"This big honcho, he disappeared a week ago. And the last time he was spotted he was with Jen."

"Oh," I said.

"Yeah. And everyone is looking for him. He stopped the flow of good meth. Word is, he's making something even better, but he's cut off any trade in it until it's done so that the tweakers will be jonesing real good when the new batch comes out."

"What's this honcho's name?"

"Didn't ask. I don't want to know specifics, 'cause I'm out of the life, remember?"

"Yeah. So I should start looking at the Cellar?"

"That's what Alejandro said. The big honcho is missing, but his little brother runs the place, slings crank out of there when he has supply. Alejandro suggests you try talking to the main bartender there, a pretty brunette named Allie Martin. Just be careful."

"You know me," I said. "Safety first."

"I *do* know you. That's why I said to be careful. Don't go stepping on rattlers, Barr. You might get bit."

"Uh-huh."

"One more thing," Juan said. "Chopo got out a while back and he's heading this way to help my brother. I know you guys did some business years ago. He might be willing to lend a hand."

"I got it for now, Juan, thanks. And tell—"

"Yeah, yeah, I'll tell her. Stay alive, man." He hung up.

A HALF HOUR LATER I paused at the front entrance to the Cellar and felt under my Carhartt jacket, first to my right and then to my left, for my six-inch Green River butcher knife and my compact .40 caliber. I walked in slowly, letting my eyes adjust to the gloom. The place smelled of piss and mildew and stale beer. There was something else, too: the acrid sweat of the strung out—a smell that reminded me of the little cantinas in Bolivia where people in the coca trade use booze to come down from the powder cloud that gets them through the long shifts. If broken souls had an odor, they'd smell like the Cellar.

A single bar on the right ran the entire length of the building: twelve bar stools, five occupied by men. And to the left of the bar was a group of tables, one of which propped up three people—two women and a guy—who looked like they were passed out. The bartender, a good-looking young woman with a ponytail, was yelling at a man whose elbows were propped on the bar. He stomped outside after the reaming, and I headed toward his abandoned seat.

The four men who remained on the stools glowered as I walked past and sat down. The bartender pretended to ignore me. After she waited the predetermined time it took to show the four men whose side she was on, she walked over and took my order. A Canadian whiskey with a cheap beer back. My version of a boilermaker.

The four men fidgeted, animated about something or other, eyes constantly searching, seeing and cringing at the spiders on the walls and the mothmen in the corners. All four tweakers were white, thin, and tall. And close to the same age. All wore baggy shirts and baggy pants, and their flat-brimmed ball caps were crooked. When they spoke it was clipped and fast and they used hand gestures that looked like bad karate. Occasionally they'd look my way, make a gesture, laugh, and sneer. One spit at my feet. I smiled, nodded, and held up my whiskey.

The three at the table must have been coming down from "a long time on the moon," as the meth heads called the time they spent tweaked. Their heads were cradled on skinny folded arms and one, the guy, snored.

"You Allie?" I asked the bartender as she pulled a bottle down from the top shelf and wiped an inch of dust off it.

"Maybe."

"You know a girl named Jen Barr?"

She smiled, a strange smirk that told me she knew a lot of things. After putting the bottle back on the shelf, she said, "I might. You a cop?"

I pulled up my coat sleeves, showing her scars and green ink. "Do I look like a cop?"

She laughed. "Everyone has ink. Cops too."

Which I couldn't argue. When I left, only sailors, bikers, and cons had tattoos. From what I'd seen since I'd returned to this country, everyone and their grandmothers had something scrawled on their skin.

"I don't care much for the law," I said. "I'm just a brother looking for his sister Jen."

"You should ask the owner," she said with that same strange smirk. "He's outside smoking, but he'll be back soon. He might know her."

"Care if I sit here and wait?"

"Be my guest."

So I sat and sipped and waited. "Who owns this dive?" I asked after I finished the whiskey.

"Brent. Everyone here calls him Spike."

"Spike?" The name made me think of a cartoon bulldog.

"Yeah. He got the name when he stopped smoking and started using the needle." She pantomimed someone sticking a syringe into a vein. "It's a stupid name. Fits him well."

"Got it." She either believed that I wasn't a cop or she hated her boss. Or both.

She walked over by the till, shook the empty tip jar, and glared at the four restless men next to me. Grabbing a rag, she started wiping down the bar and made her way back to me.

"Brent's not going to like someone coming into his place and asking questions," she said. "It's not the kind of place where you get answers."

I nodded, not showing any worry, but I was getting restless. This was taking too long. I thought I'd just ask a few questions, then hit the road with a direction. Hunting people was much more frustrating than hunting animals, because it involved talking, which I wasn't very good at. I sipped my beer, resigned myself to a long night, and thought about all the dirty little dive bars I'd been in over the years.

Allie kept wiping, trying to push a puddle of liquor off the bar. I said, "You do know her, though?"

She folded her arms and stared at me with a look of defiance that told me she was done with annoying men for the day. On *her* the expression looked cute.

"Maybe you should ask *him*," she said, looking over my shoulder.

I turned and watched a short guy with fussed-over dusty-brown hair who I assumed was the owner come back into the bar like he'd forgotten something. He strode quickly across the room, quickening his pace further when he saw me. He wore green slacks and a brown T-shirt that was too tight. There were track marks on both of his Popeye arms. The gold Rolex on his wrist wobbled as he cracked his knuckles.

"And who the holy hell are you?" he asked, his voice high-pitched and angry.

"You must be Spike," I said.

"You didn't answer my question, asshole. This is pretty much a private club. No outsiders. You're going to tell me who you are, and why you're here, then you're gonna get your ass off that stool and out of my bar or I swear to God—"

"The name's Clyde Barr," I said, pushing back on the stool a few inches. "I'm looking for someone and thought you could help. Want a beer?"

"No, I don't want no stupid beer. And I don't talk to no cops, either."

This cop thing was getting old.

"He's not a cop, Brent," Allie said. "And don't take out your being pissed at me on him. He's looking for his sister."

"Shut up, bitch, no one asked you. We'll deal with our thing when this is done," Spike, or Brent, said.

Allie threw the wet rag at Brent and walked to the other end of the bar.

"You should watch the language," I said. "But she's right. I'm not a cop and I'm looking for my sister Jen. Know her?"

"I might. She may have been that slut my brother was—"

I'd had enough. I leaped off the stool, grabbed the mouthy prick by the neck, and shoved him up against a carpeted pillar. My eyes caught movement as the four bar-stool guys rushed toward me. I'd forgotten how fast tweakers can move.